THE ORPHAN

Thief

Glynis Peters lives in the seaside town of Dovercourt. In 2014, she was shortlisted for the Festival of Romance New Talent Award.

When Glynis is not writing, she enjoys making greetings cards, Cross Stitch, fishing and looking after her gorgeous grandchildren.

Her debut novel, *The Secret Orphan*, was an international bestseller.

🐦 @_GlynisPeters_
📘 www.facebook.com/glynispetersauthor/
📷 glynispete

Also by Glynis Peters

The Secret Orphan

THE
ORPHAN
Thief

GLYNIS PETERS

OneMoreChapter

One More Chapter a division of
HarperCollins*Publishers*
The News Building
1 London Bridge Street
London SE1 9GF

www.harpercollins.co.uk

This paperback edition 2020

First published in Great Britain in ebook format by
HarperCollins*Publishers* 2019

A catalogue record for this book
is available from the British Library

US PB ISBN: 9780008374631
CAN PB ISBN: 9780008374648
UK PB ISBN: 9780008384906
US+CAN EB ISBN: 9780008363260
UK EB ISBN: 9780008374624

Typeset in Sabon LT Std by Palimpsest Book Production Ltd,
Falkirk, Stirlingshire

Printed and bound in Great Britain by CPI Group (UK) Ltd,
Croydon CR0 4YY

MIX
Paper from
responsible sources
FSC
www.fsc.org   **FSC™ C007454**

Dedicated to my husband, Peter, in our 40th year of marriage; our Ruby Wedding Year.

I love you for believing in me, for encouraging me, and most of all – for feeding me during the writing of this novel. This is your medal. x

And to my new granddaughter, Felicity Dilys Piper Smy. You came into our lives during the start of this book. My little Canadian Bunny, Meemaw loves you very much. x

PROLOGUE

Coventry, 25th December 1938

The table, laden with fresh vegetables and a rib of beef, filled the room. Chairs sat around it, seating her favourite people. Ruby Shadwell watched on as they ate and chatted about the previous Christmas, when the table had held two other elders of her family – both grandfathers.

Although both had been loved, they were also remembered for their dour outlook on life. No one banged the table for silence today, and Ruby slipped into a relaxed position in her seat. Her gran praised her parents for such a feast, her siblings drooled as her father sliced the meat onto a large platter and her mother, pretty in her new dress, trotted back and forth from the kitchen. Ruby studied her family as they moved through the day. Her father, over-polite to his mother-in-law and extra friendly to the children, with praise for her, and she even saw him kiss the cheek of her mother. He'd planned their day with great precision and not a minute was wasted.

They played games of charades after the meal and sang carols around the fire during the evening. They sat in silence and listened to her young sister Lucy recite a poem, and smiled when her brother gave a pretend snore at the end of it, earning himself a gentle clip around the ear from their father.

Boxing Day would be a day of rest too and their father had promised them a day much like their Christmas Day.

Ruby looked forward to reading a good book rather than planting out or pulling up vegetables to sell in the family shop, but she couldn't quite believe her father would honour his declaration. Contentment resonated around the room, but there was a darkness hovering over the adults too.

War loomed, but not a word was spoken about it during their special day. But once the two youngest of their children had given into sleep, the adults renewed their concerns about Hitler and his desire to hold power over Europe.

At fourteen, Ruby understood the implications of war. Her grandfathers and her father had already fought in one, and she'd witnessed men who'd lost limbs, or who choked still on gassed out lungs. Ruby knew if she sat and listened, her father often forgot she was in the room and broadened his views on the current situation. Today he didn't fail her, and she hung onto his every word. Ruby knew dark days were around the corner, but when it was due to happen was down to politicians at home and abroad. The Shadwell family could only sit in hope it wouldn't disturb the balance of their peaceful lives.

Toronto, Canada, 25th December 1938

Jean-Paul Clayton Junior watched his father dip the negative into the solution. Their darkroom housed many dripping negatives waiting to share what the two men had captured through their lens.

Photography was Jean-Paul's passion and his father's hobby, so when he'd mentioned his intention to leave the banking sector to take up photography full-time, this had not gone down well with his parents. At nineteen, although he wanted to rebel, he took their advice to continue earning and build a portfolio of work which might stand him in better stead for when he took it up as a permanent career.

Today, he unwrapped their gift to him, one which showed they understood his restlessness. He now owned one of the latest cameras and a ticket to travel throughout Canada. With news of the war brewing in Europe, his parents wanted him to have an adventure during his summer break. His sister received jewellery, which delighted her as much as his gift did him, but Jean-Paul knew his gift would never go out of fashion. A camera would always capture life through a lens and Jean-Paul intended never to miss a moment.

CHAPTER 1

Coventry, 15th November 1940

Ruby Shadwell stared out into the street, blinked away her disbelief and then looked down once again into darkness over the edge of a large smoking crater. A flash of light from the rising sun emerging from behind a cloud skimmed across scattered shards of glass, giving her an insight as to what was below. The epicentre of horror.

The place her parents and two siblings would have sat enjoying their cocoa around the fire, as they did every night. Ruby had no doubt their routine hadn't altered despite the air raid warnings.

Even if they had been in the Anderson shelter at the bottom of the garden, the scene before her would be the same. Total devastation. Her family crushed to death like ants under the foot of a human.

White-grey flakes fluttered from the sky. She held out her hand. It wasn't snow, but something like the ash from the fireplace in their house. The house which no longer existed.

Ruby wrapped her arms around her chest and shoulders and gripped hard, digging her fingers into her flesh through the woollen coat she wore. At sixteen, she could not recall a pain so deep, even when her precious grandfather had passed away. Unable to absorb the enormity of the disaster, she remained staring downwards into the crater in the hope it could be a dream. She'd even accept a nightmare. One from which her family clawed their way back to the surface. Back into her life.

Her body, freezing with the November frost and easterly wind, felt stiff and bruised.

Heavy drizzle dripped across her face and she brushed it away, her skin sore with cold, but she was unable to move away from the place she once knew as home. How had it come to this?

Walking home from Lammas Road, Ruby had witnessed the first of the bombs before a warden had grabbed her arm and took her at great speed to the public shelter underneath Radford Common.

Someone gave the time as seven-twelve when the sirens blasted their warning around the city. They ran past the group and towards the shelter, the warden shouting for them to run faster. An elderly lady stumbled and the warden left Ruby in order to help. The enemy attacked before the wailing of the siren had stopped. Ruby screamed as a bomb dropped on the rooftops of a nearby street.

A feeling more than the fear of the bogeyman forced her onwards – it sickened her to think she was streets away from the comfort of her family. Her lungs burned with the cold of the evening air and by the time she made it into the shelter, huddled amongst strangers and a few familiar faces, more bombs had fallen. Too many to count, too many to ignore.

Everyone waited for the all-clear to sound. It never rang out, but the reassurances and door-banging from ARP wardens now that the raid was over came as a huge relief. The warden seeing them out of the shelter warned people to be careful of fires and unexploded bombs, and that electricity was no longer on supply.

Ruby moved forward in the queue to leave and was stunned by what she saw as she stepped outside. Enemy bombs had proved themselves to be powerful and destructive – they'd destroyed Coventry. The people with whom she'd sheltered shouted their disbelief, many sank to their knees, but the majority screamed and ran towards their homes. Ruby headed back; her family would be frantic with worry and she needed to get onto Radford Road and back home to reassure them she was still alive.

The further she made her way back towards the centre of Coventry, the more the mangled streets disorientated her. Once she'd gained her bearings Ruby headed for Eagle Street, picking her way through what should have been darkness, but the city was lit with fires so bright, and the moon shone clear. She had no trouble seeing, although at times she wished it was dark. The more she saw, the more fearful she became of what she might find nearer her own home, and her fears were soon realised. At one point she questioned herself so much she thought she'd go mad. Bombs. Craters. Death. Was she truly staring at the outcome of human action? If only she'd stayed home. Her head throbbed.

She worked out she'd lost hours, as already the day was drifting into late afternoon. She'd lost precious family time after falling and hitting her head. She'd lain in the darkness and wasn't found by rescuers for several hours. Even without being knocked unconscious, Ruby knew the outcome would be the same. Over eleven hours or eleven days, it made no difference. She was here now, and she knew she was not insane.

Her family were dead.

She touched the bruised area on the back of her head and winced. Gingerly, she pulled her hand away and inspected her fingers, but saw no blood. Ruby walked around the edge of the crater, hoping to catch a glimpse of life – a movement or shout for help. Something, anything to prove her parents or siblings were still alive. Only devastation and darkness reflected back the image of mangled memories. Memories of a happy family life. Of a home brought to its knees by grown men in machines. Ruby had never understood the point of this war, no matter how many times her father drilled into them why it was necessary.

She thought back to when her dark-haired, brown-eyed nine-year-old brother, with his forever-grazed knees, ill-fitting socks and stick-thin legs which dangled from his baggy shorts, had announced he was going to be a soldier and fight for his country. Their mother had laughed and told him to wash his hands and eat his breakfast. With two front teeth missing, he often produced a lisped retort or a cheeky statement. Only that morning he'd teased her for having droopy drawers. James, named for their father, had been a loving soul. Their twelve-year-old sister Lucy had been a quiet, serious girl, her nose forever in a book, and her love of animals, especially cats, frustrated their parents as every day a stray would be brought home and fed. Lucy pleaded for a pet of their own, but their father forbade it and would shake his head and state they already had Coventry's largest collection of animals hovering in the lane behind the house; he could not be doing with one indoors.

How could her family's spirited energy disappear so

suddenly? In such a cruel way? Painful thoughts dug deep inside and Ruby allowed them space to run free, until a sickness clawed inside her gut.

No more walks on the common, no more hide-and-seek, where her brother would peek from between open fingers. No more listening to the soft voice of Lucy reciting a poem, or her neat and tidy mother singing a verse or two of a song from the radio. No more them. No longer would Ruby use the term *us* when referring to her family.

The dark hole glared back at her, mocking her tears, tearing her heart in two each time she blinked down in hope.

Even the sunshine had given up trying to spread cheer and waned behind clouds, refusing to dress up such a hideous sight. Ruby shivered and staggered to one side. With a glance back down into the dark abyss, she teetered on the dislodged bricks. Was she meant to jump? What was she to do? How was she meant to survive alone?

Screams and shouting filled her ears. A little girl called out for her mother in the distance, but Ruby remained rooted to the spot. The child was not her problem. Guilt washed over her. Should she make the girl her problem? Should she leave this place – the grave of her family – for there was no reassurance on this earth which would allow her to think they could be rescued. If she had not taken outgrown clothes to her mother's friend in Lammas Road, she'd have been with her family, enjoying their love, their laughter. More guilty feelings washed over Ruby. She should have been there. It was her mother's fault. Ruby's mind spun out reasons and accusations so fast she found it hard to concentrate. Eventually, she stopped and took a deep breath to gain control of her emotions.

What difference would it have made? She'd be dead instead of staring down into the centre of the planet. Either way, she'd be alone. Feeling nothing. Why didn't she feel anything? Why wasn't she crying? Slowly a fear crept into her veins. Now she was feeling something. Now she felt alone. No mother telling her off for not folding her clothes. No father reprimanding her for returning ten minutes later than normal. Never again would she hear his sermons. Ruby knew her father had loved them, but he'd struggled to express his feelings. He had good days when he made them laugh, but Ruby now realised his gloomy outlook was because of the never-ending war talk, and she wondered if he'd thought Christmas would be their last together. If he'd thought it, he'd been right, and she was grateful to him for trying so hard. Her family rarely laughed together but when they did the world was a good place to be, even during wartime in England.

Ruby pulled her coat around her as the temperature dropped, when it dawned on her she'd never hear their voices or laughter again. Disbelief set in.

Surely not? There must be life down there. She had to fight for them. Their family business, Shadwell's Grocery, the place where she'd worked day and night, gone.

'Here! My family! They are down there,' she called out.

'Get away from there, girl. It's dangerous,' a male voice bellowed out above the many sounds echoing out around the city.

Ruby turned to see who was talking, and she saw his tin hat bobbing up from a large hole in the ground. The man threw bricks and slates to one side. His plump face glistened with sweat and white vapours escaped his mouth and nostrils as he worked.

'Get away. There'll be no survivors down there. I'm sorry if they are yours, duck, but you must get away. Find somewhere safe. Don't go to town – it's bad there. Very bad. Those flames –' he pointed to a red-gold skyline '– it's the cathedral. There's no hope left here.' The man drooped his head, his voice gentle yet firm. Ruby said nothing, mesmerised by the flesh wobbling beneath his chin – a flash reminder of her mother. The man was the opposite to her father, whom her mother had often described as scrawny, and Ruby took after him. The man repeated his instructions and returned to clearing rubble, and Ruby shrugged her shoulders. Where's safe? she thought. How would she find safe without her parents to guide her?

'Get away, girl. There's nothing you can do – it's a mess. Go to a shelter. Get yourself to safety. Follow her,' a man in Home Guard uniform shouted and nodded in the direction of a woman walking with a baby in her arms, but Ruby ignored him.

She stood and watched as he pulled at pipes and bricks from the doorway of a house which still had some resemblance to a home.

A fierce hissing sound penetrated into the many noises nearby, followed by a loud explosion forcing her to the ground. Ruby fell backwards, away from the crater. It was a sign. Time for her to leave.

The man who'd encouraged her to leave earlier groaned several feet away. Ruby scrambled to her feet. Before she could reach him, he was upright and brushing his hands against his trousers.

'You still here?' he said and moved towards her, his hands held out to her. Ruby noticed the thick mud still clinging to them and kept hers to her side.

She remained silent. Her legs refused to move.

'Young woman here needs attention. Anyone? Family trapped in this one and I can't leave.'

She listened as he barked out requests and instructions. He represented life. She needed to be near him, to hear his voice above the sirens and screams. She took a step towards him.

'Gas!' someone from behind them shouted, and the

man turned their way then back to Ruby, his voice thick with concern.

'The pipes are blowing. Get away, girl – how many times do I have to tell you? Run for your life. You are one of the lucky ones. Run.'

Ruby stared at him. Lucky? He considered her lucky? Didn't he know what she'd seen? Didn't he understand?

A tremor of gas hissed, and the man nudged Ruby's back. 'Go! Now!'

He ran towards the building in front of them. Ruby heard a woman shout for help when another explosion vibrated through her body. The noise was so loud she put her hands to her head, but the sound continued to penetrate her eardrums. Ruby crouched down to stop herself from fainting. She looked towards the building just as it blew into smithereens. The man didn't reappear. The woman no longer called for help. Yet again, Ruby was alone.

Where now? As she looked around, all Ruby could feel was despair. She'd never experienced a loss so great and her heart beat fast and furious.

She stood back up and turned full circle. Her lungs choked on smoke, her eyes stung and watered, but she could still see a hell on earth. She'd heard enough sermons to have imagined it over the years, and now she stood in its jaws. Gripped by thoughts so powerful she couldn't comprehend all of them. What was expected of her now?

Jump into the pit? Or live? Jump or live? The words pounded through her head, then she leaned to one side and retched out nothing. She watched the living retrieve dead bodies for a while longer, when she remembered her grandmother.

Gran! She must be petrified.

Breathing as deep as she could, she gained control of her feelings and got her bearings. She ignored the hunger gnawing in her belly and moved with speed towards Kirby Road, where her grandmother lived. The usual half hour walk took twice the time due to the detours she was forced to make, and Ruby's calves ached. She turned into Kirby Road and saw it too had fallen foul of several bombs and no longer resembled the street she knew. Smashed chimney pots, cutlery, crockery and items of clothing were scattered everywhere. As in her own road, water flowed free from smashed pipes and added to the mess.

She picked her way from one end to the other, to where she estimated her gran's house to have once stood. Another crater. The scene before her was much like the one she had just left. Ruby's grandmother would never greet her with open arms and beaming smiles again. She'd also taken the full fury of Hitler's bombs.

'Excuse me,' she called out to a woman in uniform escorting an elderly man from a house still standing, which Ruby knew had once been his home. His arm was in a sling, the striped material bearing resemblance to a bed sheet.

'Fred?' she said and took a closer look at the old man. He and her gran often exchanged produce from their gardens. The man looked different. More aged, and frail.

'He's in a bad way. Shocked is an understatement. I've got to get him help. You're welcome to tag along,' the woman said.

'Did anyone leave here?' Ruby asked, and pointed to her gran's empty plot.

'If they did, it wasn't alive, my love. Not many did that side of the street. Sorry, sweetheart. Try the medical tent. You never know. But I'm warning you, don't get your hopes up. If not, try the gasworks. That's where the –'

Ruby flicked her chin upwards to indicate she understood, and to stop the woman saying the words out loud. The woman gave her a weak smile, her eyes loaded with sympathy.

'Come on, Fred, let's get you out of here before it's too dark to see.'

Ruby nodded her thanks, fighting back tears.

'You coming with us?'

Ruby shook her head at the woman and gave Fred a reassuring pat on his arm. 'You take care, Fred,' she said.

'Gone. All gone,' Fred said, showing no recognition, and he continued to repeat the words as they walked away.

16

Dazed, Ruby felt the overwhelming urge to run away from all she'd seen, to hide under a hedge on Radford Common until it was all over. Her life or the war, whichever ended first, but there was a chance her gran was still alive. She had no choice; she had to see if there was any news on the last surviving member of her family. She clenched her fists against her ears to drive out the mechanical and human noises pounding around her. Once again, her stomach growled with hunger and her tongue clung to the roof of her mouth. The smoke grew thicker and indescribable smells assaulted her senses; her heart pounded in her chest and for a few seconds Ruby thought she might faint.

Pull yourself together, girl. Gran might need you. She might still be alive.

All the while she walked towards the busy hub of medical tents, hastily erected food and information huts near the town centre, Ruby talked to herself. Forcing her legs to keep moving.

For over an hour she searched for her grandmother. Eventually, she found her name on a list of the dead. Her request to see her body was gently refused for her own sake. Ruby left the makeshift morgue and with a heavy heart made her way towards Radford Common with the intention of gathering her thoughts. She needed to think, away from the terrors she'd witnessed, and hoped the thirty-minute walk would help. Her young brother and his friends had made dens on the common, and for a few hours Ruby intended to make use of one. As she looked out onto the city darkness fell but it remained host to the endless glowing fires. Ruby doubted even the fiercest of flames would warm her through. She glanced skyward and saw a cluster of stars. Five. Were they her family, huddled together, shining out their love? Were they reunited – her parents, her brother, sister and grandmother? Ruby pondered the thought as she continued to stare. A dark cloud flitted across the stars; once again the lights went out for Ruby.

CHAPTER 2

16th November 1940

A frozen Ruby stretched out her legs and rubbed them warm. Born with her left leg shorter than the right, she despised the limp and cramping of the muscles it gave her whenever she'd walked too far. Today she experienced severe pain, but knew sitting still would not relieve her aching limbs. She massaged them, pleading with her legs not to let her down.

A shiver ran through her as she heard a loud bang. They'd endured another long night of explosions from buildings and gas pipes, and it continued into the new day. Endless screams echoed across the city. The bombing was the cruellest thing anyone could have inflicted upon Coventry.

She felt dirty, unwashed, and needed food and drink.

Crawling out from the small den, she made her way towards the public shelter. Bone-weary townsfolk sat propped outside its entrance. They stared at her, but she knew she was invisible to them. A nothing. Nobody's daughter. She walked on, heading towards the warmth of the city, a fifteen-minute walk towards the heat of death and destruction. Rows of weary travellers passed her by, all fleeing the devastation for fear of more bombings. On more than one occasion she was encouraged to join friends of her parents and other families. She muttered about later, with no intention of leaving Coventry. For Ruby, despite not having one, this was home.

As she walked past a tumbled house, she spotted a blanket lying across a tangled fence. She glanced around but couldn't see anyone, and tugged the blanket free. Draping it across her shoulders, she felt the weight of an honest parent bearing down on her. For the first time in her life, Ruby had taken something which didn't belong to her. She'd not been given the blanket, nor had permission to remove it, but she'd gone ahead and done it with no repercussions other than a guilty mind. The freezing air away from the town deemed it necessary, as she fully intended to return to her den after she'd found food.

Picking her way down Little Park Street towards the centre of town, the sight of the burning cathedral in the distance took her fears to another level. It looked no more than a shattered piece of architecture. Splintered shards of brickwork refusing to cave in to a power mightier than itself, it stood defiant in the raging flames. She prayed it would survive. It was the beating heart of the city. The residents were proud of their cathedral and she watched as men battled to save its crumbling shell.

On the corner of Hertford Street, Ruby noticed a crowd praying and sobbing; most were women with children clinging around their legs or held tightly in their arms. To one side of the gathering she spotted a family whose children she knew from church, standing in an obvious queue near a makeshift building Ruby hadn't seen before. They looked as bedraggled as she felt. She hesitated in her approach, and decided to join them for whatever they were queuing for, in the hope it was food.

'Hello, Jenny,' she said to a girl around her age but much shorter, making her appear younger.

'Ruby, oh, Ruby,' said Jenny, her voice soft, her left eye twitching. 'Isn't it awful? We lost our house. We're waiting to be taken to my auntie's at Warwick. We'll sleep on her floor. Mum's registering for new papers, and sending word to me dad we're all safe.'

She sniffled and her mother pulled her close. A pang of envy stabbed at Ruby and she gripped her hands together to remain in control of her emotions.

'Ruby, where's your family?' Jenny's mother asked.

'With my gran,' Ruby replied. 'Probably heaven.' She

didn't want to shock the woman but couldn't think of another way of wording her loss.

'Oh, my girl, come here,' Jenny's mother said, and smothered Ruby in a hug. She smelled of smoke and soot, and clung onto her until Ruby gently pushed herself free. It was her mother's comfort she yearned for, not a woman filled with pity and sadness.

'Do you know where I can find food? Is this a queue for some?' Ruby asked.

'You need to register your family deaths and get papers for yourself. I assume all is lost?'

Ruby nodded.

'Food can come later. Stand here – we've waited around an hour now, and no one will notice you've jumped in halfway,' Jenny's mother said.

'It's been a busy day,' Ruby said, and inhaled to fight off another wave of nausea.

Jenny reached out to take her hand, but Ruby gave a brief shake of her head. She could no longer bear the pitying eyes looking back at her. They stirred something inside and Ruby was wary of whatever emotion it was creating the dark thoughts each time she allowed herself to soften to another human's kindness. Her heart was bruised, battered beyond repair.

'I feel sick and weak. I can't focus on anything,' she said, distracting her from the rejected look on Jenny's face.

'Ah, of course. Silly me,' Jenny's mother said. 'Try over at one of the canteen vans. They've got tea and beef dripping batches. Be careful, Ruby, and don't forget, you need to get registered. Find a new home. You're too young to be alone.'

'What happens when I'm registered?' Ruby asked.

'They might find you a new family. Someone will take you in. If not, you will at least be in the care of someone until a permanent home is found for you. You need a roof over your head. It might be away from here too – safe,' Jenny's mother said, and gave her another hug.

Ruby removed herself from the well-meaning arms and gave a brief nod. 'I'll sort it as soon as I've eaten. Thanks. Bye, take care, Jenny.'

Jenny gave a half-hearted wave and Ruby left the queue and walked to the area where Jenny's mother had pointed.

Tea and a bread roll steeped in meat fat appealed far more than explaining her predicament to a form-filler at the beginning of a very long queue. Besides, she didn't want a new family, or to leave Coventry. The thought of being sent to an orphanage frightened her, and if she left the area she'd lose the sense of her family still surrounding her. And what if they'd survived and were looking for her? She needed to stay, to keep her eyes open for them. Registering might mean living miles away and the thought made Ruby shudder.

The best thing she felt she could do was to slip into the background during the confusion of the city, and find a way of surviving without leaving town. Her dream had always been to have an adventure of sorts and, although this was a tragedy forced upon her, Ruby sensed it was time for her to make her own way in the world.

She kicked a battered box away from her path. Life was going to become difficult for her, and she had already turned her mind to the important issue of obtaining food. She needed money. Maybe she could work off her purchases by washing up. It was worth an ask.

Entering an area set aside for food distribution, Ruby looked on in dismay. Queue after queue faced her, and all were longer than the previous one she'd stood in. At the pace they were moving, it would be well into the night, even the early hours before she would eat. She shifted from one foot to another, debating what to do. It frustrated her, knowing their shop had housed tins and packets of foodstuffs, along with fresh grown vegetables supplied by growers from nearby towns. Her energy was sapped, but Ruby thought about her gran's house. Although it was no longer standing, her gran had always kept a good vegetable patch. Maybe there were a few veg or fruit items left amongst the ruins and, though sad at the thought of returning to the bomb site, Ruby knew she stood a chance of finding something to eat without having to beg elsewhere.

'Oi. Where's your mask, girl?' a man's voice bellowed out a few feet away from Ruby. She knew his question was directed at her, as she had no mask to carry. Not wanting to suffer explaining her losses, she turned and saw a man in police uniform. She waved a hand vaguely in the direction ahead of her.

'I'm heading back home for it now,' she called out.

'Make sure you do. And your ID papers. Keep them to hand too,' the officer said.

Ruby rushed away. ID papers, ration book, birth certificate – anything official, her mother kept in a case under the stairs. With the flames flickering within the crater, Ruby doubted the case would have survived and realised she had nothing to show she even existed. Registering would be an impossible task and she was too tired and fearful to face more impossible tasks.

She entered Kirby Road and made her way to the small row of houses still standing. Each remaining property stood with glassless windows and shredded curtains flapping in the chill wind. The majority of the contents of one house lay strewn along its pathway, and the path she walked crunched beneath her feet. The road had a silent eeriness to it, and there was no one around. Ruby, puzzled by the fact, called out, 'Hello. Anyone here?'

Silence. The only noises from the street she stood in echoed across the flattened right-hand side, but human movement and voices no longer existed. Ruby shook off

25

the air of loneliness; she could not afford to dwell on it for fear of breaking down. She gulped as she walked over what had once been a happy house filled with love and baked cakes. Her grandmother cured many a tear with a slice of Victoria sponge and a strong cup of tea. Her beloved gran, lying cold in the temporary morgue. Ruby's throat tightened against the scream she wanted to release, but she needed to focus on regaining her strength. Her legs and hands trembled with hunger and cold.

She scouted around her grandmother's land, but soon came to realise that all was lost. Mangled blackout curtains were a stark reminder of hours spent in the house helping her grandmother with her mother, preparing the windows for war. Only the memory of evenings spent with the two women she loved made Ruby appreciate it had not been wasted time.

She spotted a few personal items, untouched by the bombs, and for the first time a smile flickered across Ruby's face. The items were random ones, but they'd belonged to her family. They were the only connection to them she had left: heirlooms. A colander, a blue glass powder pot with no lid, two silver forks, a bowl with pink rose patterns around the edge and a tortoiseshell hair comb. It was one her grandmother used to pin into her thinning grey bun.

Ruby also found coins amounting to one shilling,

which she placed into the blue pot. Twelve pennies would get her milk and possibly an egg or two if available, but it would certainly not help her clothing or accommodation situation. She decided she'd return and search for more once she'd found somewhere to live. The chances were her gran's electricity meter had burst during the explosion. No one would be collecting their payment for supply. The coins were family money; it wouldn't be theft.

Ruby crossed the road and walked up to Fred's and wondered how he was doing after seeing him so badly shaken. At least he was alive and in the care of someone; the woman she'd seen leading him away yesterday had looked kind and gentle.

Although she knew he was not home, she still knocked on the door. She called hello through the blown-out front window, but there was no response. She did the same to five other houses in the row. All residents were elsewhere. Ruby headed back to Fred's house, which sat at the end of the terrace, and went around to the back garden. She doubted he'd begrudge her any foodstuffs, and she'd pay him back when she was able. Only a small patch of turned over soil laid untouched by debris. She peered through the broken back window and door and then, taking a deep breath, Ruby stepped inside. Now she added trespassing to her sins. A shiver passed through her body as she stared around the home. How scared

Fred must have felt. Shelves swung downwards, their contents on the tiled floor. The house appeared worse inside than from outside, and Ruby pondered the safety of the walls. She took another look at the exterior and, aside from one or two roof tiles missing, the brickwork seemed sound. She listened. No hissing sounds unnerved her – no gas pipes releasing their explosive poison.

Ruby spotted a photo frame lying face down and lifted it away from a pail of dirty water. She rubbed away the grime on the glass, and a young couple from an era long gone smiled back at her. The petite young woman in the picture held a small bunch of flowers. A bride and groom, standing in the kitchen where she now stood. This house had been a home of longstanding to Fred and Elsie Lester. Life and age had taken Fred's wife before Ruby was born, but the enemy had destroyed their home – all he had left of the life they'd shared – and anger built inside Ruby's chest to the point of exploding into screams, and she feared once she started she'd never stop.

She'd witnessed a woman's face twisted with grief, receiving a resounding slap for hysteria, and another bellowing out a sound so guttural and raw Ruby knew the woman had lost her mind. She'd seen a man beat the crumbling wall of a house, his screams as high-pitched as any female. Their pain had been so deep they'd never recover, and Ruby closed a door in her heart to prevent the same happening to her. She locked in memories and her own deep pain so tight; each time she sensed an inkling of it breaking free she suppressed the feeling and replaced it with another. Now was the time for survival. She had little doubt the tears would find her further down the years, but for now she needed to focus on the positive side of things.

She made a decision there and then. Although she wasn't close to Fred, he'd been a friend of her gran's and he was alive. He deserved a home to come back to, and Ruby vowed she'd work and clear the old man's home in readiness for his return. He looked as if he'd suffered a broken arm when she'd seen him being led away, so she had no doubt, once fit, he'd want to come home. She'd repair as much as possible, as payment for her rent whilst she stayed there. Fred's home would survive, where hers hadn't.

Before she got started, Ruby spent time looking for anything edible. Her hands trembled with hunger, and nausea came in waves. A knob of bread and a thin slice of cheese with a sprinkle of grit sat on the side. A supper untouched; he'd probably prepared it before the siren sounded. She cleaned away as much as she could of the grit and dust, ate it without noticing flavour or added soot, and washed it down with the remains of water left in the kettle. Mains water appeared to be cut off, as did the electricity and gas. After finding a small torch, she set it to one side for the evening. Dragging a mattress still with a bottom sheet wrapped around it, and which she noticed matched Fred's sling, Ruby made herself a makeshift bed in a corner of the kitchen and then started her cleaning mission with fierce determination. A strange smoke-filled sky made everywhere warmer and darker than normal, and Ruby worked in a dream-like state.

Four hours into clearing broken items into one side of the garden, the light disappeared. She dragged a blown-off door from the left of the property, unsure if it belonged to the old man's house or the neighbour's, but it was too useful to be left to rot. She propped it across the window from the outside and hoped it would help block some of the cool wind building into freezing air. She'd placed the torch in the lower part of the room, finding its shadow and glow a comfort. Grateful for the two greatcoats she found hanging on the back of a door hanging by one hinge, she pulled one of them on. It wasn't too large around the body, nor too long. The second she placed on the bed. No longer hungry, just exhausted, Ruby climbed onto the bed and gave in to sleep.

CHAPTER 3

17th November 1940

'Next.'

Boom!

'Next.'

Crash!

Ruby, startled awake by loud male voices and explosions too close for comfort, rubbed her eyes and scrambled from her bed. She tried to peer from a smashed window to the front of the house, but saw nothing. She picked her way outside, but again saw nothing. Only distant noises filled the air and, satisfied it was a dream which had woken her, she gave in to nature as it begged her to heed its call. She snatched up a bucket from the yard and took it inside. Once relieved, she emptied the contents in the back far corner of the garden and covered it with soil. As she walked back through the garden, she spotted movement a few doors down, then came another explosion and, to her horror, the building collapsed to the ground. Ruby stood stock-still, her heart catching in her throat. She wanted to run or crouch, but her legs wouldn't move.

Was the enemy bombing nearby? The thought threaded fear throughout her body. She tried to take a step.

Boom. Crash.

They were getting closer and, if captured, Ruby dared not to imagine the consequences.

She weighed up the time left for her to gather up Fred's personal effects and leave before they reached the end of the row. She used the blanket she'd found and pulled several items into it, including two tins of Spam and a cabbage from the garden. She tied it with a length of rope, hoisted it onto her hip and moved to the front of the building.

'Halt!'

Without waiting to find out if the instruction was for her or the men in uniform she'd spotted near a truck at the front of the property, Ruby moved quickly, her mind settling on the best place to hide. She'd return to Radford Common. Escaping the enemy was a priority. She'd heard the adults discuss what would happen to young women if captured. Whispers of rape and abuse amongst the parishioners of their local church one Sunday remained with her. More than once she'd heard her mother whisper her fears for Ruby to a customer or two. The dread of those overheard conversations spurred Ruby on now, her legs bruised with the baggage she carried. Her hip, sore from the metal saucepans and precious colander, hindered the speed she travelled, but she was determined not to stop.

Once satisfied she had enough distance between her and the explosions, she looked about for someone to report the presence of the enemy, but all she saw were miles of shell-shocked people leaving the city.

Her weighty load forced her to stop halfway, and she took in her surroundings. Bombed car factories. Bewildered people. Smells which made her gag, some which made her mouth water; whichever way she turned there was something new to scare her, amaze her or turn her stomach.

Across the road, she heard another team of men shouting instructions to one another. They were clearing the building they stood next to and, as the bricks tumbled to the floor, Ruby felt a bubble of hysterical laughter brew inside her belly. Sudden realisation released the pent-up fear she carried. The men she'd fled weren't the enemy; they were British soldiers and workmen clearing the unsafe buildings. A sadness hit her hard and the pending hysterical laugher was soon suppressed. With the men clearing unsafe properties, it meant Fred's house would match that of her grandmother's, and Ruby recognised the fact she'd been rendered homeless once more. There was no turning back, and she made a decision to find the den she'd slept in after the bombing and trudged on towards the greensward.

Along the way she spotted many useful items flung far and wide from destroyed properties, and Ruby debated whether to collect some before dark fell; she also pondered whether it would be stealing from the dead – something she'd never dream of doing during peacetime.

Another gnawing bout of hunger reminded her of other important issues and she sat, thinking about her future. As the daughter of a greengrocer, she'd never had to consider purchasing food. Her mother was a good seamstress, and clothing had never been short for the family either. Circumstances for Ruby had not simply changed, they'd become life-altering. She needed paper and pencil to make a list of items required. For a faltering moment she considered registering herself homeless – family-less – an orphan. Orphan. A word she refused to recognise. She still had parents; they simply watched over her, not in the flesh but in her mind.

'Did you see the King yesterday?' Two women stood chatting nearby and they gave Ruby a fleeting glance as she crawled out from under the hedge.

'He cried. Cried for us,' one woman said.

Ruby brushed herself down and walked away. A crying King? Never. Some people exaggerated their stories. King George was a strong man, the head of the country. He'd never cry in the street in front of strangers.

A twist of disappointment niggled at her failure to have seen their sovereign visit the city, until Ruby decided he'd have nothing but words to offer her.

Everywhere she looked, queues zigzagged their way from one building to another. White, grey, soot-black and puce faces of worn-out Coventarians, who barely moved. The world worked around them. A loneliness sat heavy on her shoulders and she dropped to her knees, weakened by the senseless crime committed against her and her family – her city – and Ruby remained on the floor, organising her mind, her warrior instinct weakened by a heart-breaking sadness. She fought the idea of ending her own life, of leaving town to gain a better one, of joining others for nothing but company, but she couldn't bear the thought of people pitying her, and talking about her family no longer being alive. She tussled with so many emotions on the cold ground until she accepted she needed help, and resigned herself to registering herself in need. Uniformed men and women busied about the devastated areas. No one acknowledged her; she wasn't an unusual sight. Ruby had witnessed many like herself, tired, uninjured and in mourning. An everyday event for a city torn to shreds. Time and energy were spent upon retrieving and repairing. There was no time for pity.

Rising to her feet, Ruby recalled her father's best friend, Stephen Peabody. He'd definitely help her, and he lived nearby. She needed to tell him he'd lost his friend.

It saddened her to see history brought to its knees. The sight of the cathedral, now a shadow of itself, and trams twisted as if crumpled paper, protruding at all angles, upset her and as she clambered over the dark beams of what had once been a beautiful mediaeval street Ruby gritted her teeth and fought back, yet again, the nagging temptation of giving up the fight. It all seemed so pointless.

Upon reaching a building tucked away in Spon Street, she noticed the sign above the front window, *S Peabody, Accountant,* swinging on one nail. She peered through a small, intact pane of glass, amazed the building had escaped ruination by the bombs. Inside, a man bent over a desk; his head leaned on the surface, supported by his brow. A sleeping Stephen Peabody at his desk was not an uncommon sight. He often worked into the late hours.

Ruby tapped on the window. He didn't move, so she banged harder. Nothing. Walking around the side of the property, she turned the handle of the outer door and it opened. She let herself inside and rushed to his side. His hands were blue-grey and as she touched his cheek she felt there was no warmth, no breath moving his chest.

She sighed. Dead. Her father's friend, a man who had visited their home on many occasions, had joined the list of Coventry's dead. Would this nightmare never end?

Ruby contemplated her responsibility towards Stephen. He was an unmarried man and, as far as she was aware, his last living relative was a sister he'd argued with when their parents had died, and who now lived in Scotland. Pulling the curtains closed, Ruby slipped out of the door and made her way back to the main hub of activity. She found a man in uniform, clearing rubble near the cathedral. He looked familiar, possibly one of her parents' acquaintances from church. Ruby explained her discovery and the man laid down his shovel and followed her.

'Yes, girl, he's gone. Looks as if his heart gave out; I can't see any injuries. You did right, coming to find someone. Is he a relation?'

Ruby hesitated, unsure of how to describe Stephen. 'My dad's best friend. Dad's gone too.'

The man walked around the room. 'Anyone else here?'

Ruby shook her head. 'He lives alone – he had a cat, but –'

'Right, well, we need to get him moved. Are you able to stay here? Looters are creating havoc and this place will be stripped in no time if we leave it empty. I'll get the authorities to send a recovery team. Can you cope with that? We'll cover him with a blanket, so it won't be too much for you to deal with. You poor girl, you must have had a shock. Need me to get a message to your mum?'

Once again, Ruby shook her head.

'Just sit tight and they'll get to you as soon as they can.'

Ruby nodded and watched the man leave.

Sitting in the room with a dead body wasn't quite what she had planned, but it was warmer than being outside. She huddled onto a firm armchair and drew her knees up under her chin. She remained staring at the covered body for twenty minutes before a tap on the side door disturbed her dark thoughts. Guilty thoughts of being alive when so many were dead, and sad thoughts that shock had most probably killed Stephen Peabody. His house was intact whilst all around him lay in ruins, and yet he still hadn't survived.

Ruby let a man and woman inside. When they entered the room, the man laid down a stretcher beside Stephen and both gave a brief smile towards Ruby.

'Bert was right. Looks like his heart gave out,' the man said after checking Stephen.

The woman tutted and spoke to Ruby. 'You want to step outside, duck, or are you fine with us moving your dad –?'

'He's not my dad. He's . . . he's a sort of uncle.'

'Sort of uncle?' said the woman in uniform. She frowned and removed the blanket from the body. Her voice had a tone which disturbed Ruby, and her frown suggested something unpleasant.

'My dad's best friend.'

'Aha, I see. Where's your dad – want us to fetch him to see to his friend's place?'

Ruby stood up. She'd heard about fate. Her mother had often spoke about guiding spirits, and her father spoke of God paving the way forward for those in need. This was her moment of need, and finding Stephen was fate's way of showing her a safe haven.

'I'll deal with it. I'll see it's safe. His cat will need feeding. I can do that.'

The man from the rescue team gave a gruff cough, and the woman threw him a cold stare. Ruby knew why; she'd seen the stray animals feast in the streets, she wasn't a fool.

'I heard it earlier; he'd want me to look out for it,' she said, determined to give a reason for staying.

'Well, you knew him. Has he got papers?' The woman spoke to Ruby and the man at the same time.

They looked around his desk and eventually found all they needed in the inside pocket of his coat, hanging by the door.

'We'll register him. The authorities will need to come and inspect the house for safety, no doubt, and this address with be listed as empty, unless . . . are you living here? I didn't think to ask,' the woman said.

'I stay here at times,' Ruby said, and crossed her fingers behind her back. It was a small white lie. She had stayed there at times, but not overnight, only when her father or mother took their books to Stephen for him to check. He'd helped with their accounts and they had paid him in groceries.

'We'll leave that part then, and maybe your dad can sort out the necessary. We're off. Well done for being brave, not easy at your age, but girls are having to grow up fast during this war. Stay safe.'

As she heard the door click shut the house fell silent and Ruby absorbed what had just happened. Everything seemed like a story from a book. A horror story, and one from which she couldn't escape. A tear slithered down her face, swiftly followed by more until she could no longer catch her breath between sobs. She'd found sanctuary for at least another night, and this place held memories. Cigarette and pipe smoke from Stephen and her father playing cribbage. Hearing her father laugh when Stephen lost and had to forfeit a few coins, or a dram of whisky. A simple friendship which both men acknowledged through daily actions or a game of cards. Neither of them were sentimentalists, but no one who'd known them could ever doubt their strong bond, which stemmed from their first day at school. Ruby also recalled the scratching sound of Stephen's pen as he worked through the mathematics of their weekly earnings. And of how he'd helped her understand the muddle of learning her times table. He'd ruffle her hair and chortle out a 'well done' when she succeeded with a difficult sum. An uncle, as she'd told the woman? If that was what an uncle did to support a brother or niece, then yes, Stephen was her uncle.

CHAPTER 4

20th November 1940

Pulling the last of the small cupboards across the room back into their rightful place, Ruby stopped and stretched her back. Clearing the kitchen had proven to be quite a task for her, but the dust and soot from outside blew in each time she opened the door. During the day she'd cleaned and scrubbed Stephen's property, and at night she'd slept through intermittent nightmares and new noises from outside.

Whilst wiping down the last of the shelves and replacing the few china cups Stephen owned, a babble of voices distracted her and Ruby went to the window at the front of the house, but could see nothing. The drone of aeroplane engines throbbed overhead. She had learned the difference between enemy planes and friendly ones, and she identified these as British. She grabbed the coat she'd found in Fred's house and rushed out of the back door, locking it behind her. A Fire Warden stood on the pavement and Ruby could see he was watching a crowd of people walking past the entrance of the road. She saw many wore black armbands, and some carried flowers or wreaths. Another two planes flew overhead. Everyone looked skyward.

'What's going on?' she asked the warden.

'Burying our dead. Planes are out to stop the Jerries from attacking the cemetery. You should go. Pay your respects. Say a prayer for the dead. Think yourself lucky,' he said.

Shocked to think the enemy might attack the dead and their mourners, Ruby shuddered. 'Not all my dead can be buried. There's nothing to bury,' she said, her voice tightening with emotion.

'Oh, God, girl, I'm sorry for your loss. My boy –' The warden shrugged his shoulders mid-sentence and pinched his lips together.

Ruby watched his face flush red; she guessed his thoughts: *men don't cry. Put on a brave face.*

She'd heard the words said to her brother so often; she now realised it was true. From now on, she'd put on a brave face. Become a boy inside. Keep her emotions to herself. Hide from the world her thoughts. She'd 'toughen up', as her father had often instructed her brother, James.

'My gran's body was found, but I don't know what

there is to bury. I told them her name. No one said anything about a funeral, and I forgot to think about it. I'm not a good granddaughter, am I? I must go. You are right. Sorry about your son.'

Fully aware she'd not drawn breath throughout her garbled speech, Ruby ran towards the crowd. She pushed herself into a line of mourners and picked up their solemn pace towards London Road Cemetery. As they stood beside their dead, a soldier in uniform lifted a camera and recorded the despair of the living. Ruby watched him, and wondered how he could bring himself to do such a job. It seemed ghoulish – an uncaring act. She frowned at him as he lowered his camera, and he smiled at her. A soft smile from a handsome face, one which looked neither ghoulish nor uncaring. It puzzled Ruby, for she'd expected an older male to look back at her, not one with youthful features. She moved along with the crowd and, when she glanced his way again, he'd moved away towards the back of the cemetery and out of view.

The town buried everyone in an open grave of tagged bodies. There was no time to look and see if it was your loved one's name scribbled on the label in the large vat of beloved bones, huddled together after life, but there was time enough for someone to record their pain. All she could do was remain calm. Her duty was to pay her respects, shed tears and move forward at a snail's pace. Ruby returned her focus upon the words of the officials performing their last task for over five hundred residents of their city. Her city. This war was beyond cruel. Its actions were vicious, and Ruby pledged there and then to bring back a little joy to her small community, however she could.

Once home, Ruby composed herself and wrote to Stephen's sister. She'd put it off, unsure she'd want to learn of her own brother's death by post, but there was no other way. In true Stephen style, all was in an orderly fashion at his desk and she sat to write in her neatest hand. It took several attempts, but the final version satisfied Ruby enough to hunt out a stamp. She'd seen the postman tramping across town and had been amazed by how soon things were returning to normal practice. Water dribbled through the house pipes once again, and for an hour she'd enjoyed electricity. Every day the city moved one step towards recovery. The clanging of factories repairing themselves gave renewed hope. Warnings to boil the water were called out on regular occasions, and Ruby heeded the instructions – surviving was to be her tribute to her family.

Rereading the letter for any possible additions, Ruby knew once Stephen's sister received the letter and arrived she'd be without a roof over her head yet again. The letter was not a comfort to her, but she hoped it would comfort Stephen's sister to know someone from the city cared about him.

Wednesday 20th November 1940
Ruby Shadwell c/o S Peabody, Accountant,
Garden Cottage,
Spon St,
Coventry.

Dear Mrs McBrae,
   This is a difficult letter to write for several reasons. One, it is to inform you of your brother's death. You might not be aware of what happened, but we have been attacked in the most vicious way. Fortunately, if that is the correct word to use, he was not killed by a bomb, as my family were in the dreadful attack upon our city. Instead, Stephen's heart gave out with shock.
   My own family were killed, so I am the only one able to write this letter. Sadly, Stephen has already been buried. The council organised a mass grave at London Road Cemetery. I'll be willing to show you when you visit. Stephen's house is in good order despite the crumbling surroundings, and I am staying here to ensure it is kept safe and clean. I keep a bed aired in anticipation of you receiving this letter and coming to Coventry to sort out your brother's affairs.
   My deepest sympathy and kind regards,
   Ruby Shadwell, Miss

After posting the letter, Ruby took a walk around town. The queues still held strong, longer than ever. People wore an assortment of clothing, and held their heads high, the days of despair waning due to the united spirit to not allow the enemy to beat them down. The further she walked, she could see areas cleared of debris and personal items piled high in large mounds. She stood and watched lorry after lorry drive away, loaded with the city's rubbish. After seeing the same thing street after street, she headed towards the Council Office, the only place she could think of to find someone to speak to about the seedling of an idea. For the first time since the bombing, Ruby had a purpose in life and was prepared to queue for an answer to her question.

Three hours later a woman beckoned her to a small room. Efficient and tidy in her brown suit, the woman gave the impression of someone who could be trusted. Her blonde hair was neat with buoyant curls seated at the nape of her neck. Her skin, peach and blemish-free, was a stark contrast to the dirt and grime gracing Ruby's. For one moment Ruby experienced a sense of shame; her mother would not have approved of her sitting in such an important office looking like a vagrant.

'Please, take a seat,' the woman said, her voice soft and encouraging. A delicate hand directed Ruby to a chair with a gentle wave.

Ruby's feet and legs ached, and she expelled a deep sigh as she sat down across the desk from the woman.

'It's hard work getting back on our feet, isn't it? My name is Helen Morgan, but feel free to call me Helen. What can I do for you, Miss . . .?'

'Shadwell – Ruby Shadwell,' Ruby said, and watched as Helen frowned in recognition of the name.

'My entire family were killed – gone. There was nothing left of them. They were crushed beneath our house.'

The woman put her hand to her mouth and Ruby heard a sharp intake of breath. She continued talking, wishing she wasn't so blunt with her speech, but she needed to keep control of her emotions.

'I believe you knew my mother, June Shadwell, and am grateful for you seeing me like this,' Ruby said and tried not to speak in a monotone downbeat voice, but all strength and energy had left her in a dark mood. A fear of what was to come swamped any feeling of hope.

Another gasp left Helen's lips and she moved both hands as if in prayer to her mouth. 'I did know your mother. Very well, as it happens. I'm sorry for your loss. Your mother made my wedding dress several years ago. And I am . . . was a regular customer of your father's. I am blessed enough to have not lost either my home or any member of my family, and I cannot imagine how you must feel,' Helen said, and Ruby saw tears glisten in her eyes.

Ruby twisted the piece of damp scrap paper in her hand. She'd written notes whilst waiting in the street, but now she sat talking with someone she no longer needed them.

'I feel numb, lost. Confused.'

'I cannot register you here, Ruby. I'm a secretary manning the offices. Although I have more jobs every day. There's so much to be done for recovery. Everyone else dealing with reissues are out there, in the temporary buildings.' She pointed to the window.

Ruby shifted in her seat; there was nothing comfortable about it and her tense body ached. It was time to move the meeting along. Her future depended upon it and Helen had a long queue of desperate folk waiting outside.

'I can deal with the registering. I've come about something different. I've questions to ask about personal items lying around the streets.'

'Ask away, and I'll see what I can help with. Your family's items are yours to claim, Ruby,' Helen said.

'There's nothing left. Nothing. I borrowed – no, took, as I still have it, a blanket which had blown from a house. There was no one there, no house. When I went to my gran's I found a few things. Silly things, but they are mine, and it got me to thinking – what happens to all the other things lying around if no one claims them? Can they just be taken, collected and sold on, or given to those in need? I saw a mound of perfectly good items scooped up and put into a truck with mud and rubble. Such a wicked waste when so many have lost so much. I've an idea to set up a collection business. To repair, sell and, if possible, return to the rightful owners. It is something I can manage alone, and I've a feeling it would be useful to others.'

Helen stood up from her chair and walked to a filing cabinet. She tugged open the drawer and pulled out a form. She placed it in front of Ruby and tapped it with a manicured nail. Ruby sat on her hands, ashamed of her own dirt-ingrained ones.

'You will need permission from the owners of the houses if they are contactable before you touch anything.'

Ruby flinched and thought of Fred's photograph. She'd find him as soon as possible and return it to him. The last thing she needed was trouble with the police; she'd definitely be sent away from the city then.

'I'm not sure what the War Department will expect of me if the war continues. I'm not much use with this short leg.' Ruby tapped her thigh.

'We'll cross that bridge when need be; in the meantime, let's get you set up with the great idea you have. The white form is to apply for a trading licence. You are under twenty-one, but I'll act as co-owner until then. I want no payment. Your parents helped me, and it is my turn to help you. Red tape must not stop you from your dreams. Goodness knows we all have witnessed how quickly life can be taken from us.'

Helen placed the forms into a large brown envelope. 'The form will take several weeks, possibly months, to process, given the circumstances, but maybe you could collect items to repair in the meantime. To take things without permission would be classed as looting – a criminal offence, which carries a prison sentence. Sadly, there is a lot going on at the moment, and several people have been caught red-handed. Make sure you are not one of them, Ruby.'

Ruby gave a gasp. 'The blanket –'

Helen gave her a smile. 'The blanket won't be missed, and it's between you and me. Don't fret. Ruby, are you staying somewhere? Are you safe?'

Unsure whether to give her whereabouts to Helen as she was determined to remain as independent as she could, Ruby gave a tight smile. 'I'm looking after a family friend's house. He died, and his sister is coming from Scotland to arrange things.'

She gave away no more about her living arrangements, or where the house was. Helen might be kind and supportive, but Ruby could not risk being sent away from Coventry.

Helen tapped the white form on the desk. 'Fill it in and return it to me when you are ready. Think of a name for your business and put it in this box. Your name and address must go in this one. Once done, we can make you official.'

Ruby's heart gave a disappointing dip and rise. She had no formal address. 'What if I move house?' she asked.

'Then you inform us and we amend the paperwork accordingly. Don't worry, Ruby. I'll help you.'

Rising to her feet, Ruby held out her hand. Helen had helped remove the depressive mood and fired up her passion of wanting to succeed once again. 'Thank you. I'll get the form filled in once I've given my idea some more thought.'

'Good luck, and well done for being so brave. I'm not sure I'd be so clear-headed as you. We'll speak again. And I am really sorry about your family.'

Outside in the damp air, the cold nipped at Ruby's skin. A shiver ran down her spine and she gave herself a shake. Had she really just set herself on the path of a new business? And ensured she didn't have to leave the city? Helen had been upbeat and reassuring, and her confidence renewed Ruby's. She would fill in the form. She would make a new life for herself. It could be done.

She set her mind to speak with as many residents as she could. Stephen had always impressed the importance of good paperwork to encourage her father in keeping better records for the business. A task she would attend to once she and his sister had spoken face-to-face.

CHAPTER 5

25th November 1940

'Excuse me. Was this your house?'

Ruby approached a woman perched on an upturned metal bucket, staring at a partial end of terrace house. The exposed interior showed brown striped wallpaper, a badly damaged horse-hair sofa, and she could see the building meant a lot to the woman. Large teardrops trailed from her chin, and she snuffled into a grey-white handkerchief.

'I came back for my stuff, but I can't find a thing.' The woman waved her hand in front of her. 'I'm exhausted. Too tired to look.'

Ruby didn't like to say she looked worn to the bone, but that was exactly what the woman presented. A washed out, hollow-cheeked living ghost with black rings framing terrified eyes.

'I lost everything too. It's frightening, isn't it? Have you found much yet?' Ruby asked.

'Only bits and pieces, and I haven't got time to find more. I've got to get food for the kids. You stood in a queue yet? Murder on your feet, and nothing to sing home about at the end.'

'I've stood in one. Three hours. Listen, go and get food for your children. I'll scout around here and anything I find, I'll store . . . er . . . over there,' Ruby said, and pointed to a lopsided shed.

'That's very kind, but why? Why would you do this for me? A stranger?'

'We have to pull together. And I'll be honest with you. In a few months I'm getting a business licence to set up a shop repairing and selling unwanted items, or ones I've been given permission to salvage.'

'How do I know you won't take anything today?' the woman said, and gave Ruby a frown.

Ruby clasped her hands together, then wiped them down her dress. They would not warm up with the cold wind and fresh sleet falling feather-like to the ground. She held her right arm out and flexed her fingers in readiness to shake hands.

'Trust. We have to have trust between us; that's all this city has left. I promise – *promise* to help you. I have nothing in my life except this new idea. No family, and no home of my own. I have to wait for the licence, but was told I could approach people like yourself. You are the first and I'll be honest, at sixteen I'm finding this hard, but I have to survive, to carry on the Shadwell name.'

'Shadwell?' The woman rose to her feet. 'As in Shadwell the grocer?'

Ruby lowered her head; just hearing someone else mention her family name and business was painful. She held her breath for a moment. 'Yes,' she said.

'All gone? What a loss. Your dad gave me extras at the end of the week for the kids. I've four, and their dad's away fighting. Your dad was a good man. Church-goer like my mam. Girl, take anything broken and if you think you can fix it, sell it and get your shop going. Good for you. Brave girl. I'll go and get food for the little ones; you have my trust,' the woman said and took Ruby's hands in hers.

As she walked away, she turned back and called out to Ruby. 'By the way, what will you call your shop, just so I know what to look for if I find stuff I don't want, or something I need?'

'Shadwell's Buy and Sell,' Ruby replied. The name rolled off her tongue with ease for the first time. It came to her in that split second. It was meant to be and gave her a warm sensation of pride.

'Sounds a good name to me. Good luck.'

Watching the woman pick her way out of the street,

Ruby felt a strange sense of peace wash over her. She lifted her head skyward and smiled.

'There you all are. Watching over me. I know you're there; I'd never have thought of that name alone . . . Oh, and if you can think of how I might buy things with no money, I'd be grateful if you could let me know!'

With a light-hearted giggle, she blew a kiss to the clouds. Something had changed during her conversation with the woman. She'd found a friend. For Ruby, it was a crutch, something to hold onto during the dark, grey day – and beyond.

A fork here, spoons there, cracked plates, pillows, cushions, whole sideboard drawers were piling high inside the shed. No longer cold, Ruby worked with steadfast determination to find as much as she could for the family. Even a one-armed teddy bear lay, waiting to be reunited with its owner. Baby clothes made a large pile of messy washing, and Ruby didn't envy the woman the task of cleaning them. With limited water, it was virtually impossible to wash her own clothing, but Ruby debated taking them home, then reminded herself of the pact she'd made. To take them away was not an option but, then again, they were in need of repair of sorts, and she was allowed to take what she wanted according to that conversation.

Around two in the afternoon, the woman reappeared with her family in tow. She hitched a baby on her hip whilst the others, the eldest no older than six, ran around the grounds of what had once been their home. A little girl ran to the teddy bear and squealed with delight.

'Ah, you found Ted, thank goodness. Now maybe she'll sleep at night.'

They walked to the shed and the heap of broken items, and Ruby opened the door.

The woman gasped with delight. 'My word, you've worked hard. Look what you've found. I'll have a word with my brother-in-law and he'll come with his cart and take it to his. That's where we're living now. His wife never made it, and he needs help with his little ones. Seven kids between us. What I don't want, I'll know where it can be of use. My other sister has lost her home and moved back to my parents. Once she's in a new place I'll give them to her.'

Ruby walked to the pile of clothes. 'I'll wash these for you if you'd like,' she said, and lifted a tiny cardigan, ingrained with black soot.

'No, you take them. I've plenty between all seven of the little ones to keep me going. Sell them if you can. Grow that business.'

Smiling, the woman picked out a little pair of grey shorts. 'School shorts. My eldest's first pair. Someone will be grateful for them.'

A loud bang made both women jump and the children scream. The youngsters clustered around their mother, and Ruby stood with her hand over her mouth. A plume of smoke rose at the rear of the property.

'Another incendiary late for the party,' said the woman, her arms sheltering children like a mother hen under her wings.

'They never fail to make my nerves tingle,' Ruby replied.

'Nor mine. Come on, kids. Home. We have food!'

The excited group walked away, and Ruby watched on with envy. She gulped back dark thoughts and headed home herself.

Once indoors, she gathered up matches and headed outside again to light a small fire to heat a saucepan of water. She'd always be grateful to Stephen for his collection of tea, coffee and cocoa. More evidence her father had paid his bills in goods. Each packet wore the ornate *S* stamp of Shadwell's – one she was determined to use for her own business. The form given to her by Helen sat on the desk and, once settled with a warm drink, she entered the shop name in its appropriate box, using Stephen's fountain pen and her best handwriting. Seeing the words on official paper made her smile. It indicated another step towards a brighter future.

Keeping busy during the day helped Ruby, but the evenings were lonely and the night-time frightening. Planes flew overhead and bombs dropped in the distance. A few days previously, the Germans had bombed

Birmingham, and Coventry had held its breath every day since, waiting for more to fall on the factories returning to production of vital supplies for the forces. Car production was on hold, and everyone worked to defend the country.

10th December 1940

Each day, Ruby kept herself busy finding personal items for residents, and leaving them in boxes to be found should the owner return. After one particularly busy day, she returned home to find a white envelope pushed through the door. It was a response from Scotland. She marvelled at how quickly she'd received a response, tore it open and pulled out the contents.

Dear Miss Shadwell,

It is with regret I inform you that my wife passed away two years ago. I've sought advice about the property you mention, and it appears it is rented accommodation. With regard to the funeral of my brother-in-law, thank you for informing me. I have no desire to become involved in his affairs. I have written a second letter giving you the right to clear the property and sell items to fund any outstanding bills. We were distanced due to a rift between him and his sister, and I am not interested in any contact

with regard to the matter. Please do not write again, nor pass along my address to a third person.
  Regards,
  Thomas McBrae

Ruby read the second letter, written in the same handwriting.

25th November 1940

To Whom it May Concern,
  As the heir to my wife's estate, and she to her brother's, Mr Stephen Archibald Peabody of Garden Cottage, Spon Street, Coventry, I hereby give permission to Miss Ruby Shadwell, of the same address, permission to collect and sell personal items belonging to Mr Peabody (my brother-in-law), and use the money for any outstanding debts. Any monies remaining, Miss Shadwell is free to keep in repayment for her work in housekeeping the property after the death of Stephen Peabody.

The letter was witnessed and signed by the Reverend Burns of Dumfries, and formally signed by the sender. Ruby read through both a second and third time, and each time she realised she now had responsibilities beyond her comprehension. Where did you find a landlord of a property if he'd not already been to find out if the property was still standing? How long would it take for her to raise the money to pay for any rent Stephen owed?

Although she'd peeked into the odd drawer or cupboard, Ruby had never fully investigated Stephen's belongings. Now it appeared she'd been given permission to do just that, and more. Since the bombing, her life had become quite bizarre – beyond a believable story – yet here she was, living it each day.

CHAPTER 6

11th December 1940

'My, it's cold outside today, and not much warmer in here, I'm afraid. Sit yourself down, Ruby.' Helen Morgan unbuttoned her coat but didn't remove it, and beckoned Ruby to sit in the same seat as on her previous visit. Today, she'd risen early and was the first in the queue to see Helen. 'Do you have the form I gave you?'

Ruby nodded and with shyness handed the form to her. Helen looked them over and frowned.

'You have no address written down.'

'That's why I'm here, Helen. I don't know what to do. I wrote to the sister of the man living . . . well, he's dead now . . . in the house I'm staying at, and this is what I received back.'

She passed the envelope containing the two letters

from Stephen Peabody's brother-in-law. Helen ran her tongue across her lips as she read, then replaced the letters into the envelope and handed them back to Ruby.

'As I see it, all is legally binding. What does the land-lord say?'

'That's just it. I don't know who it is, and hoped you might be able to help me find out. I still have to register for a ration book, Identity card and everything else I've lost. I'm scared,' Ruby said, and chewed on her bottom lip to stop herself from crying. Confessing she was scared and speaking out about her lack of papers had taken every ounce of courage. She waited whilst Helen walked around the room, blowing on her hands as she did so.

'I understand, but I thought you were going to deal with this, Ruby. Give me your details. I'll get the paper-work sorted out for you. Where is it you are staying?'

'Peabody Accountants. He was Dad's best friend. I found him dead.'

'Not pleasant for you. I remember Stephen, and heard he was one of the unfortunates. Not pleasant at all. Right, why have you left it so long to register yourself, Ruby? It's not that difficult.'

Ruby looked down at her feet.

'Ruby?' Helen said, and sat back in her seat.

'I don't want to leave Coventry. A friend's mother told me I'd go into care or another home somewhere. I can't . . . I won't leave my family.'

Helen gave a slow nod of understanding. 'But your family aren't here, Ruby. I'm confused. At our last meeting you were ready to start again.'

'You've heard my idea. I want to keep the Shadwell name alive. To have a business just like Granddad and Dad. They were proud of this city, and I don't want to leave. If you fill in the forms I might –'

Helen held up her hand, indicating Ruby stopped talking and listen.

'It will mean you have a right to stay here. We'll put down the address you are at for now, and it can be changed when you move out. If the landlord hasn't been around to check on his property, then there's a chance he's from out of town. This is to your advantage as it will be some time before they realise the rent hasn't been paid. Or they have a private collector to collect on their behalf and, with so many dead, well, who knows, they might have not survived. Leave it with me. I'll do all I can. When I have news, I'll call on you. I promise. Do you have food in the house?' Helen asked and pushed a pen and paper towards Ruby.

Ruby scribbled down her previous and present address, full name and date of birth.

'I've plenty of tinned foods, and someone gave me milk for sorting out their property the other day. I've learned to go without it in my drinks; it was a real treat. Fresh and creamy.'

'Right, well, you take care of yourself, and please, do not think me rude, but what about clothing?'

With a shrug of her shoulders, Ruby looked down at her coat, glad it hid her one outfit.

'It's due another wash, I know, but this is all I have –' she gave a cough '– I'm wearing a pair of Stephen's underpants and a vest. I wear one of his shirts and an old cricket jumper when this is drying. I have no fire. I'm not sure about gas pipes in the street. They blow up so easily.'

'Stay here,' Helen said and left the room.

Ruby sat watching snowflakes hitting the window; it was to be another cold night and soon she would be unable to retrieve any goods from nearby properties. The Anderson shelter in the garden of the cottage made an ideal storage room, and it was already a quarter full of broken items waiting for repair.

The door swung open and Helen came back into the room and handed Ruby a bulging pillowcase.

'Inside you will find four pairs of knickers, all new. A cardigan, vest, blouse and skirt – not new but in good condition. You are a little smaller than my daughter and I'd put these in our back room for distributing to those in need. I think they'll do you a turn. And here's a small loaf to tide you over. All bakeries are closed, except for the one on Maudsley Road. My mother can share ours,' Helen said, and waggled the bag in Ruby's direction.

'I'm grateful – thank you.' Ruby took the gift from Helen and clutched it close.

'It's the least I can do. I'll sort out the papers for you and, as I said, will drop by when I have news. Now, get yourself home before the weather sets in and you get soaked. One thing before you go. Do you know if your parents had a bank account? Most business people do, but some preferred to mattress stuff and not trust banks.'

'I don't know. I counted the end of day money and handed it to Dad; after that he dealt with it. I can't recall going to the bank for him. He was a bit funny about money, so the chances are he hid it in the travel trunk we were never allowed to touch,' Ruby said.

'Hmm, shame. The bank might have held money in his name. Mind you, we'd have to prove you are his daughter and, without papers – Wait, were you christened?'

'Yes. We all were. Why?'

'It will be recorded in the parish records. Unless, of course, they were destroyed. The same with civil documents, recording your family. There will be copies – birth certificates and such. Leave it with me. One step at a time; we'll sort things out, don't you fret. Now, as I say, head home and stay warm. And you're sure you've enough to eat?' Helen said.

'Yes, and thanks. Thanks for everything,' Ruby said and hesitated. She wanted to ask more about the bank, but changed her mind. It would keep for another day; Helen had done more than enough for her, and other people were outside, waiting their turn for the next available slot.

As she exited the building Ruby noticed the clouds scudding overhead and threatening to drop more than a few flakes of snow. In her arms she clutched the new clothing bundle from Helen, and hurried home to try them on, excited at the prospect of having fresh things to wear.

A rush of memories caught up with her and she let them flow as she walked home. She recalled the pretty dress her mother had made for her sixteenth birthday in June. Green paisley with a yellow sash. She'd worn it on for the church summer party after the fete, along with white gloves, shoes and a yellow ribbon for her hair. She'd watched Lenny Barnes blink and stare at her as she'd walked towards the church doorway. Lenny often declared her as his girl, and she would retort with a dismissive put down which always ended with a wink from the tallest boy in school. When they left, he made it his duty to escort her to and from the church dances, and Ruby always ensured another female friend tagged along. Ruby had never had many close friends as she preferred her own company and attending the dances was under sufferance, just to please her mother. Her father had no say over Lenny's protection of his daughter, but always gave a speech prior to them leaving the house. Lenny had left Coventry with his parents when war broke out and Ruby missed his humour. She also missed how he'd made her feel special in her new outfit – a precious gift she'd never see again.

Before melancholy could set in, Ruby walked faster and thought of what room she needed to investigate next. She only just made it inside before a torrent of hail dropped to the ground. Winter was edging its way closer, adding to Ruby's concerns. The coal store looked full enough, but the fear of exploding gas pipes prevented her from lighting a fire indoors. On the sideboard in Stephen's office she'd stood Fred's photograph and she reminded herself to find him and return it the following day. The weather didn't invite a second visit outdoors. She had a lunch of thinly sliced bread from the small loaf with a smearing of some fruit jam she'd found in a cupboard. Stephen had certainly received a variety of gifts from his customers; she'd found pickles in old jam jars, and more tinned food than was allowed on a ration card.

After she'd eaten, Ruby made a start on the paperwork in the office. She created piles of official-looking papers to take to Helen and ask her to find the appropriate people to deal with them. Whilst she was sorting them out, she came across a file with her family name written in one corner. She lifted the many papers inside and laid them onto the table. Most were scribbled notes from her father and notifications from Stephen, all relating to the business. She also found papers from the savings bank on Hertford Street. They suggested her father held an account there and Stephen paid in money on a regular basis. It made sense and she laid them onto the pile to take to Helen the next day to see if she could find a way of accessing the account on Ruby's behalf. If her father did have money for the grocery business, she might be a beneficiary. The thought excited her and she made plans in her head as to where she would set up business in the city. Daydream after daydream kept her company as she packed away the papers. Once finished, she moved upstairs.

Ruby stepped inside Stephen's bedroom. She'd been inside before to find temporary underwear, but this time the room carried an air of sadness about it as she was to clear away his belongings. His clothing was of fair quality, with one suit barely worn. Ruby guessed it was his Sunday best. A drawer of pullovers and knitted waist-coats proved useful, as four of the seven fitted Ruby and she kept a dark navy one as another warming layer. Socks were also placed in a pile for her own use, as were a pair of brown corduroy trousers and a set of braces. Working on the bombsites, Ruby often scraped her knees and the trousers would be ideal for workwear.

With the clothes sorted into piles, she wrapped and

tied them with old newspapers, took them downstairs and placed them to one side for the outside storage room. On the top of the pile she placed Stephen's brown fedora hat, but almost immediately changed her mind and put it back on its hook. It seemed disrespectful and Ruby hoped the landlord would make good use of it, as it looked relatively new.

A loud bang and crash startled her as she carried the last of the packages down the stairs and she lost her footing on the bottom step, causing her to stumble to the floor. The noise came from outside and she listened in the darkness of the hallway to deep muffled voices outside the door.

Looters!

Ruby remained on the floor, afraid any movement would alert whoever was outside to the fact there was someone inside. After a minute or two, it dawned on her to make herself known, and then word would be out that Garden Cottage was not empty. She had no candles and the light faded fast, but she recalled seeing an oil lamp in the corner of the second downstairs room, just off the hallway. She crawled into the room, feeling her way around until she touched the lamp. She went back to the kitchen, found matches and lit the lamp, keeping it low. Persuading her shoulder-length curls to settle under Stephen's hat, she slowly opened the side door and lifted the lamp.

'Who'sa'?' she called out in a gruff voice, the deepest she could muster, and made the two words roll into one. It hurt the back of her throat, but she held back the tickling cough which threatened. She banged a saucepan lid against the edge of the lamp, unsure why, but hoped the noise would add to the threat she tried to offer the intruders.

She saw two shadows at the bottom of the pathway leading to the garden; both loomed large and masculine. Ruby, not wanting to get into a physical confrontation, went back inside, leaving the lamp on low at the kitchen window and the hat on her head. If the men were looking for trouble, it was best they thought a man was inside. The thud of their feet running past the door told her the ploy had worked and she let out a breath of relief.

Then she stopped. She'd lit a lamp and the house hadn't blown up. She glanced over at the fireplace. She'd cleaned and prepared it in readiness for when it could be used. The fire would be so helpful for many things and, before she talked herself out of lighting it, Ruby struck a match and held it to the paper in the grate.

A large pan of water sat on the flames and Ruby's clothes waited in the sink for a dousing of hot water. A wooden clothes horse propped around the fire overnight would dry them in no time. Ruby placed a tin bath beneath them to catch the drips. A scraping of washing soap would help with the soaking process, and give her another change of clothes. Helen was a kind soul and, yet again, Ruby felt guided by a parent in the right direction. She lay by the fire on a makeshift bed; the heat was not to be wasted.

As she drifted off to sleep, Ruby thought back to the days of working for her father, and of chatting with customers whilst tidying the shop. She yearned for those days again, even a stern lecture from her father on how to present the produce in their crates and how to safely stack tins on their shelves would be welcomed. News of her licence couldn't come quick enough.

CHAPTER 7

12th December 1940

'First in the queue again, Ruby?' Helen said and gave Ruby a beaming smile.

'Second today. And thank you for the clothes; they fit me well enough. I found a couple of Stephen's pullovers and look –' Ruby opened the front of her coat to show off her ensemble.

'Very . . . um . . . chic,' said Helen, and both laughed. Ruby's clothing was a mishmash of colours, but warmth and comfort came first. Stephen's socks were long on her legs and the skirt fell calf-length and between them they kept her legs from freezing.

'What's that you've got there?' Helen asked, and pointed to the packages in front of Ruby on the desk.

'Papers I found in Stephen's office. I think they need

to be seen by someone with knowledge of accounts and passed along to the relevant people. This pile is mine.'

Ruby waited for Helen to sit in her seat across from her and she unravelled the string holding her package together.

'They are to do with Dad and the business and, would you believe it, he had a bank account.'

She passed the papers one by one to Helen, who read each one and placed them to her side. When she'd finished glancing over the last one, she looked up to Ruby and then back at the paper in her hand.

'Have you read these, Ruby?'

'Some, but I haven't read them all properly.'

'Well, as you say, they are your dad's, and they do relate to business. Two businesses, in fact. One the grocery shop, and the other as a landlord – Stephen Peabody's landlord. Garden Cottage belonged to your father and, according to this, he rented it to Stephen.'

Ruby frowned at Helen and took the paper from her. She read it and laid it back down on the desk. 'My dad owned the building – is that what you're saying?'

'I am. He did.'

'How come we didn't know?' Ruby said, and ran her fingers through her hair. 'Mum never mentioned it, and I went there for lessons enough times. Are you sure it isn't that Stephen owned the grocer's and we paid him rent – wouldn't that make more sense? I know we paid rent. I heard them talk about it often enough.'

Helen shook her head. 'It's there, in ink and binding. Stephen paid your father rent to live in the house. It was probably never mentioned as, with no disrespect, Ruby, it's not the sort of thing children need to know. It does mean we have to sort your papers out and we find out about getting your inheritance sorted officially. There's money in the bank, according to these. They are statements of the account. Stephen was a good tenant and paid on time.'

With a shudder, Ruby stood up and began pacing the floor. 'It does explain why the landlord's not been around for rent. I've waited for them to knock on the door.'

Helen gave a smile and chuckled. 'In a way you've been waiting for yourself, Ruby.'

Ruby responded with a grin. 'I suppose I have, but I'm not silly; I know I have to prove who I am and that it was Dad's place. What happens if I can't?'

Helen tidied the papers and took a brown file from her drawer; she placed the papers inside and wrote Ruby's name across the front.

'I have a good friend, a solicitor. I'll track him down and ask his advice – with your permission, of course. But, in the meantime, say nothing to anyone. Sadly, there are a few ruthless people taking advantage of the vulnerable since the bombing. Keep yourself to yourself. If you need help, come here or this is my address.' Helen scribbled it down on a piece of paper and handed it to Ruby.

'Thank you. This will change my life. Help my plans. If Stephen was alive, he'd explain and I know he'd look after me. Thank goodness I went to find him or I'd never have known. I'm not traceable, have no papers, nothing.'

'Ruby, if I am right about this, you will have a lot more than you realise right now. You will have premises to sell from, and a home. And again, if I'm correct, a tidy sum of money in the bank. I suggest you go and stand in a food queue today; fresh bread and milk arrived in town and there'll be a scramble for them. You won't need a ration book; take this letter from me if you are asked for any type of paperwork. It explains your situation.'

When she left Helen's office Ruby knew she'd found a friend, not just an official body willing to help, and she allowed some of the fear she held close free with a large sigh.

CHAPTER 8

20th December 1940

'Hello, Fred,' Ruby said, and sat beside the frail man staring out of the window. His lank grey hair drooped over his weathered face, and his hands trembled in his lap.

Ruby had tracked him down to a private lodging in Cheylesmore, after a day spent checking medical tents, the morgue and finally the hospital, where they'd told her he'd been taken in by a friend of one of the nurses.

'Fred, do you remember Gwen Blake, your neighbour from Kirby Road?'

With slow movements, Fred turned from the window and faced her. His arm was no longer in a sling, but his face bore the scars of recent wounds.

'She was my grandmother. I'm June's girl, Ruby. June Shadwell, her daughter?'

Fred's hand reached out for hers. His eyes filled with tears. 'Gone. All gone. I saw her fly,' he said and he gripped her hand tighter.

Ruby realised he'd witnessed her grandmother's death, and sat in silence whilst the old man allowed his tears to fall. She watched his lips tremble and the pain of what he'd witnessed flow with each tear.

Men do cry, but it takes death to free their pride. There's nothing I can say or do for him.

'Ah, you found him,' the woman who'd let her into the house said as she brought in a tray of tea. 'Got you a cuppa, Fred.'

Rising to her feet, Ruby helped clear a small table for the woman to place his cup.

'He's rather sad, I'm afraid. I think he saw my gran die, and I've reminded him.'

The woman touched her shoulder. 'It might help him to sleep better now he's shed a tear or two. All this brave face nonsense. If you've been through hell, why on earth can't you show it?'

'I feel the same, but sometimes we have to hold back and be strong for others,' said Ruby.

They shared a smile and sipped their tea in silence. Fred reached for his cup.

'That's it. A nice hot cuppa will make it better,' the woman said.

'Is he going to stay living with you?' Ruby asked.

'For a while,' the woman replied, 'but I can't have him here for ever. He needs a better home than this one, but I'll do my bit until it is found.'

Fred slurped his tea and held out his cup for more. Ruby obliged.

'I've brought you your photograph, Fred. I rescued it from your house,' Ruby said as she poured the tea. She waited until he'd finished his drink and handed him the picture, wrapped in an old tea towel.

Fred blinked, looked at the package and back up to Ruby.

'It's a special one, I could tell. Your wedding day?' she asked as she unwrapped the picture.

He snatched the photograph from her hands and stared at it, then stroked the glass front. His hands trembled. Looking back at Ruby, he clutched it to his chest and continued looking out of the window.

'He hasn't said a word since he arrived. You've done him some good,' the woman said.

A sharp snore from Fred made them both smile.

'It's done the trick,' said the woman.

'Where will he go from here?' Ruby asked. She watched Fred's chest rise and fall as he settled into a peaceful snooze.

'I've no idea. He doesn't appear to have family. You're his first visitor, aside from my friend at the hospital.'

'This war is cruel,' Ruby said. 'I've a lady, well, she's

a friend now, helping me with important things. I can ask her about Fred's future for you. Can I visit again next week?'

'God willing, yes,' said the woman.

Ruby frowned.

'If the enemy allows us next week. I'm fearful every day I open my eyes.'

'I know what you mean, but I'm not focusing on that any more. I'm going to build myself a future. Hitler won't stop me,' Ruby said, defiance in her voice.

'Ah, the optimism of youth. I bet your parents are proud of you,' the woman said.

'They were, and I'm sure they are watching me grow stronger each day, but we just can't communicate it in words, only thoughts.'

'You've lost them. Both of them. I'm that sorry . . . Oh, you poor girl. Me and my big mouth.'

'It's painful, but I need to talk about them. I say things and get upset because I've embarrassed someone, but it's the way I cope. Don't be sorry for me. I was lucky; they gave me a good start in life. I'm building a business to carry on our family name,' Ruby said with pride.

'Time for another cup of tea? I'd love to hear your plans. Aside from Fred, some days I don't get to see many people for a natter.'

For another hour Ruby sat explaining her idea, and left for home with a small basket of bric-a-brac to sell once she opened Shadwell's Buy and Sell. The woman applauded her idea, and Ruby walked home with another spinning inside her head.

25th December 1940

The tiny Christmas pudding sat on its plate in front of Ruby. She sliced it across the middle and placed a portion into another dish. The smell made her mouth water as she poured a small dribble of watery custard. Although she'd called it a Christmas pudding, it was more like a marmalade suet sponge.

The smell transported her back to the previous Christmas. No matter how hard she tried to ignore the memories, she could not help but think back to the days she'd spent embroidering a tray cloth for her grand-mother, a pinafore for her mother, wrapping a twist of fudge, hidden inside hand-knitted mittens for her siblings, and restoring a pipe stand for her father. She'd sanded and polished it until the perfect grain of wood shone. His face had lit up when he'd seen it, and he'd immediately placed his four favourite pipes in the appropriate holes and stood it beside the hearth. Every gift offered to her family had received a rapturous shout of glee. Ruby, in turn, had received a new hair ribbon and band, a pair of pink lace gloves which frilled at the wrist, a small bottle of peach perfume and a small raffia handbag.

She remembered the smells of the day, the laughter, the joy of listening to the King give a slow, deliberate speech of reassurance about the onset of war. They had stood united in the best parlour and held hands. When he'd finished, they'd hugged each other. What she'd give to have that day again. The fear had been there still, but so was her family.

Today, her Christmas was shared with Fred, who sat snoring in his chair by the fire. He'd moved in with her two days previously. She knew she'd taken on a great challenge, especially if she had to find a new home for them both, but he represented the last link with her grandmother, and he needed her just as much. They'd enjoyed a meagre meal; she'd purchased a small piece of beef with his meat ration.

She watched him sleep, grateful for the occasional snore reminding her she was not alone. He looked so peaceful and she wondered when she'd sleep for more than two hours of a night without waking herself from a bad dream. She envied Fred.

'Pudding, Fred,' she said and gave him a gentle shake of the shoulder.

He gave a yawn and broke free from his snooze with a last snort, rose to his feet and sat at the table. 'Looks good,' he said.

'Simple but filling. Next year we'll have a proper plum pudding with creamy custard,' Ruby replied.

'This is tasty enough. Better than nothing,' Fred said and shovelled a large spoonful into his mouth.

Ruby remembered he'd probably been without during the Great War, and so her pudding effort was appreciated. She opted to do the same and appreciate what she had in front of her.

'You're right; it is tasty, and better than nothing. Fred, there's a bottle of rum in the cupboard; I found it when I cleared out papers. Would you like a tot? I know Dad enjoyed one at Christmas, and recognised the bottle, so I suspect it was a gift to Stephen last year.'

Fred scraped his spoon around his dish and ate the last spoonful. He leaned back in his chair. 'A small rum would be acceptable, considering the day. Thank you. And Ruby, thank you for your company. You remind me of your grandmother – generous and thoughtful. You look like her too, but a taller version.'

Handing Fred his drink, Ruby giggled. 'I think everyone was taller than Gran. She was a tiny thing.'

'Feisty, though. I've seen her chase off a grown man for ill-treating a dog, and that man ran for his life,' Fred said and laughed.

'She loved animals, but would never keep one as a pet.'

'Talking of pets, did you hear that cat again? I thought I heard a meowing in the yard earlier this morning.'

'Not since yesterday. I'll keep an ear out. Stephen had a cat, so there's a chance it ran away after the bombing and has found its way home. Ooh, look, time for the King to say his piece,' Ruby said and turned on the radio. They both stood as the National Anthem played. When the King spoke of Christmas being for children, no matter where they might be, the words hit Ruby hard.

At the end, Fred gave a huff of indifference. 'A happy Christmas. We've coped, but can't say either of us, nor any of them poor buggers – excuse the language – fighting are having a happy one, and some won't ever again. Words are all very well, but this war needs to end. We were told it would be over by now. What's the point of carrying on living? Politicians. Pah.'

He drained his glass and Ruby held back from offering him another. His flushed cheeks and fired up temper told her she'd been generous enough the first time around.

'It's tough for us all, Fred, I agree, but we have to find a way forward. Tomorrow, I'm going to write a list of the stock I've collected. I'm going to label it all with the street and, where possible, the number of the house I found it, so if anyone claims it as theirs I can give it back. If not, I'll sell it on. You can help and polish a bit of brass for me, and I'm sure you're a dab hand with a screwdriver and paintbrush. We'll make it work, Fred. Me and you, we'll get through this.'

His aged hand with its long bony fingers laid across hers. He gave her a wan smile.

'I'll try for you, Ruby. I'll keep going for you.'

CHAPTER 9

12th January 1941

'Will it never warm up, Fred?' Ruby opened the door into the house as she spoke. Fred followed.

'I don't think there's been a warm day since November. Everyone says the same. Jimmy the barber wore gloves to cut my hair yesterday. Roll on spring . . . What the . . .?' Fred stumbled into Ruby, forcing her forward, and she just managed to prevent herself from dropping her packages.

'It's too icy for you to come with me today, Fred. Stay home. Work on that old clock I found. What on earth is that?' she said, pointing to a large moving mound under a blanket by the fire.

'It's a ruddy cat,' Fred said, lifting the blanket to reveal a large tabby cleaning itself.

'It's Stephen's cat. She's come back! A warm welcome home to you, Tabs! I saw a couple of rats roaming yesterday. If you do your job, then you get to warm by the fire.'

'Size of that belly, it's either eaten one of them already or it's going to produce a family in a few months.'

Ruby went to the cat and touched its rounded under-belly. 'In that case, she can live in the shed, not in here. I've a box and rags. Do you really think she's pregnant, Fred?'

Fred nodded and picked up the cat. 'I'll put her out and make her comfy. Not a fan of them myself but, with the number of rats running around, you're right, it can earn its keep.'

Ruby watched him leave the house. She knew his words were hot air. He cooed and coaxed the cat as he walked to the shed and she knew she'd have a job on her hands getting him to part with the kittens when they arrived.

Every day she went out salvaging and if Fred didn't go with her he sat at home repairing or cleaning their findings; they worked well as a team.

Word had reached others that Ruby intended to set up shop, and not a day went by without being approached to buy something. With limited money, she encouraged them to wait until she was formally trading, but they were welcome to store and add the item to her catalogue.

The catalogue grew on a daily basis and Ruby kept her fingers crossed she'd be approved for the licence.

February saw her dream come true.

5th February 1941

'Fred! Fred! It's arrived. The licence has arrived!'

Ruby trod with care along the icy path to the shed, where Fred was seeking out his next project. She pushed open the door and he beamed up at her.

'Who's a bright button this morning?' he said and pulled out a box of various bits and pieces.

'We're in business. Shadwell's Buy and Sell has a licence to trade. Isn't it wonderful?'

Fred grinned and took the paper from her. 'This is the best news we've had for a long time. Well done, Miss Shadwell. I suppose we'd best clear the room you call the office and open up that front door area.'

Ruby nodded. 'I also think we need a proper workshop section for repairs, but we'll make do in the back room for now.'

After a day of reorganising, Ruby and Fred sat relaxing by the fire.

'A job well done today, Fred,' Ruby said and leaned back in her chair.

'Certainly was. Any idea when you want to open the shop?'

'According to Helen, the bank has authorised a small payment to help me get back on my feet. She's agreed to be my guardian until I'm twenty-one; isn't that wonderful?' Ruby said. 'I'll be able to open by Valentine's Day. Oh, Fred, I'm so happy for the first time in a long time.'

Fred struggled to his feet and saluted her. 'Ready for duty and proud of you.'

Ruby jumped from her chair. 'Come here, you silly fool.'

Scooping him into a great hug, Ruby felt a sudden rush of human contact, something she'd missed since losing her family. The embrace of another gave her hope for the future.

'I'm officially adopting you as my granddad,' she declared.

Fred eased himself away from her arms. 'If I'd been blessed with a granddaughter, what a wonderful thing it would have been to have one like you. I'm honoured and return the gesture,' Fred said and cuffed away a tear.

Guilt washed over Ruby but she quashed it as soon as she could. Her family were still her family; she'd now added an extension – someone who needed a family of his own. Companionship was vital to their recovery and Ruby intended to make Fred's last few years as comfortable as she could. The enemy hadn't beaten them; it had given them a new path to follow.

14th February 1941

'Ready?' Helen asked Ruby as they stood admiring the new shop contents.

A nervous Ruby nodded her reply.

'Let them in – most are nosey buggers' said Fred.

'Fred! That's no way to talk about our customers,' said Ruby, and flicked her hand across his ear in jest.

'Oi. Cheeky.'

Helen held up a pair of scissors and pointed to a length of yellow ribbon across the doorway. 'Here we go then,' she said and pulled open the front door.

A crowd of eager faces, the majority with dark circles under their eyes, stood in eager anticipation.

'Hello, everyone. Thank you for coming along to support Ruby today. I'm sure you'll agree she's shown initiative with her new business venture, and those of you who knew her family will want to wish her all the very best. It is now my great pleasure to announce Shadwell's Buy and Sell open,' Helen said and cut the ribbon.

In true British style, the queue moved patiently into the large room, oohing and ahhing as they browsed the items on display. Ruby stood back and watched with pride.

A large woman approached her. 'Ruby, I noticed the tags. This was my old house; this dish was my mother's.'

A rush of pleasure ran through Ruby's body and she opened a large drawer in the desk now sited at the far end of the room, housing a large till Helen had purchased as a gift. Ruby pulled out her book and ran her finger down the pages until she found the code number which matched the tag.

'Yes, here it is,' she said and crossed out the item using a ruler and pencil. Neat and tidy was her father's motto, and she intended to keep her books in such a way.

'How much?' the woman asked.

Ruby shook her head. 'Gracious, nothing. It's yours. I'm happy for it to be returned to its rightful owner.'

'Well, you aren't going to make much money doing that, duck. Let me pay you something; you had to do the dirty and dangerous bit of retrieving it for me. And all the hard work of cleaning it and storing the darn thing. It's ugly but it was my mother's, and we haven't got much left to call our own.'

'A penny. I'll take my first penny from you,' Ruby said, and in a louder voice she called out to the others in the room. 'If you find your address and an item which is yours, I'll take a penny for my efforts. If it isn't yours and there is no label, then it is the price marked.'

A buzz of voices shared their approval.

Helen smiled at her and walked over to the desk. 'I must go. I'll call in at the end of the day and see how many pennies you've earned.'

The woman with her dish placed a penny in front of Ruby. 'Good luck to you. I'll be back when I get paid. I've a fair few things needed for my new home.'

Fred kept Ruby supplied with cups of tea and a sandwich at lunchtime. By the end of the working day, he came to her and saw the last of the customers leave. 'I'll pull the blinds and turn the sign. Helen will come around the back. I'll have a sweep up and tidy whilst you count your pennies. What a turnout, and you look exhausted.'

'Tired but happy, Fred. So many items returned to their rightful owners, and they were so thrilled to have them back. It made my heart sing whenever anyone clutched something tight to them and declared it as a family heirloom.'

Fred clicked the lock above the door and turned the key. 'When you gave me my photograph I felt like that, Ruby; you gave me something of my past but also my future. You did the same for a lot of folk today. Well done. Now, get your books in order, for I think tomorrow will be another busy one for Shadwell's.'

CHAPTER 10

March 1941

With her business growing and the joy of reuniting people with family items, Ruby quickly gained a reputation as someone to be trusted.

The scrapman, Bill, proved to be a friend and reliable source of trading. He'd bring her salvageable items in return for her unwanted goods. No money changed hands. Slowly, the house filled to the point of bursting.

Helen heard of a building where the owners wanted to let it out as they were leaving the city. She'd spoken on Ruby's behalf and a peppercorn rent was agreed. The couple were impressed – and touched, by Ruby's efforts and kindness. Another chapter in her life was about to begin, and Ruby embraced it with great enthusiasm. Her leg ached, but she struggled through the pain. Once the physical work was over, she'd have the opportunity to rest.

Bitter winds didn't stop Ruby's enthusiasm on moving day. Once again, Helen and her ribbon and good wishes were called upon to decree the doors of Shadwell's open. Chamber pots, saucepans and jewellery came and went, all recorded and ninety per cent paid for this time around.

Just as Ruby went to turn the closed sign, a small voice called out, 'Wait up missus.'

Ruby grinned back at the boy through the glass. He waved his arms and his grubby face made her heart lurch. His eyes wore a worried look and Ruby swung open the door and ushered him inside.

'What can I do for you, young man? Are you hungry, lost, need help?' Ruby said as she knelt down to look him in the eye. Her hand resisted the urge to sweep the curl of red-brown hair drooping over one eye, leaving the deepest chestnut one free to look back at her.

'Me auntie's lost everyfing 'cept this,' he said.

'Ah, you are selling, sir. Well, that is serious business. Let's go to my desk and have a look at the goods,' Ruby said, adding a teasing note to her voice.

The serious-faced child clambered onto the seat facing hers. He knelt to see over the top. Ruby guessed him to be no older than five years, and it was obvious he'd suffered during the Blitz. He had a bruised cheek and a healing cut across his eyebrow. His bottom lip sported a scab from another gash.

'Show me. What are you selling? Your auntie's, you say?'

The boy nodded and handed over a silver bracelet. It was a narrow band with intricate markings depicting a vine twisting its way around the bracelet. Ruby thought it beautiful.

'It's very pretty. Your aunt must be sad to part with it; I know I would be. I'm not sure of its value, though. I might have to get a professional to take a look and then give you the fair price.'

With a quick shake of his head, the boy reached for the bracelet. 'She needs food today. And she's got rent to pay. We didn't get bombed out and the landlord wants his money,' he said.

Ruby found him older than she'd first thought. 'How old are you?'

'Six,' the boy said. Ruby hid a smile as he lisped the word. Two missing top teeth didn't help him with pronunciation.

'That's a great age to be. Do you think your auntie might be better off keeping it and having a word with the landlord? It seems a shame she should sell her jewellery –'

Ruby stopped in her tracks as the lad burst into tears. She rushed to his side and knelt beside the chair. 'Whatever's the matter – er . . . what's your name?'

'T-Tommy, miss. Tommy Jenkins.'

Ruby handed him her handkerchief. 'Why the tears, Tommy?'

'I'll be in bother if I don't take back some money. We're living with her and she's strict. Nasty to me mum. We moved 'ere from Isle a Dogs when Dad joined up. We 'ave to stay 'ere now 'cos 'e wrote an' asked me auntie. I 'eard me auntie say she 'ates me mum for it, 'cos her brother married an Irish woman. She don't like kids neiver, so Mum 'as to move out soon. We ain't got money though.'

As she looked at him, cuffing a snotty nose against a rough black jacket too short in the sleeves, Ruby came to the conclusion that this was a moment when she had to make a serious decision. Children of this age shouldn't have to hear cruel words against their parents. Nor should they be homeless. Tommy was carrying the weight of the world on his shoulders.

'I've never heard of the Isle of Dogs, but I bet you miss your old home. I know I'd miss this place.'

'It's in London. I come from the capital city of the country. Learned that at school on me first day. I miss it every day,' Tommy said between sniffles.

Touched by his story, Ruby turned the bracelet around in her hand. She liked it for herself and, although she had no idea of its value, to the child it meant far more. He'd not get into trouble and he'd eat. She could afford to treat herself, and had already considered creating a collection of her own for any future family she might be lucky enough to have – when she was married and old enough, it was her dream. To settle down. Coventry was too important to her to leave. The spirit and blood of her family had been spilled here; it stained the soil of a beating heart which Ruby clung to, for her sanity.

'I'll give you two pounds. If it isn't a fair rate your aunt will know and come tell me, I'm sure. She sounds a tough one. Now, tuck it into your pocket and dry your tears. Run along – it was nice to meet you, Tommy. Stay safe.'

The child scrambled from his chair and gave her a grateful smile. He looked nothing more than a raga-muffin, but Ruby fell for his charm. As he scampered away down the street, she watched him and knew she'd done the right thing, but her heart broke as she remem-bered another young boy. His gangly legs splaying out as he ran towards her with his arms wide open in read-iness for a swooping swing. Ruby snatched at her chest and a small cry of angst left her lips before she could quell the pain. The loss of her little brother and sister had sneaked up and nipped at her heart when she'd least expected it, and seeing Tommy had opened a raw wound.

'You all right there – are you hurt? Can I help?'

A startled Ruby looked over from where the voice projected itself; it wasn't an accent she recognised. She saw a young man in uniform step into the doorway. He beamed out a smile, one which begged to be returned. Ruby dried her eyes and gave a half smile.

'Tommy –' she pointed to the back of the little boy, jumping over bricks '– reminds me of my brother . . . he's dead.' Unsure why she'd confided that snippet of her private life, Ruby gave a brighter smile, not wanting to put off a potential customer. She'd seen the camera around his neck, and recalled his face from the community funeral. 'Can I help? I'm closing shop for the day, but can stay open a few more minutes if you want to browse.'

The soldier stepped closer, and held up his hand. 'I won't keep you. I just wanted to ask if you knew when the next bus leaves town. I've missed my train.'

Ruby closed the ledger she'd written inside when she made her sale to young Tommy, and gave a short sigh. 'I'm afraid you've missed that too.'

'Oh. Really? I was due to return to London tonight.'

'I don't recognise your accent as a London one,' Ruby said.

The soldier gave a laugh. 'That's because I'm Canadian. From Canada.'

Ruby, irked by his last remark, replied with deep sarcasm. 'Really? Is that where Canadians come from?'

With both hands up in surrender, the soldier gave another of his beaming smiles.

'Forgive me. I wasn't being patronising.' He put his arms down and held out a hand for her to shake. 'Jean-Paul Clayton, but you can call me John – my friends do. My family stick to the formal.'

Ruby took his hand and felt his firm grip. 'Ruby Shadwell. Nice to meet you, John.'

His fingers wrapped around hers and she looked into his face; he gave a slight wink and Ruby sensed a warmth rush through her skin. She hoped her face was not as red as it felt. The man was handsome, and Ruby doubted there was a woman who would argue it wasn't the case. His eyes shone, and their handshake lingered beyond what was usual for two strangers meeting. Ruby was disappointed when he pulled his hand away and pushed it into his pocket.

'I'll have to find somewhere for the night if that's the case. A guest house, bed and breakfast. Maybe you know of one?'

Unable to think of a place in Coventry which would not be full or destroyed, Ruby suggested one or two she knew of out of town, with only a twenty-minute walk. It was windy, but not raining. Weather a soldier could handle.

'I'm grateful to you, Miss Shadwell.'

Ruby watched John walk away. Then he turned around, waved for her to stand still and photographed her in the doorway. When he lifted the camera for a second time, she giggled and closed the door, retaining her own image of him. Of one of the most handsome men she'd ever spoken with – the first male she'd ever noticed as desirable. His photograph of her would be black and white, but her image of him was filled with colour. Brown eyes, dark hair, neatly cut, tanned skin and a white smile beneath full lips. A sharp jawline, tapering to a neat chin, with a slim neck and not a sight of a protruding Adam's apple. His voice was velvet-smooth and natural, not forced to be suave, and the way he'd thanked her was as much a caress as his fingers might have felt on her cheek. It was deep, with a husky tone. She'd heard and looked up in a dictionary the word sensual, but now she understood its physical form.

Ruby felt shaken by the way a young man, in his twenties at most, she guessed, had affected her heart rate. She felt daring and in need of a small adventure. He'd brought something new with him, a slight air of mystery, and she wanted to learn more about him. It wasn't every day she got to meet someone from another country. She turned the key in the lock and called out to him. 'Soldier . . . John. John Clayton – wait. I'll walk you through the streets to the main road. It's not easy to find your way out of the city.'

After she said the words Ruby felt a little foolish. Here was a soldier who'd found his way from another country to Coventry, and she expressed concern about him trying to find his way to the end of the road. This time she knew the blush was there, burning beacon-red and showing him her naïve ways.

'That's mighty kind of you – thanks,' John said, and Ruby liked him even more for not dismissing her as a foolish girl. She tried not to rush and stumble as he waited for her to join him.

'Is Canada safe from the war? From the bombs? I haven't got a clue who's attacking who, and where in the world. Ignorant but, to be honest, it's enough dealing with what's going on here, in my own city – country,' Ruby asked as they picked their way through the bombed-out streets.

'We're in it, but nothing like this. I cannot imagine Toronto being brought to its knees like Coventry. We are a resilient race, and I'd like to think we'd handle it as well as you all have, but it frightens me to even consider we'd suffer an attack on such a scale.'

The silence which fell between them gave her a chance to suppress the string of questions she wanted to fire at him, but as they trod closer to the point she'd have to turn around and leave him, she couldn't retain her curiosity any longer.

'I saw a picture of Canada once. Nothing but snow for miles, and so deep! I've never seen snow so deep! Is it like that every winter?' Ruby exclaimed, lifting her arms to show an imaginary heap of snow above her head.

'It gets cold, I'll grant you that. Colder than Britain – Scotland. Double figure minuses. I ski when I can, but sometimes even I baulk at the depth of snow and the cold.'

Taking it all in, Ruby envisaged herself trying to ski, and laughed. 'I can't imagine stepping out in such temperatures, let alone enjoying a sport in them. I'm definitely sure I'd not like the cold, but I do love the spring. Is Canada seasonal?'

'Yes, and springtime is my favourite season – in both countries. Britain has such glorious spring days, and I love to sit and take in the calm it brings with it. I witnessed the prettiest spring in Yorkshire; it will stay with me for ever.' John's voice sounded wistful, and Ruby wondered how much of the fighting abroad he'd seen. She didn't like to ask, and let him continue talking without interrupting; she found his voice soothing. 'Maple trees in Canada bud and bloom, and tell us the winter has long gone. I miss walking through Allan Gardens. A visit to the greenhouses can transport me to a warmer place on a damp day.'

'You'll have to drop by the shop and tell me more about where you live. Fred would love to chat with another soldier. He fought in the last war, and I know he'd share one of his stories too.'

'I'll take you up on that, Ruby. Fred – is he a friend or your grandfather?'

'Kind of both, I guess . . . yes, both. Since Christmas.'

John pulled a face, suggesting he did and didn't understand. Ruby just smiled back.

'What did you do, before the war?' she asked.

'Banking. Mundane work. It paid well enough, but photography is my dream. I want to own a shop with a gallery, to capture the beauty of the world we live in – after the war, of course. I want families to gather and smile back at me once more. All I see at the moment are haunted faces.'

John's voice faded away with his last sentence. Ruby understood only too well that vision.

'You'll do it one day. I wanted to own a shop, and look at me, sixteen and a half and a business owner,' she said with pride in her voice.

'It's yours?' John's voice held an impressed tone.

'My name is on the licence, yes. I have a guardian, Helen. She keeps my legal things – legal.' Ruby shrugged with the words.

'Impressive. A hard worker with brains and beauty. I'm in good company.'

Unsure of how to handle the compliment, Ruby gave a quiet giggle. 'This shop, or gallery of yours – will it be in your home town in Canada?'

'Probably not. I've family to consider, but Britain has captured my heart too. It has such history and incredible architecture. I feel a connection with my ancestors here.

When the war is over, I'm going to make the biggest decisions of my life, I'm sure, but I'll definitely choose England if I ever choose to leave my home.'

'Lucky England,' Ruby said with a cheeky grin. The flirtatious words slipped out before she had chance to suppress the thought.

'Lucky me, if all the girls in England walk you to the end of the road.' John's reply was followed through with a wink.

Ruby sensed another blush, but had little control. She flicked her hair and said nothing.

At the junction, she stopped. A sinking feeling in her gut told her she'd enjoyed the last of his company, and she pointed out the direction for John to take.

'This is us, then. Turn left after the postbox. I know of four guest houses along that road, and I'm sure there'll be a space for you. If not, return to Garden Cottage, Spon Street, and Fred will help find you somewhere.' Ruby didn't like to say she'd find him a space in her home, it was far too forward for a first meeting, and for a young girl to suggest to an older man.

'Thank you, Ruby. I'll see you around.'

John held out his hand, and Ruby didn't hesitate to shake it goodbye; she wanted the physical contact with him again.

'I hope so. I really would love to learn more about Canada in the springtime.'

She watched him stride away. Tall, well over six foot; his back was upright and straight and his body swayed with a relaxed rhythm. He walked with a purposeful stride, not a swagger.

'Drop by the shop any time,' Ruby called after him.

'Will do,' he shouted back.

Ruby smiled to herself. She'd gone out of her way to walk with John and, although her leg ached and she still had to walk home, it had been worth the effort. He fascinated her with his quiet, calm ways. Other soldiers she'd met walking through town were loud and leery. John behaved with good manners, and she was reluctant to let him disappear without finding out more about him. What little she'd learn she'd live with and what she didn't know she'd make-believe.

CHAPTER 11

When Ruby arrived home she noticed Fred seemed quiet and distant. He didn't chat during their evening meal as normal, and only seemed half interested as she relayed the story of Tommy, and of John seeking accommodation. She didn't mention she'd walked half a mile in the wrong direction with a stranger. Although she was tempted, just to get a reaction from him.

'Are you feeling all right, Fred? You seem unusually quiet tonight,' she asked when he appeared to not be listening to another of her stories of the day.

'Would've been our anniversary today – fifty-five years. Mine and Elsie's,' he rattled off and picked up his plate and took it into the kitchen.

Ruby put her hand to her mouth, saddened and annoyed with herself; she'd not noticed Fred's mood first thing that morning.

'Tell me about her,' she encouraged. 'How did you meet and fall in love? Only if you want to, of course. But you know I love a great love story.'

'She chatted as much as you do. S'pose that's why we get along. Don't take this the wrong way, but to me she was the prettiest girl alive and you are a looker, Ruby, so that will tell you how beautiful she was,' Fred said with a soft smile.

'I know she was. I saw your wedding picture, remember? She was tiny too. I'd tower above her,' Ruby said, pleased Fred had relaxed and cheered up a little.

The rest of the evening was spent chatting about Fred and how he'd met his wife, Elsie, when he worked at a bicycle building factory and she worked the canteen trolley.

It was love at first sight for both of them, and they'd courted for several years before committing to marriage. A marriage which lasted two years before Elsie was struck down with a disease which baffled the doctors. She'd lost weight and soon her mind wandered. Fred said she became spiteful and it broke his heart, as she was the gentlest of women. They were never blessed with children, and Fred never found another woman who would be fitting to take Elsie's place in his life. When he finished speaking Ruby understood how love could last if you had the right person in your life. The thought of love at first sight fascinated Ruby and she'd often deemed it impossible – until John had walked into her life and she'd got an inkling of what attraction towards the opposite sex felt like. It amused her that whenever she thought of walking out with a man, the image was now of Jean-Paul Clayton. His name was a mouthful when said in full, but sounded so romantic whenever she sounded it out in her mind. In such a short time he'd turned her thoughts from war to romance, and Ruby enjoyed the distraction.

'Let's clear this away. Pudding was tasty, by the way – clever idea, sweetening the rhubarb with the mashed carrot,' Ruby said and picked up the dessert dishes.

'And then it's your turn to tell me about your family. Your grandmother was quite a character. I was fond of her as a friend. I miss her humour, but often hear it in you. Your mother had her ways, but gained a more sober side to her after she married. Like your father,' Fred said.

Settled in their usual seats for the evening, Ruby sat and began sharing her memories.

'Life was busy with the shop, and Dad's love of the church. Mum joined in the women's groups, and I can remember her making the costumes for a show in the community hall when my grandfather was alive. He was dressed as a rather large elf; Gran was a smaller version. It was quite a shock, as my grandfather was a stubborn old man, with little humour. Goodness knows how Gran got him to dress up. Dad didn't go for the funny side of life, and Mum tolerated his moods. But, with this particular show, she stood her ground and he had to help with making the background for the stage. He was good at that sort of thing.'

Fred rubbed his chin in thought. 'That was your mum's dad?' he asked, and Ruby nodded. 'Wasn't his father an artist as well as a greengrocer? I think I remember your gran saying he was away with the fairies at times. Might explain your dad's stern outlook on life.'

'Grandfather Shadwell was a miserable man. Never had a kind word to say to me or Mum, and would never let the two youngest near him. Dad said we must show respect, but it was hard to be pleasant to an unpleasant person.'

Fred gave a 'hmph' sound, banged his pipe against the fireplace brickwork, sucked against the stem and refilled the bowl with a scoop of tobacco, lit it and drew in and puffed out.

'I think the last war – and this one will do the same – it changed men. Women held us together, but we had to defend them and the country. An enormous responsibility, especially for the young. The married men with families – well, it tore them apart inside. When they say no news is good news, that isn't true for a soldier fighting in mud and blood.'

Ruby watched another spiral of smoke escape his lips.

'I would have thought it would make them soft-hearted, not mean.'

'Depends on what they saw. I know when I fought, thoughts of my own safety never existed. I fought for family back home, but had to become tougher to cope.'

Ruby gave a slight shake of her head. 'I can't imagine how that must have felt. The Blitz has given me a little insight, but to have to shoot someone face to face, and when you've not a violent bone in your body . . . frightening. I've become tougher, thanks to our enemies, and had to grow up faster than planned, but I'm not convinced I could kill. I'd be useless on the front line.'

'I hope you meet someone who will be kind and let you soften again. When this war is over, grab life with both hands and never look back. Hold onto the memories but don't let them drown your future. I've learned it isn't being disloyal. It's a compliment to those gone before us, that they gave us something to live for – to remind the world they once existed,' Fred said, his voice gentle and with a smile creasing his eyes.

Ruby's heart went out to him; he gave her guidance with lessons he'd learned the hard way.

'Some existed only five months ago. Sometimes I pretend they've gone on holiday and will burst through the door spilling sand from their suitcases and sharing shells from the beach. In my mind they're in Cornwall, just a few hundred miles away.'

'Ah, that'll come when you have children of your own. You wait. We'll go to Cornwall together. Why Cornwall? Have you been before?'

Ruby rose to her feet and went to the sideboard across the room – a room transformed into a cosy retreat from the busy shop. Both she and Fred had cases with their valuable papers and treasures beside their beds but, other items she came across, Ruby kept in a drawer she'd named her 'one day' drawer. Inside were images of clothes she'd like to wear, of houses she'd like to live in and places she'd like to visit for a holiday. On one of her searches she'd found a magazine which featured sandy beaches in Cornwall, and it sat in the drawer. Scruffy, torn and singed around the edges, it represented Ruby's partial image of her future. She'd yet to consider who she'd share the future with.

'I found this. Look, doesn't it look beautiful? One day, Fred. One day I'll let you walk me down the aisle too, so I can have my children to take with us, but for the moment we'll make do with this picture. I'll cut it out and frame it for the wall, over there. It will fill the gap. What the . . . what's the matter? Fred, are you ill?' Ruby asked and rushed to Fred's side. Without speaking, he continued to sob into his hands. A heart-wrenching sound escaped his lips and Ruby held him close. 'Tell me. What's wrong – are you in pain?'

Panic raged through her body. Her heart rate speeded

up as she clung to him. His sobbing continued and his breathing came fast and furious. His body sunk into hers, limp and sapped of energy from the emotional outburst.

'I'm sorry, Fred. We shouldn't have talked about Elsie. It's all too much for you,' Ruby said and a teardrop rolled from the end of her nose onto his head. She released one hand and wiped it away. Fred's arm reached up and he laid his hand over hers. Slowly they separated. Ruby was relieved he'd stopped crying.

'It's you, not Elsie. My tears are for you,' he said and blew heavily into a large handkerchief.

Ruby rocked back onto her heels as she remained kneeling beside him. 'Me? I made you cry? I'm so sorry, Fred. It's the last thing I'd ever do. What did I say wrong?' she whispered, scared of what his reply would be as she went over the conversation in her mind.

'You want me to walk you down the aisle,' Fred said.

'Of course I do. You are my granddad now; it's your duty,' Ruby said, adding a flippant tone to her voice in the hope of pulling him from his miserable state.

'I'm old, Ruby. You are only sixteen,' he said and held up his hand. 'I know, seventeen this year, but you are still young, and have a long way to go until marriage. We have to be realistic. Don't hold onto me as part of your future. I am your here and now.'

Sitting on the floor and pulling her legs into a more comfortable position, Ruby stared up at him. In such a short time they'd formed an incredible bond, and now he'd reminded her of their age difference – of what life could do to them at any point. To be parted from him would be as painful as losing her own flesh and blood. No words could cover over the truth in what he said, so she sat in silence.

They allowed the silence to wash over them until Fred found the strength to stand up and stretch his legs. 'We needed this evening. It helped,' he said and left the room.

Reminded of his words about grabbing life and of how the war destroyed happiness, Ruby curled into a ball and as she thought of her future it reduced her to tears – the tears of a child moving into a woman's world. A world with an unknown outcome. A time in her life when nothing made sense, and fear rode over hope, and hope over fear. She had a knot of anger where only a short while ago there had been calm and a sense of well-being. The war had tainted her world yet again, and Ruby struggled to see how she could ever move on with her life – how to find love without the pain.

CHAPTER 12

7th April 1941

Ruby stared out of the window. An overcast grey sky slowly gave way to a few rays of weak sunshine, then quashed them as fast as they arrived. A shower fell and cleared up in minutes. Spring struggled to show itself, but the garden had burst into life and Fred worked tirelessly to grow food.

Picking up her bag and a thick cardigan, Ruby went in search of Fred. He was never far from the garden or the cat and her kittens. The kittens had been born during a spring storm and Fred sat with Tabs the whole night. From that day, Tabs followed him much like a dog would its owner, and now the two kittens tagged along. It was a comical sight.

'Fred, I'm off. Are you coming down to the shop with

lunch or shall I take something with me?' she called out, but got no response. Then she heard Fred talking to someone in the shed. Puzzled, she pushed open the door.

'And this one is called Patch. See, it's got a black patch behind its ear –'

'Oh, hello. I wondered who Fred was talking to,' Ruby said, and smiled over at Tommy, stroking the white kitten with a black blotch on its back.

'I found him loitering outside at the end of the jetty.'

'Eh, jetty? We ain't near the seaside. I was down there,' Tommy said, and pointed down the side of the house. 'Down the alleyway. It was a bit nippy.'

Ruby frowned at him. 'What do you mean about being near the seaside? A strange thing to say.'

'Jetty – 'e got 'is words in a muddle. 'e meant alley, that bit there.' Tommy pointed to the side walk way.

'You make me laugh. That's its name – the jetty. It's an alley where you come from and a jetty here,' Ruby said.

'And you mek me laff. Laff. Why don't you say larf and make?'

Fred laughed so loud the kittens scampered off. 'Listen to the pair of you. The war of the accents.'

'Yours is funny,' Tommy said indignantly.

'We'll beg to differ. I take it you've come to tell me your aunt is unhappy with her money for the bracelet.'

Tommy jumped to his feet and held out his hand to

the struggling Fred. They looked a comical pair, but it touched Ruby to see the boy had manners and was thoughtful.

'Nah. She's given me summat else to sell. Said you was genrus.'

'That London accent is something else, boy. Slow down and I'll understand you by the end of the day,' Fred said, and ruffled Tommy's hair.

'I've just realised. What are you doing here, Tommy? How do you know where I live?' Ruby asked.

'Saw you in town the ovva day, and followed you. Don't know why. Just did. I was bored out me brains.'

'You should have shouted. We could have had a chat. Why are you so bored?'

'Auntie kicks me out when Mum goes queuin'.'

'Walk with me. I'm heading off to the shop. You can tell me about your life in London,' Ruby said and lifted the kitten from his lap. 'Let this one feed from his mummy now.'

She smiled at Fred over Tommy's head. 'Bring lunch around twelvish, please, Fred? Put extra in; we've got a guest. Carry this bag for me, please, Tommy?'

'Yeah. Put summat for me in the lunch bag, Fred. I might be 'angin' around if she gets me started on a job.'

Ruby laughed. 'You are the guest, Tommy, but you're also right about earning your lunch. Come on, no dawdling.'

By the time they reached the shop Ruby had learned the difference between a batch and a bread roll. Bread rolls were proper rolls, eaten in London – Tommy would not accept the word batch for one – and Ruby couldn't understand how people in London ate eels in jelly. She'd learned most Londoners lived next to the King of England, and had trains running underground. For a young child, Tommy had a wealth of knowledge and used all the air in his lungs to get it across. Ruby didn't have an opportunity to speak until they'd unlocked the shop's front door.

'Before we get busy, show me what you have to sell today.'

From his pocket, Tommy pulled out a tatty scrap of cloth and opened it to show off a pretty brooch. It was inset with pale blue stones and was shaped like a silver bird.

'This is beautiful,' Ruby gasped.

'Me auntie says it's gotta go. So whatcha gonna give me?'

'I'll give you another two pounds. It's worth more, I'm sure, but I'd have to get it checked over. Maybe, if your aunt –'

'Nah, I'll take it – the two pounds, I mean.'

'I'll add another to that if you'll stay and tidy a shelf or two, and sweep the floor for me. It will help Fred out too. And tomorrow I'll take you to the Memorial Park and you can help me turn over soil and plant veggies. I volunteer on a community project up there – on the allotments. It'll keep you out of your auntie's hair and earn you a coin or two. What do you say?'

Tommy shrugged and turned his head to one side, giving her idea some thought. 'I ain't comin' if it's rainin',' he said.

'I ain't goin' if it's rainin',' Ruby said, mimicking Tommy's accent.

'Oi, you ain't takin' the mick, are you?'

Ruby laughed. 'I wouldn't dare, Tommy. I wouldn't dare. Can you reach the Open sign?'

''Course I can. I ain't no shorty. Me legs are longer than me mates' – the ones in London. I ain't got any 'ere.'

'What – legs or mates?' Ruby teased.

'Now you're bein' silly,' Tommy said. He turned the sign and opened the door to a woman waiting outside. 'Mornin', missus.'

The woman stared at him walking back to Ruby and glanced up to Ruby with an amused look on her face. 'New member of staff, Ruby?'

'Hello, Mrs Price. Yes, this is my helper for the day, Tommy. He usually lives next door to the King, in London, but he's staying with his auntie here in Coventry. Fred will be by later. He's fixed your watch.'

Ruby pulled a chair out from the back room and

offered it to the large woman she'd first met when clearing her yard near Eagle Street. Her husband never survived the blast of a gas pipe, and her daughter lived the other end of the country. Ruby had helped her compose a reassuring letter to send to her daughter to let her know her mother was safe and not to try to get to the city. Fred had taken to talking with her and a deep friendship had formed. They were two friends in the last few years of their lives, juggling with the struggles of war and ageing.

'Ta, duck. My feet are killing me. Chilblains. It's so cold in my place. I can't light a fire.'

Tommy moved around the room with a brush and dustpan. 'I can teach you. Me mum showed me,' he said.

'That's kind of you, little man, but what I mean is I'm not allowed. Too many broken gas pipes in the area, and my chimney is badly damaged.'

'Ah, you need a good chimbly for a good fire. See, the kindlin' won't fire up,' Tommy said and carried on sweeping, unaware the two women were struggling to remain composed. Beatty had resorted to ramming a fist into her mouth and Ruby was bent double in the pretence of looking for something by her feet. Eventually she couldn't control the laughter any more.

'I'll make us a nice cuppa, Mrs P. Back in a minute.'

'Call me Beatty, for goodness' sake. You make me sound old.'

When Ruby returned with a tray of drinks and three biscuits on a plate, she saw Beatty reading to Tommy. It was a calming moment of normality. It seemed a shame to interrupt them.

'Tommy, carrot juice and a biscuit?'

Tommy scrambled to his feet and took his glass and biscuit from the plate offered.

'Ta,' he said and sat on the floor with his legs crossed.

'Beatty?' Ruby said.

Beatty nodded and took her cup and saucer. 'Tommy can have my biscuit,' she said.

'It's his lucky day. I was going to give him mine, but we'll put them back for another day. They might not have rationed them yet, but they are hard to find at the moment. Fred enjoys a bit of baking and he'll be here with lunch soon. I have a feeling there will be something made with carrots coming our way. There's not a day goes by where we don't get treated to something carroty,' Ruby said and giggled.

'Rationing is going to get tougher, so I hear. Clothes next, apparently. That's where you'll do well, collecting and repairing. Don't give them all to the ragman,' Beatty said and slurped her tea from the saucer.

A customer entered the shop and Ruby greeted her. 'Feel free to browse, and there's the notice explaining the tags attached.'

Tommy rose to his feet and put his crockery on the

table. He took the outside broom and swept the front pathway. 'Hello, Fred.'

Ruby watched as the pair greeted each other. One as tall as the broom, the other as thin.

'Friends for life, that pair,' she said to Beatty.

'Don't let the lad get too attached. Fred's old, and –'

'Please, Beatty, don't,' Ruby said and held up her hand to stop Beatty from speaking.

'Be realistic, girl.'

'Tommy is only here for a short while. He'll be long gone by the time age has taken Fred from us. Let them enjoy each other's company.'

'True enough. Goodness knows we have so very little to take comfort in at the moment. Who am I to prevent a friendship? Ignore me. I just worry for Fred, that's all – and you.'

'Don't worry about me, Beatty. My life is ticking along and, thanks to Fred, my lonely days are a thing of the past. I never mixed much, but it is nice to have someone moving around the house.'

'I know what you mean.'

The rest of the day was spent cleaning and pricing new items and by the time Ruby turned the Closed sign she had no regrets about setting up the business. Tommy left with his money tucked into his pocket and Fred returned home to heat the oven in readiness for his meat and potato pies.

Ruby decided to visit the ruins of her old home on her walk back. It would be the first time since the November bombing and she was unsure whether she'd make it all the way to the crater or whether the pain would still be too much for her to bear.

CHAPTER 13

Clearing teams still moved around the city streets and the noises drowned out birdsong; there was nothing beautiful left to lift their spirits. As she approached the vicinity of her old home her nerve faltered. She saw that it had been fenced off, and it irritated her to have a barrier between her and her family. Undeterred, Ruby lifted the barbed wire and wood to one side and entered the area marked as dangerous by several signs. Once through, she dropped to her knees, scouring the area for a hint of her family, for something to make her understand the sickening reality of it all. She sat dangling her legs over the edge of the deep hole, unafraid of falling in, but hoping familiar faces would draw her to them and comfort her in the darkness of their new world.

A movement from across the site caught her attention and from the corner of her eye she spotted a man in uniform. Her heart pounded with excitement. It was John Clayton. He stood with one leg on the ground and the other balanced on a floored chimney pot. He lifted both arms and held out a black box. Each time she moved she was aware of the camera covering his face. Ruby remained seated, talking to her family. Let him take his photographs. Let him record her anguish and share it with the world. If he could take pictures of a young girl breaking her heart over the death of her family then he was as hard as the pilots who had dropped the bombs. She had no time for the likes of him when others were tearing their hands to shreds trying desperately to right the wrongs.

She kept her eyes on the crater, not wanting him to see the tear snaking its way down her cheek. Once she'd composed herself, she turned to face him. He lifted his hand in greeting and made to move in her direction. Ruby shook her head and held up a hand to prevent him from coming to her. She stood up, moved away from the hole in the ground and scooted under the barbed wire. Halfway across the bombed-out street, she saw him disappear behind a wall which had once been the interior of the house belonging to a pair of newlyweds. Ruby recalled the laughter from the house when the couple had been decorating. They'd moved in four days before the bomb had dropped and killed them. On display was their chosen colour and wallpaper in the latest fashion. Wasted. Destroyed.

As she turned behind the wall she saw John leaning against it as he smoked a cigarette and when she gave a slight cough he glanced her way. His facial expression was not what she'd expected. A deep sadness stared back. He looked tired, and his jawline showed a hint of growth.

'Hello, Ruby. How are you?'

'Well, thanks. You?' Ruby knew her voice was clipped and over-polite, but she still smarted at him photographing her at such a private time.

'Tired. Seen a few things I can't un-see that keep me awake at night, but I'm happier for seeing a friendly face. Although, is it a friendly face?' John asked, and mimicked Ruby's scowl.

'Did you take many?' Ruby asked and pointed to the camera.

'A few.'

Ruby gave him a tight-lipped stare and crossed her arms with displeasure. 'It was a private moment.'

'I'm sorry if I invaded your privacy. I didn't think until it was too late. When you turned around, I could see I'd been wrong to photograph you here,' he said, his voice soft and genuine. Almost a whisper.

'Why? Why did you feel the need to take pictures of my grief?'

John moved to his camera, perched on a concrete slab, and lifted it to his face and, before Ruby could prevent him from taking the picture, he'd clicked the button.

'It's my job,' he said, and discarded his cigarette, grinding it underfoot.

Ruby watched and shuddered as his large black boot snuffed out the red glow. All thoughts of ants and the enemy were swiftly suppressed.

'Job? But you're in service uniform, and is it right to do that –' she pointed to the camera '– when the person is in front of you? Shouldn't you ask first?' Ruby could hear the indignation in her voice.

John raised an eyebrow and gave what Ruby took to be an apologetic smile. 'We record the war. I'm recording it for the army – the Canadian Army, to be precise. I'm part of the Canadian Military Headquarters, based in London. They decided, as I'd missed my train, I could stay around here and record the Blitz damage a while longer.'

'Why here? I know why for Coventry. I mean England.'

John took another photograph, this time of smoke spiralling across the rooftops of the houses ahead. Rooftops without roof tiles, chimneys unable to accommodate fires. He turned back to speak and Ruby saw his job was more than just taking photographs; it was a passion for remembering what might have been before the destruction.

'It needs to be on record. Another war? We never expected it, and we have lessons to learn. Folks back home want to know what's happening over here. Many are originally from Britain, or their ancestors were; some of mine came from England, which is why I wanted to see it for myself.'

Ruby noticed his voice remained soft, almost apologetic.

'Will they see me – in your collection?' she asked, her voice also soft. There was an air of calm around them and, although she'd been angry before reaching him, she was now curious about the kind of work he carried out.

'They will.'

'But, as I said, it was a private moment with my family.'

John looked about and then looked back at Ruby. His face wore a puzzled crease across his brow.

'They're not here. They've gone. They're at the bottom of the crater . . .' Ruby pointed to where she'd sat when he first saw her. 'It might be fenced off, but that land used to support my home. My parents, little brother and sister are crushed beneath it all. The Shadwell family plot is not in the cemetery. Gran is, but the rest are here.'

John's shoulders sagged as he expelled a breath. He put his hands behind his head and paced up and down in front of her.

'I'm so sorry, Ruby. Truly. I never gave it much thought when you said you were alone and had built your own business when we spoke the other day.' He pointed to her legs. 'I noticed you limp quite badly. Is that how you injured your leg?' His voice was loaded with concern.

'No, I was born with one longer than the other. Or shorter, whichever way you like to say it.'

'There I go again, me and my big mouth. I'm sorry for being so rude,' John said, and Ruby saw his face flush with embarrassment.

'Believe me, others have been just as rude.' Ruby dismissed his words with a wave of her hand. 'This job you do, it captures the horrors of war. Not easy, but do you ever know what you are looking at?' she asked.

'Not always. There are times I've wanted to know but dared not ask, or I'm alone, with no one to explain,' he said.

'I did wonder. I can help you here, as the wall you've leant against was the home of a bride and groom – married just a week. The wallpaper is the latest one in green. Now look at it, spattered with soot, water, mud and . . . well, their blood. Photograph it, keep it to remind you of Eagle Street, Coventry, England. The place you saw inside of me – '

Ruby's words came in a rush and she sensed the heat in her cheeks. It was time to leave before she embarrassed herself in front of the man who made her heartbeat skip and jump whenever he looked at her.

'I must go. Fred, my grandfather, will be worried. It was nice to meet you again. Take care.'

Ruby walked away, hoping he'd not stare after her and just see her limp. For the first time in her life she resented the notion that a man would consider her a cripple. Wanting another sneak look at John, she turned back to give a polite wave goodbye and smiled when she noticed he was taking photographs of the wall. He was a listener, a man who understood emotion – qualities Ruby admired.

CHAPTER 14

8th April 1941

Grabbing her case and yelling for Fred to get his, Ruby raced to his room. The siren blasted out the warning of enemy planes heading their way; the ear-splitting sound was exhausting. Adrenalin pumped around her body and her nerves tingled with fear. She tried not to show it, and knew Fred felt the same.

The sirens gave out their eerie whine and alerted them on a regular basis now the winter weather had passed, but no one took them lightly. Ruby and Fred always headed for safety, and tonight was no different.

As fast as Fred could walk, they headed to the Anderson shelter, now fully cleared of her collected items. Once settled under blankets, they waited for the all-clear.

'That young Tommy is a bit of a character,' Fred said with a chuckle.

Ruby laughed with him. 'He certainly is, and his accent, well, if the King sounded like that, no wonder they wanted him to have speech lessons.'

'Do not disrespect the King, Ruby,' Fred reprimanded.

Knowing it was wise not to respond, Ruby sat in silence. Outside was a different story and she and Fred moved closer to each other as the first bomb echoed out around the city. The walls of the shelter vibrated. Bomb after bomb dropped, well into the early hours. Memories of the last time they'd experienced such a violent attack churned around Ruby's insides. Fred trembled as they held each other close. It was not the time to hold back the fear; they needed to claim comfort from another human being.

Once the all-clear sounded, they ventured into the garden, not knowing what they might see. The house stood firm and they looked at each other and sighed out their relief, but exhausted and terrified of what they might see beyond the walls of their sanctuary.

'Well, we were lucky this time,' Fred said, and opened the shed to let the cats out. They meowed around his legs.

'Nice to be wanted,' Ruby said. 'I must go, Fred to see . . . out there – the shop.'

'You go. I'll follow on.'

More fires, craters and devastation greeted her once she stepped out onto the main area of Spon Street, and Ruby dared not breathe for fear of inhaling some of the thick black smoke surrounding her. She coughed and choked her way to the shop. One pane of glass had a minor crack, but Ruby could see no other damage. She touched the door. It was warm from the fire burning across the street. Once inside, she found every pail and bucket on the shelves and in the storeroom and filled them with water. Once filled, each one was placed outside the door. Satisfied she'd got enough to make a small impression on the fire, she grabbed them one at a time and threw the contents over the shop front, and then the flames across the road.

Flashbacks of the events of November found Ruby needing to stop and catch her breath every few moments. Everywhere she turned there were desperate faces staring back at her, their eyes willing her to say it was a dream – another nightmare. She threw bucket after bucket of water onto surrounding land and buildings, working with her eyes directed away from people, their pain unbearable. Hitler's men had unleashed their political rage against the innocent yet again. Who were the enemy? Ruby refused to believe ordinary men would carry out such cruel and violent acts against women and children. However, life had forced Ruby to enter adulthood at a rapid pace and the naïve girl she'd once been no longer existed. Of course these sorts of things happened. War forced the commandment of *love thy fellow man* to one side; enemies suffocated them under the clouds of ash, suppressing independent thoughts and bringing survival of the fittest to the fore. War brought out the worst in those who wished to rule, but those whose only wish was to continue living a simple life – she saw the best of them come into play. The enemy had a job to do and, unfortunately for Coventry, they were doing it rather well.

Once satisfied she'd saved the exterior of the shop, Ruby went inside and locked the door as she waited for Fred to arrive. She could not face seeing the fresh devastation brought to her city. She washed her hands in the sink and fluffed her hair, which she'd noticed was sitting beyond her shoulders with a hint of a curl at the bottom. No more sitting on a kitchen chair whilst her mother cut it to the base of her neck, admiring its rich auburn colour. For months Ruby had simply tied it back or scooped it under an old cap of Fred's – an image captured for ever by a wartime photographer – and every day she cringed at what her mother would have thought. Baggy trousers, an old sweater and cap were not exactly her idea of a sixteen-year-old's attire. Ruby was past caring and wore whatever was practical when working.

'Well, well, if it isn't young Tommy,' she said as he and Fred tapped on the door. She pulled it open and Tommy ran inside, full of life and excitement.

'Did you see them bombers flyin' over last night?'

'No, I did not. I was inside my shelter with Fred. Where on earth were you if you saw the planes?'

'I . . . um . . . I . . .'

'Did you sneak outside?' Fred asked.

'N . . . yeah. I snuck out when me mum and auntie weren't lookin'.'

Fred and Ruby exchanged concerned glances. Neither believed the boy and Ruby was alerted to the violent blush spreading across the boy's face.

'Where do you and your family live, Tommy? I take it the family are safe?' she asked.

'Yeah. Don't you worry 'bout us, Rubes, we're fine. We need a bob or two, though. Got this to sell. Was me Gran's,' Tommy said and held out a hat pin.

Ruby took it from him. 'Your family have lovely things, Tommy. This is too good for me. Isn't there a jeweller you can ask for a proper price?'

'Me auntie said I'm to only come to you. She said you are honest,' Tommy said and his flushed face remained staring up at her. His grubby fingers, with nails chewed to the quick, picked at a cuff of his equally grubby jacket. The term 'street urchin' had sprung to Ruby's mind the first time she'd seen him, and today he suited the title.

'Listen. I need to speak with your aunt and explain she could earn more elsewhere. I try to be honest, but feel I'm cheating her out of much needed cash. Do you understand?' Ruby spoke with a firm voice. It had no effect on the chipper Tommy.

'You ain't gotta 'splain. I ain't fick. Me auntie will 'ammer me to bits if I brung a stranger 'ome,' he said and with pleading eyes looked to the plate of biscuits.

'Right, well, this will be the last piece I buy from you, Tommy. If she wants me to take her pretty things, she'll have to come herself. School is where you should be, lad. Fetch a glass of milk and two biscuits, sit here with Fred, whilst I go to check on Beatty. Fred, you all right looking after the shop? When Tommy's finished eating, he's going to go home. Right, Tommy?'

Tommy frowned, bit on a biscuit and chewed.

'Tommy? Home when you've finished,' Ruby said.

The boy nodded.

'I'll see he goes, Ruby. You check on Beatty. She'll be scared witless after last night. It's bad out there again,' Fred said.

When Ruby arrived at Beatty's house she saw the elderly woman standing by her gate. Ruby waved, but Beatty simply dabbed her eyes with the corner of her apron with one hand and propped herself against her gate with the other.

'Beatty . . .' Ruby said as she approached.

'Wicked . . . Wicked, that's what they are,' Beatty replied, and continued to dab away the tears.

'I take it you aren't hurt? We're not hit. Shop has a

cracked window, but Fred will sort it out for me. Beatty, come back with me for a while – for a bit of company,' Ruby said.

Beatty didn't argue; she walked back to her front door and pulled it closed.

Linking her arm through Beatty's, Ruby listened as her friend talked about life before the war, of baking bread and cakes without wondering whether she had enough ingredients, and enjoying a good Sunday joint of beef. Cheap cut, slowly cooked over a batch of potatoes. By the time they'd reached the shop, Ruby's salivary glands were working double time. She pushed open the door, relieved to see Tommy had left for home, and pleased to see three people browsing the shelves. Fred was serving a fourth.

'We'll go out back, Beatty,' she said and encouraged her friend through to the rear of the shop.

'Fred's in his element. He's a kindly soul,' Beatty said and stood by the door, watching as Ruby removed clothing items from a clothes horse. 'Here, let me fold them. You go and sell something –that's where you belong.'

Back out beside Fred, Ruby nudged him when the customers left. 'Beatty was not in a happy state when we met. Go easy on the teasing today. I think she's terrified and covering it up with endless chatter about the past.'

'Leave Beatty to me. She'll be all right. We'll get her to eat with us and relax a bit.'

They ate and chatted until daylight started to hint at giving up.

'I'd best go and get some sleep.' Beatty rose to her feet.

'I'll see you home,' Ruby offered.

'You go back to Garden Cottage. I'll walk with Beatty and get some air. I've only walked a few yards today,' Fred said, pulling his cap onto his head.

'Make sure you come right back. No wandering off down the pub,' Ruby said and laughed. As often happened, the laughter caught on and all three enjoyed a light moment.

'I'll send him right home, Ruby. Never fear.'

Fred chuckled. 'Women!' he said in jest.

Ruby stood by the uncracked window and watched the pair walk away; once they were out of sight she locked up.

Back home, she went to the bookshelf and ran her finger across the selection of Stephen's books she'd kept back when clearing out his belongings. The titles she wasn't sure of, she'd put outside the door for people to take away and they'd gone within a day. Eventually, she stopped trying to choose from the titles, closed her eyes and touched a book. *Jane Eyre* by Charlotte Brontë was to be her evening read. Tonight, Ruby realised it was the first time she'd had time to sit alone without worries of where her future was heading, and she focused upon the orphan Jane Eyre and thanked the stars above she did not have a cruel aunt. At times thoughts of Tommy and his aunt threatened to distract her, but she suppressed them and concentrated upon Jane's story.

The hint of a high-pitched sound startled her enough to jump to her feet, and Ruby ran upstairs and grabbed both hers and Fred's bags. She clattered back downstairs and out of the door to the shelter. Her heart pounded. Fred. Fred was not home. *Please keep him safe.*

She pulled the shelter door to one side and ducked inside just as a scream from above pierced through the evening sky. Voices, horns and sirens filled her ears and Ruby's resolve to remain strong left her. She slammed the door shut and lit the oil lamp Fred had secured to the ceiling. She curled up on a bench and pulled blankets around her. Even if she'd remembered to snatch up her book from the floor indoors, she knew she'd never have settled into reading it whilst another attack raged over her head.

A spider meandered along the wall beside her. It spun a web and scuttled down to the floor and, as she watched, Ruby wondered if it knew what was happening in the world. What she'd give to be that spider at that moment. Carefree.

'Ruby! Ruby!'

Startled from her daydream, Ruby jumped from the bench and answered the banging on the door. She recognised Fred's voice above the hideous sounds surrounding them. She lowered the flame of the lamp and opened the door. 'Quick, inside! Beatty!'

'She's hurt,' Fred said and guided their friend into the shelter.

'What happened?' Ruby asked.

'The siren started but we were closer to her house than the shelters, so we moved as fast as we could towards the jetty behind her house to get to the garden shelter, when boom – the house went down like a house of cards.'

Ruby settled Beatty into a seat and increased the flame to give more light.

'A flying brick caught her forehead. She didn't faint. I knew there's no point in going to the hospital – it was hit last night. Did you hear? We were told by Beatty's neighbour.'

'Never. They bombed a hospital?' Ruby said, shocked to the core to think the already injured faced upheaval – or worse.

'Keep your head up, Beatty. We've got a box of bits here and I can patch you up a little. I don't think it's a large gash.'

Beatty, unusually quiet, simply nodded. Shock had paled her face and the small trickle of blood stood proud, congealing like a black piece of artwork.

'I can't believe they're here again,' Fred said.

'It's exhausting,' Ruby replied.

The walls of the shelter vibrated when an explosion nearby hurled everything it touched into the air and it clattered to the ground again.

'That was close,' Fred whispered.

Ruby heard the fear in his voice and reached out to touch his hand. 'We'll be fine, Fred. Tucked in here with the comforts you've given us. A proper little palace.'

Beatty remained silent. It unnerved Ruby.

'Beatty. How're you doing?' She knelt down and stared into blank eyes. Beatty never blinked or said a word.

'It's as if she's here in body but her mind is outside somewhere,' Ruby said.

'I saw a lot of men like that during the last war. Some snapped out of it, but others stayed shell-shocked. We both know how it feels, and poor Beatty was frightened the moment the sirens started. She acts tough as old boots but she's a big softy once you get to know her.'

Ruby nodded. 'We'll look after her; she can move in with us. I'll make up a bed in the back room using the spare mattress. We can turn it into a bedroom for her.'

'That's a grand idea. She might not want to stay but, looking at her now, I think she'll just go wherever we take her.'

Gentle snores soon hinted her companions were

sleeping and Ruby allowed herself to relax for the final hour of the attack. Blurry-eyed she woke to silent skies. She peeked outside as dawn rose to herald another day. Ruby shuddered when she saw the outcome of the night raid. The shed and back buildings of the shops behind were badly damaged. The cat and kittens sat on the shed roof, which lay on the floor, waiting to pounce on a rat scurrying past them. Again, a pang of envy crept in and Ruby scolded herself. She had a job to do and no time to feel sorry for herself. She'd committed to Fred and Beatty. To care for them.

'Fred, come on, sleepyhead. Time to take a look at the damage. They were close.'

Surrounding Garden Cottage, the world hurried by and Ruby acknowledged people moving in different directions around her. Luck was on her side this time. Her home had survived another night.

She and Fred guided Beatty inside the house. Ruby opened the bathroom door and directed Beatty to the facilities, and softly closed the door behind her in the hope Beatty would respond to her surroundings. Fred stood guard and Ruby tugged a few pieces of furniture around the back room, dragged down a spare mattress, pillows and bedding. By the time she heard a flush of water from the bathroom, Ruby had managed to create a temporary haven for Beatty.

Beatty appeared from behind the door and Fred took

her by the elbow and guided her towards Ruby. His tender words of encouragement were touching and Ruby knew he thought of Beatty as more than a friend. It pained her to see him look so worried.

'She'll be all right, Fred, I'm sure. Beatty, take a rest on the bed – your bed. You can stay with us.' She helped Beatty move onto the bed and covered her with a blanket. 'You rest.'

A hammering on the back door broke the silence of the house and Fred hurried to answer it whilst Ruby closed the door on Beatty.

'Fred – Ruby there? Safe?' Helen's voice rang out from the doorway.

Ruby rushed to greet her. 'I'm here. I'm safe.'

Helen stepped inside. 'Thank goodness. When they said your shop had taken a direct hit –' She stared at Ruby. 'You don't know? Oh, Ruby, I'm sorry. Come here.' Helen pulled a sobbing Ruby into her arms.

Fred closed the door behind him and pulled on his jacket and cap.

'I'll go and see what the damage is, Ruby. You stay here with Beatty.'

Ruby stepped away from Helen. 'No, Fred, I'll go. You stay here. I need to see it for myself. Thank you, Helen.'

'I'll go with her, Fred. I'll make sure she's not in any danger.'

*

Gaping holes where there had once been a row of shops stared back at them and both Ruby and Helen gave small squeals of horror. Shadwell's Buy and Sell no longer existed. Much of its stock rose skyward as smoke, whilst flames licked their way around it in a monstrous fashion.

Helen pulled Ruby to her and held onto her trembling body. Before she passed out, Ruby heard Helen call her name, but she was not able to stop the faint. She welcomed the darkness, embracing the floating sensation and feeling of peace which came with it. Ruby no longer cared about watching fires, listening to the cries of frightened people or the radio reports of how brave they all were in Coventry. She no longer wanted to be part of the world in which everything that brought joy into her life was destroyed by men with their fingers on a button, snuffing them out at will. Undoing all that they fought to rebuild. No, Ruby wanted to stay in a dark world of warmth and comfort. With only the beat of her heart settling into a slowing pace within her chest. This was a space where nobody could destroy her faith in mankind, where she could give up the will to live and join her family, find their spirit in the calm.

Gradually, Helen's voice faded into the distance and Ruby shut out life outside of her cocoon. She felt the physical shaking of her body but blanked out voices as soon as they called her name. And then she came round.

Death wanted nothing to do with her, and Ruby felt its rejection in the deep breath which surged through her lungs. She coughed and gulped in more air, blinking her eyes and trying not to look in the direction of the shop. Several pairs of concerned eyes stared back at her, and a man held out his hand and pulled her to her feet. She staggered slightly and Helen moved to support her.

'You gave me such a scare, Ruby. I've never seen anyone so pale and lifeless. I thought . . . Well, never mind what I thought – let's get you home. There's nothing for you to do here.' John's warm breath touched her ears. His voice brought comfort over Helen's anxious questions.

'Is she hurt? You know her? Is she hurt?'

'She's coming round fine. I'm John, her friend. I heard this area was attacked, and thought of Ruby.'

'I'm Helen, her friend and guardian. You are kind to think of her – poor thing, she's in shock. Come on, darling, let's get you home.'

John helped Ruby to her feet and put a supportive arm around her shoulder. Helen grabbed Ruby's left hand. She looked at them both, then back at where the shop had once stood.

Accepting she'd never rebuild the business there, Ruby allowed her friends to guide her away from the scene, whispering words of encouragement in her ears. Numb and unable to speak, Ruby stumbled home knowing she had their love and support to get her through the next few hours.

Helen pushed open the door to Garden Cottage and called for Fred. The moment Ruby saw him she gave a small smile.

'I'm afraid it's all gone,' Helen said. 'And madam here gave me the fright of my life. She passed out and at one point I was convinced she'd passed away. This is her friend, John.'

'Nice to meet you, lad. Come and sit down, Ruby.' Fred fussed around her and Ruby gave him another soft smile.

'She's not spoken since she came round, Fred,' Helen said.

Fred bashed life into a cushion and placed it behind Ruby. 'It's going to be a quiet house then, 'cos I've got Beatty in the same way in the front room. This one,' he said, pointing at Ruby, 'made her a room to live with us, 'cos her place is gone too. I might do a bit of singing and see which one tells me to shut up first,' he said, and Ruby heard the teasing humour she loved so much. It wasn't fair on Fred to be waiting on her and Beatty to rally round.

She gave another cough. Her throat felt sore with dryness. 'What does a girl have to do to get a cup of tea round here?' she said, her voice croaking out the words.

'There she is. There's my girl. One cup of tea coming up. Helen? John, you stopping for one?'

'Let me help, Fred,' Helen said and followed him into the kitchen.

'You're in safe hands here, Ruby,' John said as he sat on a chair beside her.

'Fred is a good man – they are all dear to me. The war brought us all together.' Ruby smiled with a nod towards the kitchen door.

'It brought us together too.' John's voice was barely audible, but Ruby saw something in his face which expressed far more than words.

'It did,' she whispered back.

Fred and Helen re-joined them, armed with warm drinks, and the moment to talk more alone passed.

Fred tapped on Beatty's door. 'Tea's up, Mrs P,' he called out before entering.

''bout ruddy time too,' came the reply from inside the room.

'And there's the other one. I knew it was too good to be true. That's me peace shattered for the evening,' Fred said with good humour.

Ruby put down her cup and rushed into the room. 'Thank goodness, Beatty. I've only just recovered from my bout of shock, but thought you never would. You gave us quite a scare.'

'Sorry, duck. I can't believe what happened in front

of me. It took my breath away. I was stunned,' Beatty said and handed her cup back to Fred. 'That went down well. Thank you.'

'Same with me last year, and now with the shop,' Ruby said.

'No! The shop's gone too?'

'All gone, the lot of it.'

Beatty looked over at the doorway. 'And who are you, young man?'

Ruby turned and smiled at John, standing tall at the entrance of the room. 'That's John. He's Canadian, and a friend – be kind.'

Beatty chuckled. 'I must say, you are a pleasant sight after such a shock. I can see why Ruby befriended you.'

'Beatty!' an embarrassed Ruby chided her friend, who stood looking an equally embarrassed John up and down.

'I'm glad she did, Beatty, or I'd have missed the opportunity of meeting you, Helen and Fred. She's mentioned you all.'

'Ah, so you've met more than once then?' Fred questioned John, then looked at Ruby.

Ruby, not wanting Fred to question John on his moral duty and other things she suspected Fred wanted to reel off, changed the subject. 'I'm going to be lost without the shop. It's a nightmare. We're living in a nightmare.'

Beatty held out her hand and Helen put a comforting arm around Ruby's waist.

Ruby took Beatty's hand in hers. Beatty's large fingers wrapped themselves around her slender ones.

'You're a survivor. You'll start again. We'll help. Probably find a lot of stuff in my place when it's safe to go back. Where I'll go from there, I don't know,' Beatty said.

Ruby waved her arm around the room. 'You will stay with us. It's not much, but it's yours. We don't bite, do we, Fred?'

Fred laughed. 'Not many teeth left to do that, Ruby.'

The atmosphere of doom and gloom lifted, and Beatty manoeuvred herself to the edge of the bed.

'I've got my mask and my handbag has my papers inside,' she said and pointed to the sideboard where Ruby had placed her things.

'If you allow me to put your name down on the homeless list, Beatty, it can help when you need somewhere of your own.' Helen stepped in from the doorway as she spoke.

'I'll need details of your old property, and can get the ball rolling for you.'

John gave a polite cough, and all eyes went to him. 'I have to go. I'm glad you are safe, Ruby.'

Before Ruby could move, Fred went to John and snatched up his hand, pumping out a vigorous handshake.

'We'll be forever grateful to you, young man. Ruby

needed help and you thought of her. Kindness goes a long way. Stay safe and come visit again. Thank you.'

An echo of thank yous joined Fred's, and Ruby went to John.

'Fred's words are mine too. Thank you for helping me and Helen. Be careful out there – it's going to be back to what it was like in November.'

John lifted her hand and they moved away from Beatty's room and prying eyes.

'I'd like to see you again, Ruby. I'm alone here, and enjoyed your company when we first met.'

'I'd like that – very much. I've only got them –' she tilted her head to the bedroom

'– and I'd like to hear more about the world outside of Coventry. Come and visit any time.'

John reached out and lifted a small curl winding its way down the side of her face.

'Your hair is a beautiful colour. It reminds me of the maple leaves in the fall, before they turn bright red.'

Ruby put her hand to the curl and moved his hand away from her face. She was fully aware that if Fred saw John's attention to her he'd prevent her from seeing him again. He'd become the protective father figure and, as a minor, Ruby would be expected to comply with the rules of good behaviour.

'Thank you. My mother and gran had the same colouring.'

An over-exaggerated cough came from the doorway, and Fred and Helen stepped into the room.

'Helen's going now, Ruby. I'll see them both out,' Fred said.

John gave a gentle nod. He'd been dismissed by a higher ranking officer; the regimental tone of Fred's voice made it quite clear.

'Yes, sir. My duty is done here. Maybe our paths will cross another day,' John said, and Ruby knew full well he'd visit again.

'Perhaps. Stay safe, soldier,' Fred said and held out his hand.

'Thank you for helping us, John,' Helen said and also shook John's hand.

After a flurry of goodbyes and handshakes, the house fell silent.

Thousands of incendiary bombs had dropped over Britain throughout April, and for three nights at the start of the month Coventry experienced another attack from the enemy. Ruby dreaded turning on the radio. London residents had also suffered huge losses, and her heart went out to them. News reporters spoke of the resilience of the British, of how they rose each day to face whatever the night raids had inflicted upon them. She thought of Tommy and his family. He'd hinted about returning to London, and she wondered if he and his mother had survived the nightly attacks.

During May a few unsettled times were endured, but by the middle of the month there were several nights where the enemy hadn't flown over and disturbed the British people. Coventry took a deep breath, vowing to double its production of wartime supplies to support the defence. Factories whirred out sounds of reassurance that things were moving forward. People worked longer hours with a stubborn determination. A lesson had been learned, and one was to be taught. Coventry would not bend to the will of the enemy. Ruby's household held the same view.

Beatty, now settled and recovering, busied herself each day with running the home. She'd shush Ruby when she told her to sit and let her take a turn, and barked out instructions to Fred to remove his boots and leave them by the door. A limited sense of normality returned for Ruby, giving her a sense of place. She was nearing seventeen, and still wondering where life would lead her.

Life in Garden Cottage slowly took on a routine and when the weather changed for the better they planned to enjoy the evenings outside in the hope the sky above would be free from those driven to bring them to their knees.

After flicking through a magazine gift from Helen, Ruby had taken to wearing her hair rolled in a more adult way. The new style and interest in what colours suited her made Ruby the butt of Fred's teasing that they were for a certain soldier. Ruby enjoyed the banter, but sometimes he earned a well-humoured clipped ear from Beatty.

Since meeting John, Ruby noticed she drew attention to herself more, and her sensitivity to her limp was no longer an issue. Beatty declared Ruby to be a blossoming woman, and it described how Ruby felt. She experienced her first whistle from a group of soldiers brought in to assist with restoring the city. Ruby caught the eye of one of them and when he winked at her her stomach fluttered and she giggled. Something changed for her that day, and she looked at the world through fresh eyes. She wanted to be part of it, and to contribute to its future. To feel more alive than she'd done for months. So, when Helen mentioned that a girl, Katie, from her office had asked if Ruby would like to attend a local dance, Ruby accepted.

31st May 1941

Scrubbing the dirt from her hands, Ruby turned them over. Chipped nails and scuffed skin were not the mark-ings of feminine hands shown in the fashion magazines. With a sigh, she scrubbed them again. Red raw was not a great look either.

'I'll have to wear gloves,' she said to no one in

particular. Fred was with the chickens, and Beatty sat rewinding wool from a jumper too small for her. Her skill would produce another for Ruby from the rewound skein.

'I'd knit you a pair, but I'm afraid they won't be ready for this evening,' she said and laughed.

Normally, Beatty's laugh was infectious, but today nothing made Ruby smile. Although keen to experience her first dance, nerves overpowered the excitement.

Katie had proved herself to be a good friend when she'd arrived with a dress for Ruby to wear. Helen had guessed Ruby's wardrobe was limited to basic wear, and Katie volunteered a dress in emerald green with a full skirt, which Ruby enjoyed showing off when she gave Fred and Beatty a twirl. It was complemented by a small bolero-style cardigan gifted by Helen.

The dance was still another two hours away and Ruby ached. A busy day volunteering on the park allotments and digging out new ones in Radford was not ideal before an evening out.

'Maybe I'll send a message to Katie and go another time. Give my hands a chance to look less like a farmer's,' she moaned to Beatty.

Beatty laid down her knitting and gave such a loud sigh Ruby jumped. 'No more excuses. You've seen how short life is just lately. Those service men hoping to catch a glimpse of a pretty girl are not unsavoury types

– not all of them. Some are scared young men who are convinced today is their last day. And you stand there and complain about your hands?'

With a harrumph sound, Beatty left the room and went to join Fred. Ruby watched as the pair settled into a conversation, and she guessed it would be about her.

By the time they came in from the garden, Ruby was ready to meet Katie outside the aerospace factory hosting the dance.

'Ah, changed your mind? I will say you make a pretty picture. Looks lovely, doesn't she, Fred?' Beatty said.

'Scrubs up nicely,' Fred said with a nod of agreement.

Ruby, embarrassed by the attention, fidgeted with her gloves. 'These are no good. They make my hands itch.'

'Then don't wear them, but for goodness' sake cheer up. At least look like a girl who is going to her first dance. I remember my first. I –'

Not wishing to delay meeting Katie by hearing the long version of one of Beatty's stories of her younger years, Ruby gave them both a peck on the cheek. 'I'll see you in an hour,' she said.

'I'll bet more on two or three,' Beatty replied.

'Before midnight, Cinderella,' Fred called out.

Katie waved at Ruby and Ruby forced a smile and waved back. Halfway to the factory she'd debated returning home, but curiosity got the better of her and she decided to at least see what a wartime dance felt like. The dab of lipstick on her lips felt sticky and annoyed her, but she resisted the temptation of wiping it away.

'Oh, Ruby, you look so pretty in that dress,' Katie exclaimed. 'I just knew it was the right colour and style for you.'

'And you look like a film star!' Ruby replied, not exaggerating.

Katie had a beauty about her which, although Ruby could see she wore a lot of make-up, gave a natural glow.

'Come on, let's get inside. I'm dying to show you off,' Katie said.

Ruby shuddered at the thought; to be paraded around was not her idea of fun. Drinking a lemonade in the corner, watching the dancing, was more her style. Dancing. How she wished she'd learned to dance. Her days with her parents had been filled with many things, but dancing had not been one of them. Ruby didn't know *if* she could dance in a formal way, due to her leg.

Music blasted out the moment they opened the doors – or, rather, a stern-faced man opened it for them.

'Evening,' he said.

Katie gave a side flick of her head in acknowledgement. Ruby copied and hoped she looked just as calm and sophisticated.

'Isn't it wonderful?' Katie said and pulled Ruby closer to her side.

Whether she heard Ruby's reply of, 'Yes,' or not, Ruby never found out. Katie moved across the dance floor towards a group of young women and beckoned Ruby to follow. Introductions made, Katie then headed to the table, where a display of drinks were on offer. They took lemonades and found a table on one side of the room. Katie barely got chance to sit before a man in khaki whisked her onto the dance floor. Ruby watched Katie offering up half-hearted protestations and finally sank into the arms of the soldier as they waltzed around the room. Katie returned to the table for a sip of her drink and no sooner had she placed her glass on the table, she was whisked off again. Ruby's foot tapped out the tune as she watched. Four times she witnessed the same, but each time the man asking Katie for a dance was a different one.

A youth with a face attempting to grow hair asked Ruby to dance, but the halitosis with a hint of alcohol, and his inability to stand without swaying, put her off. She apologised and pleaded a sore foot. No one else asked. After an hour and a half she was bored and wanted nothing more but to get home to her book and relax. Preening and pampering herself was not a pleasure for Ruby; it was a chore, and not one she wanted to repeat. When Katie returned to the table, Ruby pleaded a head-ache and gave Katie a hug. Katie, in turn, gave her a peck on the cheek and moved deftly into another dance.

On her way out, Ruby turned back to look into the room and knew she'd done the right thing by leaving Katie to her attentive admirers. The noise and crush of bodies was too much for Ruby to bear and she slipped out of the door into the street, enjoying the rush of cool air on her body.

Once back home she went to her room and took off the dress and placed it onto its hanger. A tap on the door alerted her to Beatty's keenness to find out how much she'd enjoyed herself. Slipping on her comfortable dressing gown, she shoved her feet into her slippers and picked up her book.

'Didn't expect you back so soon, duck. Have fun?' Beatty asked as Ruby stepped out into the landing.

'Happier here with this,' Ruby said and waved her book in front of her. 'It was exciting, but not somewhere I'd go again. Katie's still there. She loves dancing, but her feet will hurt in the morning. I saw a few boots step on her toes.'

'Shame you didn't enjoy yourself, Ruby. Maybe when things are settled more, or you are older,' Beatty said.

'Or maybe not. I loved the music, but it was too loud. I wonder if my ears have become over-sensitive due to the noises from the bombs. Or I just like softer music. I didn't feel calm as I do when I listen to the radio,' Ruby said and walked down the stairs. 'A good book and cocoa. Good company and a comfy seat. That's all I need.'

Beatty gave a laugh. 'Well, don't look for it in Fred. He's soundo on the sofa. I'll make us cocoa and maybe you can tell me about some of the dresses you saw. Clothes rationing is due soon and I suspect some of those dresses will be altered, passed around and lent out until they fall apart.'

Ruby settled into her chair and hoped the sigh she held inside didn't escape. The last thing she wanted was to talk about dresses. She wanted to escape into the world of *Jane Eyre*, but Beatty deserved her attention and it would have been mean of Ruby to plead tiredness and go to bed.

Another hour of chatter finally brought the first of the yawns from both her and Beatty, and Ruby grabbed the opportunity to say goodnight and settle in her room. She lay on the bed and pulled up her covers. It was too late to read, and she pondered over Katie's companions. Each one had looked at Katie with adoration. The hope in their eyes made Ruby wonder whether they'd get the kiss they obviously hankered after, and whether Katie was a girl to give away her kisses. Ruby doubted she'd give her kisses away so easily, although the thought of kissing John Clayton was tempting, and Ruby fell asleep with that thought on her mind.

CHAPTER 15

15th June 1941

Downing tools and waving goodbye at the end of the working day, Ruby headed home. Working on the allotments was satisfying, but she missed working in her own shop. Some days she thought about reopening, but other days she knew she'd never cope with disappointment if it was bombed and taken from her again. Ruby felt there was only so much loss she could take. Voluntary work on the land brought with it a sense of duty to the country, and Ruby convinced herself her decision was the right one.

As she turned into Spon Street, she spotted Tommy sitting outside her home. Perched on large concrete slabs, he looked tiny. He turned her way when she called out to him. 'Well, look who's here. We're honoured.'

'Rubes!' He called out her name with a whoop of joy

and ran to her, tugging at one side of the handle of her basket.

'That looks 'eavy. I'll 'elp,' he said.

'Thank you. How are you, Tommy? Was it dreadful in London?' Ruby asked, and immediately reproached herself for asking such a blunt question.

Tommy scuffed his shoes along the pavement. 'Mum 'n' me 'ad to come back 'ere to me auntie. That's getting 'eavy; give me something and I'll carry that instead.'

Ruby put down the basket and took out a small box for him to carry. 'Ah, the reason for the sad face. Auntie giving you a hard time?'

'Gave me anover brooch, but your shop –' he said and broke off, looking up into her face. Ruby wanted to reach down and wipe away a smudge of dirt from his cheek. He looked dreadful. A bruised jawline in the last stages of healing looked painful. Another above his eyebrow looked more recent. She crouched down and stroked it, and he winced.

'I bet that hurt when it first happened,' she said.

'Blown up in London for that one.' He put his hand to the fading bruise. 'Clumsy me mum said when I fell over the uvva day,' Tommy replied, and turned away from her touch.

'Come and see Fred. It's my birthday today, so come and have a bite to eat. Beatty lives with us now, and she makes enough food to feed an army.'

Ruby was amazed at how well Beatty coped with their rationed food supply.

'There'll be enough for a little belly,' she said.

'Can't. Auntie wants money from us and Mum sent me out wiv this.' He held out a silver picture frame, small and delicate.

Ruby took it from him and turned it around in her hands. Another pretty trinket.

'I don't do it any more, Tommy. I don't have a shop any more; I'm just collecting things Fred can repair at home,' she said. Her voice ached with the pain of saying the words which hurt her so much. Until she'd seen Tommy sitting waiting for her, she'd felt content with her life. Now she realised she missed saying she was the owner of Shadwell's.

''ow can you just stop? It's not fair. Wivout your shop, we don't get money for the rent and stop me auntie from bein' nasty to me mum,' Tommy said with the petulance of the child he was. Ruby had to remind herself he wouldn't understand her thoughts on the matter.

'It's hard to explain, Tommy. And I'm sure there are other places you can sell your things. Let's go inside.'

'Nah, you're all right. I've gotta find a buyer for this or I'm in bovva – again,' Tommy said, waving the picture frame, and kicked a stone away. 'See ya. 'appy birfday.'

With his head down, Tommy walked away from her

and Ruby put aside her thoughts that she should help him financially. It wasn't her trouble, or her job to keep buying his goods. His aunt and mother had a responsibility to the child.

'Come and see me tomorrow, Tommy,' she called out. It hurt her when he never turned around.

Ruby pushed open the door and dropped her basket in the hallway. She could hear Helen's voice in the living room, and Beatty's laugh booming at something Fred said. She tidied her hair in the hall mirror and stopped when another voice joined the mix. John. He'd kept his promise to visit, and Ruby couldn't have asked for a better birthday present. She took control of her fluttering emotions and pushed open the door.

'Well, this is a nice surprise,' she said and smiled when John stood up. 'At ease, soldier,' she teased, and turned to Helen. 'Hello, is that a new cardigan I see?'

Helen touched the sleeve of the cardigan. 'It is. I made it from the wool I bought from Shadwell's before . . . well, before.'

'Fred tells me it's your birthday, Ruby,' John said, moving the conversation onto a lighter subject, for which Ruby was grateful. The loss of the shop still pained her.

'Seventeen today,' Ruby replied.

'So young.' Helen and Beatty sighed out their words at the same time. Ruby looked from one to the other and held up her hands as a sign of apology, then followed it up with a giggle.

'Older in mind than your body though,' Fred muttered.

'Fred.' Beatty gave him a withering look. Ruby knew behind his words were a hidden warning.

'And you are older in mind than in body, Fred. We make a good team.' Ruby went to him and kissed his cheek.

'Careful, girl. It'll be your turn before you know it. Age has a way of sneaking up on you.' Fred responded with a pat of her hand.

'I've a lot to learn, see and do before age catches up with me.'

Ruby looked at John.

'Visiting gardens in Canada might be something I'll achieve after the war. Or playing on a Cornish beach, or riding a camel in the desert. Or I'll simply remain here and help rebuild this city. And, as exciting as those first things sound, I like the thought of remaining here. Who knows what the future will bring?'

Beatty rose from her chair and walked towards the kitchen. 'It might bring sweet treats. Our friend here –' she pointed to John '– brought us two chocolate bars, and I've cut them into slices for us all to enjoy.'

She returned with a plate of chocolate treats and gasps of delight escaped the lips of all, except John.

'They threaten rationing in my home, but it hasn't

reached my mom's ears yet and she sends food parcels so often I'd be greedy not to share.'

He waved away the plate when Ruby held it out to him. 'I've one left back at my digs. You enjoy them.'

'It's kind of you to think of us, John,' Ruby said and handed the plate to Helen.

'I always think of you.' John left a short gap before speaking again, but Ruby understood the message he sent her way. 'You are now classed as my English friends when I write to my parents. I've told them about the way you've all come together, and of the bond between you all. I suspect the next parcel to me will include a little extra for you guys.'

Fred tapped his pipe on the fireplace, and John looked over at him. 'Reminds me of my pops; he's a pipe smoker. The noise sounds the same. The sound of a man about to enjoy five minutes.' John laughed, and Fred gave a suck and puff of agreement.

'How long have you been part of the war, son?' Fred asked.

John leaned back in his seat and Ruby took pleasure in seeing him relax in her home. He looked as if he belonged amongst them.

'I joined up the day Prime Minister Mackenzie King announced we were at war with Germany. Seven days after you. Pops is too old, but does his bit at home. My mom didn't speak to me for days, but soon realised she'd

164

best do so as I wasn't going to be around for long. I got sent to London in the October.'

'Any regrets?' Fred asked.

'None, sir,' John said, directing his answer to Ruby.

Helen gave a discreet cough, bringing the attention back to Fred's conversation.

'Do you have brothers or sisters, John?' Ruby asked, finding a way for them to remain looking at each other.

'I have a sister. Older by two years. She's working in Halifax to help build ships. Quite different to the typing job she used to have.'

'Oh, that's interesting,' said Helen and she shifted forward in her seat. 'My sister-in-law lives in Halifax. I didn't realise they built ships there. It's more wool factories – or was.'

'Ah, this is Halifax in Canada. Nova Scotia, to be precise. Our aunt Mary lives there, and Marsha is staying with her. According to her letters, she's doing well, although the work is tough.'

'Well, if she ever moves into making chocolate, let me know and I'll visit her,' said Beatty as she popped another slice into her mouth.

John laughed. 'I'll remember to let you know, Beatty.'

'Fred, I have a bottle of Scotch to be shared, if you'll join me. You ladies too, if you enjoy a glass. I picked it up in Edinburgh during my last posting.' John rose to his feet and went into the hallway. Ruby followed. His greatcoat hung at the end of the coat hooks, and it surprised Ruby she hadn't seen it when she'd first arrived home.

'It's good to see you, Ruby. How are you doing?'

'Coming to terms with what's happened, and rethinking what I want to do now.'

'Whatever you do, it will be for others. You have a good heart, Ruby Shadwell.' To her surprise, John leaned forward and kissed her cheek. He stepped back, lifted a bottle from his pocket and waggled it in front of her. 'Best go and soothe the guard dog. Fred's watching us like a hawk,' he said and walked back to the others.

Ruby stood for a moment and placed her hand on her cheek. John had filled her heart with happiness, and made the day more enjoyable. A day she'd wanted to forget, but now would remember for ever.

The following morning Fred nursed his head from too many celebratory tots. The smell of bacon wafted around the house and Ruby enjoyed a slice, accompanied by an egg from the now steady supply from their hens.

'I meant to say. Young Tommy was outside when I got home from work last night. Trying to sell another trinket of his mother's. The aunt wants money again, although he looked underfed. He'd been to the shop and he took it rather badly to hear I'm no longer trading. I did shout for him to come and see me today, but he ignored me.'

Beatty placed a plate of food in front of Fred, who immediately pushed it away.

Ruby scraped the contents onto her own plate and carried on eating. 'Waste not, want not,' she said.

'Don't talk with your mouth full,' Fred retorted and left the room.

Beatty and Ruby exchanged an amused giggle.

'Poor Fred – one too many last night,' Beatty said. 'Your friend John soon won him over. Nice young man.'

'He'll be fine, and yes, John is good company. It's Tommy I'm worried about. He looks worse than last time you saw him.'

Beatty cleared the plates but said nothing, and Ruby readied herself for work.

'Maybe he'll turn up today, but don't worry about the likes of Tommy; he's a tough little button – a street child from London. I met a few when I visited my husband's family. They were a tough crew. Hearts as big as plates, but fought each other and the world on a daily basis,' Beatty said.

'I'm sure you're right. Only I keep thinking about the life my brother enjoyed at that age, and it wasn't as tough.'

Beatty wiped down the table as Ruby went to the door. 'Your brother didn't have to survive the war, Ruby. I know that sounds callous, but you understand what I mean, and the way I mean it.'

Ruby nodded. Beatty was right. Her brother might well be dead and a victim of the war, but Tommy was every bit a victim too. She made up her mind to track down his mother and offer her support in some way.

She also had something else to consider – getting a new job, rather than voluntary work. She'd applied for many, but always the same response sent her into raging rants. This one was the latest, and had the same effect. She held the letter, waving it around, reciting each word over and over until they blurred into one.

'According to this, I'm not old enough for a lot of the work and my *medical condition* prevents them from allowing me to enter other types suited for those of my age. What is it with people reminding me I'm only a seventeen-year-old *and* a cripple, Beatty? I'm willing, hard-working and able. More able than some I know!' Ruby slammed the letter onto the table, and Beatty remained standing at the other end with her hands clasped together under her ample bosom.

'Stop calling yourself a cripple, and I know you're not a girl to sit around and mope, so why start now? Fate has paved a way for you to rethink what you might like to do next. How about asking at the factories for work? They're working flat out to get orders completed. Age shouldn't be a problem there. Speak with Helen.'

'I might. Thanks for listening, Beatty.'

'When you come back we'll measure up for a skirt

from your birthday material Helen gave you. Time you had a treat. Just don't be so hard on yourself.'

Walking around the city, Ruby marvelled at how much work had gone into clearing the destroyed buildings. Word was out that plans for a new town centre were back on the table; Ruby looked forward to seeing it fresh and new again, but knew it would be years before all signs of the destruction would be erased.

Planes continued to haunt them with their flights overhead, but once the sirens sounded the all-clear the residents of the city returned to their daily tasks. Conversations in the food queues were often about persuading family and friends to return here to live, but several families reported they'd settled down in new towns. Volunteers visiting the city settled into temporary accommodation and new friendships blossomed. Accents from around the country – and world – were heard on every corner and Ruby loved to listen. She entertained Fred and Beatty with attempts to copy some of them.

Today, she heard the familiar accent of Tommy and went to walk towards him but stopped when she saw him chatting with a couple standing beside an empty shop. The man gave frequent nods, whilst the woman stood quietly to one side. As she moved her head, Ruby noticed a gash running down the side of her jawline. The woman tugged at the edge of her headscarf every now and then, in an attempt to hide it. *Scars will be worn by many around the country, and a headscarf won't ever cover some*, Ruby thought to herself, and was grateful she'd not suffered such a nasty injury. She hesitated about approaching them to say hello when Tommy drooped his shoulders and looked to the floor. The man appeared animated and clenched his jaw as he spoke to Tommy. No doubt the boy had got himself into bother again, and it was not the right time for her to interrupt, so she turned around and walked away. She had other things to attend to that morning; it was time to face the new path Beatty spoke about, and Ruby made up her mind to pay Helen a visit.

The queues to her office were not as long as they once were, thanks to various organisations taking up the reins and handling the multiple problems facing the residents. Mulling over where she might like to work whilst waiting for her turn, Ruby chose to go for a more physical post than office work – creating something to help the city get back on its feet.

'Ruby, what a lovely surprise! What can I do for you – or is this a social visit?' Helen said and moved from her desk to give Ruby a hug.

'I'm here because another letter tells me I am a young cripple. I feel useless, Helen.'

Ruby put the letter on Helen's desk, dropped into a chair and gave a self-pitying sigh.

'Oh, Ruby, I'm that sorry. What a disappointment for you.'

'I wondered if you'd help me find work in one of the factories. I need to feel useful. I help on the park allotments but it doesn't fill the day. I miss the shop. Fred and Beatty suggest I reopen, but I'm not ready. I want to earn a living though. They send their love by the way – Fred and Beatty.'

Helen pushed Ruby's letter to one side and smiled.

Ruby grinned. 'Sounds right, doesn't it – their names together. If it wasn't for the war, they'd never have met. They are happy in their daily lives and I love how we've got a home together. Providing Hitler leaves us alone, that is. Do you think there'll be work for me, Helen? It stops me thinking when I'm busy.'

Helen jotted down a few words on a scrap of paper and put it to one side.

'Come back in a couple of days, Ruby. I'll ask about for you. Or, if I hear anything, I'll drop by after work. In the meantime, think about setting up the business again. You can afford to do it, and I'm surprised you haven't.'

'I do think about it, but it broke my heart losing the shop, and I'm not sure I'm ready to start again. And is it useful to the war effort? That's something I ask myself all the time now.'

'Listen to me,' said Helen. 'There's a need. People are

struggling to get back to normal. Life will never be the same for any of us, but if there's a way they can buy on the cheap and rebuild a home, then I consider that important war work.'

CHAPTER 16

''Ello, Rubes. Ow you doin'?'

Tommy's voice interrupted her thoughts of John as she turned into Spon Street. He sat on the concrete column as before, and swung his legs against it, banging his worn-out shoes.

'Tommy – great to see you again. I saw you with your parents this morning; I didn't realise your dad was home,' Ruby said and waved to the boy.

Tommy scratched his head and Ruby immediately thought of headlice. Her hand went to her own head and she struggled to refrain from scratching her own scalp.

'Stop scratching; you'll make your head sore,' she said.

'I ain't itchin'. I was thinkin'. Ah, you saw me in town,' Tommy said and grinned back a toothless smile.

'Have you lost another tooth, Tommy Jenkins?' Ruby

teased. Seeing Tommy's smile lifted the dull mood she'd carried home with her.

Tommy poked his tongue through the gap in his teeth.

'Fred's round the back if you wanted to speak with him,' Ruby said.

'Nah, already seen 'im, gave 'im a clock t'fix for me uncle. Fred's good at fixin' stuff. And I came to see you. I went to the park, but they said you ain't working there no more. What you doin' now?'

Ruby shrugged but said nothing.

'I've found you a shop,' Tommy said and jumped down from his concrete seat and offered her another toothless grin.

'You've what?' Ruby said and laughed.

'Oi, I ain't kiddin'. Me uncle . . . well, 'e knows a bloke hoo knows anover bloke and 'e's lookin' to rent it out. Me uncle knocked 'im right down wiv the price, and when I told the bloke 'bout your place 'e dropped it more. I got the keys for you to have a butcher's.'

Tommy pulled out a set of keys and jangled them in front of Ruby. She stared at him in disbelief. Like her, Tommy appeared older than his years. How could a little ragamuffin think of such a thing?

'What do I need a shop for? I had one, but there's no call for that sort of thing now. It's not helping the war effort either.'

She watched, amused, as Tommy stood with his feet

apart and hands on his hips. His stick legs hung from beneath his shorts. Her heart went out to him; he tried so hard to make her happy.

'Why would you go to such an effort for me, Tommy?' Ruby asked and crouched down to his level.

He took his hands from his hips and shoved them into his shorts pockets. 'Why not? You're me friend an' I wanna 'elp.'

Ruby was touched by his thoughtfulness.

'I'm applying for a job in a factory, Tommy, but it was very kind of you to think of me.' She looked at his crestfallen face and quickly added, 'Clever too. Getting the price reduced. You'll make a great businessman when you're older.'

Tommy jangled the keys. 'Just take a look. Me uncle will be ever so disappointed if you ain't even looked inside,' he pleaded.

There was something about his voice, strained with a hint of desperation, that caused Ruby to refrain from saying no again. She flicked the keys with her finger and watched them swing in the air. Tommy slipped them from his hand and hooked them on the end of her finger.

'Go on, you know you want a nosey.'

He was right. Curiosity had got the better of her and Ruby clutched the keys in her hand.

'You're wrong, you know. 'Bout not bein' war thingy, your old shop. It 'elped loads of people – 'elped me.'

Ruby said nothing as they stepped into Hill Street, on the corner of Bond Street, and faced the shop front she'd seen Tommy outside that morning.

'Good spot,' Tommy said and held out his hand for the key. Ruby stood back and looked at the double windows either side of the door. A pang of nostalgia for Shadwell's Buy and Sell washed over her and, for a second, she gave in to imagining the items she'd once collected, on show in the window. When the door swung open she saw ready-built shelving of different levels and her imagination soared. Tommy moved to the back of the shop and opened one of the two doors. Ruby followed and they walked into another room of equal size to the first, with wooden rails propped against one wall. The third room was only slightly smaller and a tatty desk and filing cabinet shared its space: an office. Beside that and in a small hallway was a door marked WC. Upstairs was one bedroom, a bathroom and kitchenette, with a shabby sofa pushed under a window –a large, bright and airy living space.

'It's grand, ain't it?' Tommy said, more a statement than a question.

Ruby didn't argue. She couldn't. Tommy was right; it was grand. Not in the sense of luxurious, but she knew Tommy meant grand as in suitable.

'It's ideal,' she said. They went back into the main shop area and Ruby fought excitement – trying to suppress it over her need to carry out war work.

'When this war is over, if it is still empty, I might consider this for –'

'When will that be, Rubes? When will the war be over?'

Tommy stood in front of her with his arms crossed and one leg draped over the other as he tried to look stern.

'Stop trying to make me do something I can't do any more, you monkey. There's more important things –'

Tommy gave an exaggerated yawn, and waved his hand over his mouth. 'Me uncle said it's important. Me auntie told him about you.'

'It's difficult, Tommy.'

'It's difficult, Tommy,' Tommy repeated, his voice sneering and childish.

'Stop it. Lock up and return the key,' Ruby said. Unsettled by the feeling the property had instilled in her, she snapped at Tommy. She laid the blame on his shoulders, then felt foolish for allowing a child to invoke such emotions over an empty shop.

She went to the door and opened it, ushering Tommy outside. 'Keys,' she demanded and held out her hand.

'I'll do it,' Tommy said, and turned the key inside the lock.

'I know you're disappointed, Tommy, and I appreciate the thought.'

'Just go away,' Tommy said and began walking away.

'Tommy! Don't sulk. Tell your uncle I appreciate the thought.'

'Ain't bovvered. See you around.'

The hostility in Tommy's voice, despite his age, startled Ruby and she tugged at his arm. He tried to shake her off, but she held firm – not tight, but enough to prevent him from running from her.

'I'm going home, Tommy. Come with me. Don't be angry with me. You're a little boy – don't worry about me; worry about something else. Not a silly grown-up.'

Tommy shrugged off her arm. 'I 'ate you! You don't wanna 'elp people. Only yourself. You've made Fred sad, didya know?'

Stunned by his outburst, Ruby stood stock still and stared at him. His grubby face was scarlet and a white line appeared across the top of his lip where he pinched them together so tight.

She knelt down beside him. 'What do you mean, I've made Fred sad? Why are you so angry with me, Tommy? It's only a shop.'

Winding the keys around in his hands, Tommy stared at the ground, his rage subsiding. For a small child, he had many adult traits and Ruby wondered again what his home life must be like. Not pleasant if he was constantly wanting to be with her or Fred. He was a lonely child caught up in a violent war, afraid and confused.

'Listen. Let's go to mine and speak with Fred. Let him tell me why he's upset, and we will talk about this place. Maybe someone else might be interested.'

'It's only for you, me uncle said.' Tommy's voice although calmer, faltered. Ruby could see he struggled not to cry.

'We'll talk about it at mine,' Ruby repeated and held out her hand.

'Ain't a baby. 'old your own 'and,' Tommy said and headed back in the direction they'd come.

A bemused Ruby followed.

Back at Garden Cottage, she called Fred in from the garden.

'Ruddy weather. No rain for weeks. Hard as nails. Hello again, young Tommy,' Fred said as he washed his hands.

'We need a chat, Fred. Tommy here,' she said and ruffled Tommy's hair, but was rewarded with a grunt, 'got a bit upset earlier and said I've made you sad.' Ruby pulled out a chair from under the table. 'Sit down and tell me why. He also said I only think about myself. And at the start of our time together that was most definitely not true. However, on the way home I was given the silent treatment and had time to think, and I feel Tommy might be right. I've been selfish.' Ruby gave Tommy a smile. He looked to the floor, his mouth downturned.

'Made me sad?' Fred said and looked at Tommy.

'Apparently so,' Ruby replied.

''e ain't gonna tell you, but I will,' blurted out Tommy.

Ruby pulled out a chair for him to sit on. She called Beatty from upstairs, where she was changing bed linen, and Ruby sat down herself.

'We will get this cleared up, once and for all. Beatty, please join us. There is a bit of a to do going on, and I'm in trouble with Tommy,' she said.

Beatty sat down and looked around at them all. 'My, there's some serious faces here today. Right, get on with it. I'm busy.'

'Tommy told me I only think of myself and I've made Fred sad. I want to know why,' Ruby said and sat back in the chair with her arms folded.

'I think Tommy is referring to when I said it saddened me that you haven't reopened the shop.'

Tommy sat bolt upright. 'You're sad 'cos you ain't got nuffin to mend no more. That's why I bringed round the clock, so you could fix it and be 'appy,' he said.

Ruby rocked in her chair, thinking. Fred sat with an embarrassed look on his face, and Beatty chased a crumb with her finger across the table.

'I can see I've been the topic of conversation. Your faces say it all. Why hasn't anyone spoken to me about all of this before? Did you know about the shop in Hill Street?'

Fred's face reddened. 'Tommy said something about getting you into a new shop. His uncle could fix it. I said it would never happen. You'd never leave.'

Ruby stared at him and then at Tommy. 'Tommy, I think you need to go home. Leave the shop keys here, and tell your uncle I'll bring them round tomorrow. Where does he live – are you all living together or, now your daddy's home, do you have your own place?'

Tommy jumped down from his chair. 'Ain't none of your business. What you want 'em for anyways?' he asked as he put the keys on the table.

'I'm going to take Fred and Beatty to have a look. I've a lot to think about. Leave us to it and I'll speak to you tomorrow. In the morning.'

After Tommy left, Ruby spoke with Fred and Beatty. 'Why didn't you tell me you were missing the repair side of things? I'm sure we could have found space here for you to work. Beatty, if I've been selfish and not helped where I should, I'm sorry.'

Beatty pulled a face and slowly shook her head. 'You've worked as hard as the rest of us around here. Don't fret over a child having a tantrum. I don't understand the boy – always hanging around here. I wonder if he's always wanted a big sister. Oh, listen to me. I'm sorry, duck, I didn't mean to upset you. Thoughtless.'

'You haven't upset me, Beatty. It's fine. As for Tommy, that child has me worried. He's latched onto me and I'm concerned his home life isn't a happy one. What can we do for him?'

Ruby saw Fred smile. 'What?' she said.

'You were worried about not thinking of others, and that's all you do – fret over other folks. Listen, there's nothing we can do for the boy; we just have to be around when he's wanting a chat. He's like you in a lot of ways.'

Ruby frowned at him. 'What do you mean, like me?'

'Thinks of others and likes the company of adults.'

Beatty got to her feet and rested her hands on the edge of the table. 'Talking about adults. This business with the shop. It's a bit odd his uncle didn't come with the boy and explain himself. I understand he'd approve of your business – we all do; I miss having a nosey around and meeting others for a chinwag – but to leave it to a kiddy? Strange, if you ask me. What do you reckon, Fred?'

'Same,' said Fred.

'Man of many words. Ruby, what do you know about the boy's family . . . this uncle?'

Ruby shrugged. 'As much as you two. Tommy seems to want to please him, and me, but is frightened of his auntie. They live with her, and whether this uncle is her husband, I don't know. I thought I saw his mum this morning, with a man I assumed was his dad, but it appears it was his uncle. I wish I'd introduced myself now.'

'Are you going to set up a new Shadwell's?'

'Come with me. Come and have a look. I got goose bumps when I saw it. It's big. If you both think I ought to start again with Shadwell's, then I'll do it. I told Helen I wanted a factory job, but I know I'd be unhappy. She said I've money enough, and I think I should use it to set up something new. I want you to be part of it again – both of you.'

CHAPTER 17

10th July 1941

Unlocking the back door to the shop, Ruby stepped into the silence. Looking around and seeing the shelves stocked, waiting for another day of customers to decide whether to buy or sell, she enjoyed a moment of pride.

Tommy's face had lit up when she'd refused to hand over the keys and teased him until telling of her plan to reopen the shop. He'd run home to tell his uncle, who'd sent details of when the rent was to be handed to Tommy, and a vague promise to visit when he was on leave again.

Adjusting to Tommy's strange family ways of working, Ruby chose to stop nagging Tommy for details of his home life. He filled a gap for Ruby, and when she found a boxed game of Ludo and Snakes and Ladders she put it to one side with a promise they'd play a game on a rainy day.

Her new skirt fitted her petite waist, and she wore it with a white blouse. Beatty complimented her eye for style. This gave Ruby an idea for the second room, and Fred created a small cubicle with a curtain for privacy. Second-hand clothes were displayed on the rails now fixed into place around the room. The clothes rationing regulations of June made this room a popular one from the moment they'd opened the doors five days previously. Beatty worked on a pile of repairs in exchange for coins or goods, and Fred worked his magic with mechanical repairs. Between them, they kept an eye on the shop floor when Ruby walked the streets in search of abandoned items. She reinstated her agreement with the rag man, and Ruby knew Tommy's outburst was the best thing to have happened. She felt useful once more.

Today, she planned to work in the office. Fred had rubbed down and stained the table, using the dregs of the teapot. A rub of beeswax brought the wood back to life. Beatty had re-padded and covered the chair and old curtains from the cottage draped the window, which faced south, and made the room a cheerful place to work. Ruby placed the new ledgers and pens on the desk and smiled at the pile of scrap paper notes left for her by her friends. She had a busy day of book-keeping ahead and looked forward to meeting Tommy's uncle; according to Tommy, he was going to pay a visit when he'd finished some important business. Tommy, in the meantime, had errands to run for his uncle, but promised to return to sweep the floors at the end of the day. From the day the doors opened, Tommy lost his sour attitude and his bubbly personality returned.

Fred and Beatty worked with the customers and Ruby loved to hear the natural banter between the two. She stretched her arms above her head and went out into the shop to see how business was doing.

Whilst rearranging a row of china cups she noticed a man about to enter the shop. He stood out from the regular customers. His suit, a blue serge pinstripe, was smart, as was the wide-brimmed navy hat on his head. Ruby looked at his shoes, highly polished black brogues. He smoked a cigarette and tossed the last of it into the gutter. When he stepped inside the shop his eyes darted from one shelf to another before he settled his stare on Beatty.

Ruby watched from the far side of the shop. Tommy's uncle – it had to be him. The man was of average height and build but his face was lean, with a jutting jaw; he sported a thin black moustache across his top lip. He pushed out his chest and held himself tall – Ruby would say peacockish, if there was such a word – as he approached Beatty, behind the counter.

'You must be Ruby – the one the kid goes on about,'

the man said to Beatty as she looked up to face him. His voice held the hint of an accent, but not the same as Tommy's.

'And you are?' Beatty asked.

'Not important. I'm here to say I'll be leaving soon, and the boy will be my mouthpiece. As I said in my message, he'll collect the rent and take it to my sister. She's been a customer of yours, and will be again. The boy helps us out.'

Ruby listened as Tommy's uncle spoke in a rasping voice. His words were clipped, and he didn't come across as the patient type.

Ruby gave a polite cough and stepped forward, holding out her hand. 'Actually, that's Beatty. I'm Ruby Shadwell. I'm pleased to meet you at last, Mr – I'm sorry, Tommy never told us your name.'

'He's no need to tell it, but if you have to have a name, it's Earl. I take it you heard what I've just said. Bit young to run a business, aren't you?'

Ruby doubted Earl was his real name. His eyes were a steel grey and unfriendly, and he showed no intention of shaking her hand so she put it into her skirt pocket. It surprised her to think he'd negotiated a deal on the property, just on Tommy's word and for a stranger. He came across as a man who'd have enjoyed lording it over a female, much as he did now.

'The war makes some of us grow up faster than we'd

like, Earl. I look younger than I am, and a lady never gives her age,' she said, adding a hint of theatrical attitude.

'Spiky. You speak your mind. Good. You need guts in business. You gave a good price when the boy traded with you, I'll give you that. Honesty earns respect. I repay honesty. The war has ruined some, and others have clawed back to shake things up a bit. We're the shakers, me and you,' Earl replied, waving a freshly lit cigarette at her.

'Thank you, but I'm not a shaker. I've no intention of shaking things up. I want a quiet life with a thriving business,' Ruby said.

'Ah, but you've already joined the club, Ruby. You've shaken up the buyers and sellers – I know – I sell. I hear rumours of unrest.' Earl's voice was menacing and his face serious, but suddenly he burst out laughing. 'Gullible. Look at the pair of you. I don't listen to, or hear, rumours. I start them. You are my rumour this week. I've spread the word you're back in business. Brace yourself, Ruby Shadwell. Good luck.'

Without waiting for a reply, he turned on his heel and left the shop. Ruby and Beatty stared at his back and then faced each other in disbelief.

'Did that really just happen?' Ruby asked.

Beatty made a whooshing sound and waved her hand high. 'There he was, gone.'

They both laughed at the ridiculous way he'd behaved. Ruby stepped around the shop, mimicking his strutting walk.

'As for that chin –' Beatty said and stuck out her jaw.

Ruby gasped through her laugh. 'Call me Earl. I don't listen to rumours, I start them. What an arrogant man,' Ruby said when she caught her breath.

Fred came from the back room.

'You missed a treat, Fred. Tommy's uncle, home on leave – Earl,' Ruby said.

Beatty put her hand to her forehead. 'Fools. He's not in the forces – no uniform. Government office worker. Pinstripe suit.'

'Spy, I bet. He was so cagey about his name.'

'Earl what?' Fred asked.

'He didn't give a surname,' Ruby replied.

'There's your answer. He's an earl of somewhere. Like Beatty said, government man in a pinstripe.'

With a loud tut, Ruby put her hands up as if in protest. 'Have you seen the state of Tommy? How can he be the nephew of an earl? The man's a dreamer. Probably bottom of the pack in his unit, and gets a kick out of playacting the tough man when he's on leave.'

Beatty grunted her approval at Ruby's statement. 'And I still can't work out why he's keen to give Tommy what he wants for a friend but doesn't look after the child's needs. Still, we can't judge what we don't understand.

They must do things different in the capital,' she said with a sniff of indifference, and lifted a flask from a basket behind the counter.

'Beatty, there's a kitchen upstairs; you don't have to bring tea from home,' Ruby said with a giggle.

'I am not climbing stairs to put the kettle on and then bringing cups down. No, thank you. I'll save my breath and bring a flask. If my friends drop in, I could be up and down those stairs all day. Want one, Fred?'

Ruby left Beatty fussing over Fred and went into her office, where the sunshine flowed through the window. She sat at the desk and pondered over Beatty's comments about the kitchen upstairs. Thanks to Beatty's loveable nature, she'd drawn in a few local women and in the past two days the shop became a meeting place. They chatted and knitted together, age no barrier.

'That's it!' Ruby shouted.

'Problem?' Fred called out.

'No. Stay there. I've an idea.'

Ruby returned to the shop, smiled at her friends, looked inside the room with clothes and back into the main area again. 'Back in a mo,' she said and ran upstairs.

An idea had formed and she ran back to her friends. Breathless with excitement, she waved her hand in a random fashion until she'd calmed enough to speak. 'I want to create a meeting room. Out the back. In the office.'

Beatty laid down her knitting. 'Pardon me?'

'We could bring the kitchen downstairs and you can brew up down here. Somewhere for your friends to stay for a knit and chat, and the office can go upstairs. We can make a storeroom and repair workshop for Fred.'

Beatty picked up her knitting again and cast on a stitch. 'I can't charge friends for a cup of tea,' she said.

'Encourage them to bring a twist of tea so our rations don't run dry, and maybe you can sell some of the things you all make. Raise money for the troops. Set up a group. Someone might be a bit lonely and like the idea of sitting in the company of others,' Ruby said.

Fred laughed. 'Do you really want to alter this place around?'

Beatty's needles clacked in the background, then she laid the project down again. 'It would be useful, having the kitchen down here. And Ruby's right – I see women wandering around in a daze every day. Some are in temporary lodgings. A place where they can drop in, chat and be of use, doing something for our troops – yes, I think it's a grand idea, duck.'

Fred struggled from his chair. Ruby had a sneaking feeling he was trying to prove a point. 'Not sure how much I can do nowadays. Garden's enough for these knees and this back, but I'll have a go.'

Ruby put her hands on his shoulders and gave a gentle press downwards. 'Sit down. I'll get someone to do it for us. One of the customers is bound to have a family member in the trade. I've earned enough to pay and, besides, it's lovely having you around, Beatty. You're good for business. I'll share the chores at home and free you up to work here on a more regular basis.'

'I scare them off, I suppose. I'm happy – it will mean I'll be free to do the repairs in peace,' said Fred, teasing.

By the end of the day plans were scribbled down and a builder promised for evening work, after his main task of restoring private properties for bomb victims.

As she climbed into bed Ruby's thoughts and dreams drifted into happier times.

CHAPTER 18

3rd September 1941

The summer flew by and soon the days settled into cooler and darker evenings. The war entered its third year, and people spoke of nothing else. Precious sleep continued to be disturbed by nightly sirens, and Coventarians wanted revenge. News of war took over their lives, and no one dared predict the end for fear of disappointment.

For Ruby and her new family, life still continued along an even path as they strengthened their emotional links into something more solid in order to cope. Financially they were stable.

Thankful for a hardworking builder, Ruby stood back and admired the pretty room she and Beatty had finished creating that morning. The ugliness of outside could not touch the delicate pastels inside Ruby and Beatty's

Meeting Place. Fred had created the wooden sign now hanging on a hook beside the door of the newly decorated room. Both women clapped as soon as he showed them. Eager to involve Beatty in the project, Ruby had agreed to Beatty's favourite colours, green and pink, and the calm shades gave a feminine feel to the room. As she'd told Fred, men were welcome, but Ruby knew the visitors would predominantly be women.

Tommy arrived to inspect the finished work, and whistled his approval. As he strolled around the room, looking very much out of place, Ruby smiled inwardly. He copied his uncle in most things. Having met Earl, Ruby understood the influence he'd have over a boy of Tommy's age. It still irked her that he kept his nephew looking on the shabby side. Probably a lesson for Tommy's mother, who Ruby desperately wanted to meet.

'Tommy, bring your mum for a treat with Beatty and me one afternoon. We'd love to meet her.'

Tommy picked a petal from a rose in one of the four vases on each table in the room.

'She's busy,' he said.

'Always? Surely she must have a few hours to spend with you, Tommy.'

'Nah,' he said and moved out of the room into the shop.

Ruby followed. 'Well, mention it, at least,' she said, no longer willing to force the subject on a disinterested child.

'Yeah, but don't think she'll bovva. Here. I've got somethin' from me auntie,' he replied, and held out his hand.

A shiver of impatience ran through Ruby, but she held back from saying anything and took the small box from his hand. 'That's lovely. Oh, it's a tiny painting.'

Ruby beckoned Beatty as she walked into the shop, laden with a basket of her freshly baked pies, and wrinkled her nose with approval. 'They smell good. Tommy can have one for lunch. Look at what his aunt has sent today.' Ruby held out the box.

'Was your aunt a lady or someone rich, Tommy? She has perfect things, and they look expensive,' Beatty asked him as she guided him to a seat before handing him a pie. 'Sit there and don't make a mess.'

Tommy's mouth was full before he could reply to her question, and Ruby got the impression he had no intention of answering. The question was a valid one. Beatty was right; his aunt's things were nice. It crossed Ruby's mind that Earl and his wife might have seen better days, and the war had brought them harder times, hence the selling of their goods. When they'd first met, Tommy had mentioned rent and a landlord. Maybe they'd fallen from grace and sold a grand house.

As her imagination ran away with her, women ventured into the shop and she sat back, allowing Beatty to usher them into the new meeting room. Gasps of pleasure and excitement rewarded both of them, and Ruby gave herself a virtual pat on the back. Everything was falling into place. A good place.

She watched Tommy pick at the last of his pie and lick his lips; the boy had very little in life, and he appreciated every crumb. Now was the time to help him with something else.

'Tommy, a lady came by with some of her son's outgrown clothes and asked if I knew a lad they might fit. Do you think your mum would be offended if I gave them to you? They look your size and you've grown so fast these past few weeks, I'm sure she'd be grateful but, not having met her, I can't be certain.'

She didn't tell him she'd been holding back on items each time they were brought in and put them to one side, waiting for his next visit.

'Don't think she'd care eiver way. Me auntie'll be pleased, always moaning I cost a lot. I'm off. Me uncle wants 'is money and I ain't to dawdle.'

'Your uncle? I thought he'd returned to his unit?' Ruby questioned Tommy and watched the boy's face flush a dark shade of red.

'I meant me auntie. It's all the same, ain't it?'

Tommy's response was hostile and defensive. Ruby chose not to say anything.

'Mind how you go, Tommy. See you again soon. Hope the clothes fit.'

The last sentence was said with feeling. Tommy's

clothes were not fit for purpose and she longed to see him in fresh ones.

Tommy's voice rang out about an hour later and disturbed the peace Ruby enjoyed inside her office.

'Get off me! Oi.'

Beatty's voice now joined in with Tommy's. 'What is going on here? Leave the boy be, let him go! I'm closing up – go, shoo.'

'Ouch!'

Ruby tried to ignore the clumping sound, and returned to her books.

'I ain't a sack o' coal.' Tommy's voice lifted several decibels higher.

'Kindly leave, both of you. I'm shutting shop. Out!' Beatty shouted, and Ruby could no longer ignore the chaos beneath her room.

With a sigh, she laid down her pen and went to investigate. When she stepped into the shop all heads turned to face her. Beatty, Tommy – who sat on his backside on the floor – and John. Her heart skipped a beat, as always whenever she saw him. She prayed the warmth rushing throughout her body didn't force forward a blush. She turned her attention back to Tommy and Beatty.

'What on earth is going on? I'm working, and the noise from here isn't good for business. Beatty, I'll deal with Tommy. You head home. I'll see you later,' she said, then turned to John. 'Hello again.'

John stood over Tommy. 'Hello, Ruby.'

'I'm happy to stay,' Beatty said, her head moving from one to the other.

'Hello again, Beatty,' John said, and Ruby watched him as he charmed Beatty with one of his heart-winning smiles.

'I'll leave you to it. See you later, Ruby,' Beatty said and waved to them before leaving the shop. Ruby waited until she heard the door click shut before she turned and looked down at Tommy.

'Tommy, what are you doing on my floor?' she asked and flicked her fingers upwards as instruction for him to stand. She then turned her attention to John. 'I assume you are the cause of him shouting out in pain?'

Tommy jumped to his feet and spoke before the man had an opportunity to say a word. ''e clipped me ear. I didn't steal a fing. I didn't!' he said and ran to Ruby's side. To her surprise, he grabbed her hand.

'I saw you. A quick dip of your hand and the woman's basket was lighter by four sausages.' John wagged his finger at Tommy as he spoke.

'It was me auntie. She told me to run to 'ome to me uncle wiv 'em,' Tommy protested.

Ruby moved her head to John and raised an eyebrow, waiting for his response.

'So why did you drop them when I shouted?' John said and slapped a package onto the counter, in which Ruby assumed were the sausages.

Turning back to Tommy, Ruby tilted her head in question. He looked to the floor then lifted his head and stood back upright, with his chest puffed out. "Cos you give me a scare, that's why. I'm only a kid. Pick on someone your own size, mate.'

Ruby tried not to laugh at his attempt to scare a member of the armed forces.

John turned to Ruby. 'I'm not sure of what is going on here, but Tommy could do with a fresh set of clothes, and a better lie to tell next time he's bringing home supper, or he'll find himself in deep trouble with the law. As for being your son, you could have told me. I'm surprised, I will admit. I'll walk away, Ruby. Take care and thank you for befriending me when I needed it most.' John's voice was clipped and far from friendly.

Before Ruby could put John right about her relationship to Tommy, he was gone. She stood open-mouthed in amazement and stared after him in disbelief.

'What might I ask just happened there, Tommy Jenkins? And don't even think of lying. And why on earth did he think you were my son?'

'I didn't nick a fing. I ain't no tealeaf.'

'I see. So gaining four sausages for nothing from a woman's basket without her noticing is legal trading nowadays, eh?'

Puffing out his chest again, Tommy glared at her. 'You weren't there.'

'But your auntie was. I take it she didn't see John chase after you and try to get her precious goods off you. The ones you were innocently taking home for Uncle. I'm not stupid, Tommy. Answer me.'

'I told 'im I lived 'ere. 'e was 'urting me arm and me auntie's 'ouse is a long way away. I said you wus me mum.'

Ruby threw up her arms in resignation. 'I give up. Take yourself home and stay out of trouble,' she said and walked to the door.

'What about the sausages?' Tommy asked.

'They will be cooked, sliced and shared out in the community room tomorrow. And you need to stay away from trouble.'

Tommy's hand reached out for the packet. 'But I –'

Ruby tutted. 'No *but* about it, just get yourself home. I need to lock up and head home myself. Try going to school, Tommy Jenkins, and wear some of the clothes I gave you.'

Nudging him out of the door, she looked about for a sign that John was still around, but there was no one in the street. She went over what he'd said and felt a flush of anger rise. Just the thought of her looking old enough to have a child Tommy's age made her wonder what he thought of her. A loose woman, maybe?

CHAPTER 19

26th September 1941

Trying to avoid getting her toes crushed in the crowd, Ruby stood on tiptoe.

'Can you see him?' Beatty said, nudging Ruby in the ribs.

'Hold on, and stop nudging me – it hurts,' Ruby said and stretched her neck forward.

'He's walking past now. Quick, eyes centre and you'll see him. Wave your flag.'

Beatty did as Ruby said, and Ruby dodged the stick of the Union Jack flag her friend waved with great enthusiasm.

'I see him! Yoo-hoo, Mr Churchill!' Beatty called and Ruby burst out laughing.

'He can't hear you, Beatt!'

'Oh, he can! Mr Prime Minister, over here. Oh, look, he's waving at me.'

True enough, looking splendid in his top hat and puffing on a cigar, Winston Churchill waved Beatty's way.

Ruby groaned. 'We'll not hear the end of this, Fred,' she said and turned to her friend on her left, grateful his enthusiasm for flag-flying didn't reach the level of Beatty's.

After witnessing the historic visit outside a factory producing aeroplane parts, a noise cut through the applause of the crowd and Ruby froze. She grabbed hold of Fred's wrist and twisted her head skyward.

'Planes. Fred, planes. Quick, let's get out of here. Beatty, hurry.' Ruby, frantic with fear, tugged at Beatty's sleeve.

Fred stroked her arm and Beatty rammed her flag into her handbag, grabbing hold of Ruby, who was now shaking with panic.

'It's a flyover. A display. Oh, darling girl, it's fine. It's all fine. You stay, Fred. I'll get her home. Look at her, she's petrified, and no wonder.'

Beatty held onto Ruby and guided her to the end of the street, where it was empty of people.

Ruby stopped walking. 'I . . . I . . . I . . .' she sobbed into Beatty's shoulder.

Beatty patted her back and made soothing noises.

'It was unexpected. I know. Hush now. They've gone. They didn't think, I'm sure they didn't think. There, there.'

Able to let go and catch her breath once more, Ruby took a step backwards. As she did so, a figure across the road captured her attention. John lifted his camera and a smidgeon of annoyance reared inside Ruby. Once again, he'd taken a photograph of her at a vulnerable time.

'I'm sorry, Beatty. The noise of the plane took me by surprise, and now you've missed waving goodbye to Mr Churchill. Go back to Fred. I'll head to the shop and open up.'

'If you're sure you feel better. Calmer? Promise?'

Ruby embraced Beatty. 'I'm fine. Go. Don't hurry back; enjoy the day with Fred.'

Ruby waited until Beatty was no longer in view and crossed the road. She looked in the direction John had walked, but could see no sign of him. Knowing what he did for the war effort, and seeing him take another photograph after his sweeping statements a few weeks before, made her feel a little like a specimen in a jar – something to be ogled at whenever on display – and he'd encroached upon her moment of grief without asking more than once. Another glance across the flattened land showed he'd moved on elsewhere and she moved back onto the cleared streets towards her shop.

Her heart sank when she saw Tommy sitting on the doorstep.

'Did you see 'im?' Tommy called, shading his eyes from a shaft of sunlight straining through the cloud.

'Who?'

'The guvna, the big man. Winnie,' Tommy said.

'Our Prime Minister. Yes, I saw him.'

Tommy leapt to his feet and his toothless smile appeared as he cocked his head to one side, placed his hands on his hips, and proceeded to mimic Ruby.

'Our Prime Minist – er. Yesss, I sawwer *H*im,' he said.

Ruby pushed past him and unlocked the door. 'My morning hasn't started well, Tommy. My mood is not at its best, so I suggest you run off and take the mickey from some other poor soul who's had the pleasure of your company since you graced Coventry. Now, get out of my way! Goodbye.'

She shoved open the door, closed it before he could step inside and put the Closed sign on show. Ruby was in no mood to deal with Tommy, or purchase a trinket of his aunt's. Someone else would have to suffer his cheek from now on. It was time he found another friend to annoy – one of his own age. Besides, today would have been her brother's tenth birthday, and the last person she wanted to share the day with was a boy with a toothy grin and a cheeky manner whose blood didn't run through her veins.

She tried not to see him press his face against the glass, nor cave in when he pulled both bottom eyelids down with his forefingers and push his nostrils upwards with his little ones.

She hastily scribbled a note for the door: *In Honour of the Prime Minister's visit, we are CLOSED for the day.* The moment she taped the notice to the door, Tommy's face peered up at it and she watched as he picked through the letters, deciphering the words she'd written.

His fist hammered on the door. 'Oi, Rubes. You feelin' ill? I spelled the word Closed. You never close this place.' His voice filtered through the letterbox and Ruby gulped down verbal instructions for him to leave her alone. The more she played to his need for attention, the more he would seek it out.

She sat in the meeting room against the wall, her legs drawn up to her chin. For all the cheerful days she'd enjoyed since 15th November 1940, this one overpowered them. She'd tried so hard to wave a flag and cheer on the Prime Minister, but sometimes she held the inner belief that politicians had let them down – let Coventry blaze for the good of the rest of the country. Other days, they were her heroes. Today a little boy, mourned by his sister, might have run free on Radford Common, or begged for a twist of aniseed. Today his personality was at the forefront of her mind. Today James lived.

'Stop, James. Leave your sisters alone.' Her mother's voice rang out around the yard, and Ruby pictured the scene – one in which she'd once played centre star and heroine.

'Mummy, they were teasing me as much!' his lisping voice protested.

'Just look at the state of all of you. Potatoes are for picking, and then mashing. Not the other way around. Behave, and please don't ruin the crop. Lucy, put that book down and help your sister. Ruby, keep him under control.'

To Ruby, that was one of the greatest challenges in her life. No one could control James, but he could be loved and she'd done so from the moment he was born; bribery helped with keeping him out of trouble. He'd once climbed over the churchwarden's wall and scrumped plums from a tree and Ruby caught him selling them on the corner of the street as cheap excess of their father's stock. She'd made him take the money to the church and put every coin into the paupers' box. She'd never told her parents, and James never let them down again. Any time she asked him to do something, he did so without grumbling.

James, her beloved James. He'd have loved her shop, and the contents. Lucy, dear Lucy; her duty today would have been to recite a poem or sing a song at teatime. Each birthday celebration, Lucy had enjoyed sharing a snippet of literary interest for them to discuss before bedtime. A simple life, but a contented one. Now, for them, no longer a life, and Ruby had to find contentment without them. She placed her hands over her ears and hummed out a tuneless song to block out Tommy's persistent door-banging.

CHAPTER 20

'Oi, Rubes, I'm really worryin' now. Gonna get Fred.'

Tommy's determination to get her attention by kicking at the base of the front door now distracted Ruby from her stroll down memory lane. She could not afford a new door.

In one way Tommy saved her from gnawing pain, but in another he'd fragmented her thoughts and shattered them forever. Thoughts never returned in the same format; they often bled out a little of the true facts and ignored important things when the mind could no longer retain a memory.

'You'll never forget me, but he needs you, Ruby. Help him. Only you can.' James's voice interrupted her thoughts.

'James . . .' she whispered into the silence of the room. Nothing.

'Rubes.' Tommy's voice turned to a whine – a noise she could no longer ignore. Present day life overrode a past she clung onto, and a whining child never failed to disturb the peace. Especially one using her family's pet name for her.

'Stop your hammering, Tommy Jenkins,' Ruby called out. She stood up and went to the door. The moment she turned the key in the door she froze. Tommy's uncle stood beside him. His painted moustache and black greased slicked-back hair were more prominent than she recalled. His eyes held false smiles. His nicotine-stained teeth parted in a fake grin. She'd witnessed them before, but today they were more prominent. There was an air of arrogance oozing from him, and it irked Ruby when he pushed his foot into the doorway to prevent her from closing the door.

'Ruby... We meet again. Tommy here was quite worried about you. A good job I was passing. I noticed your sign. A businesswoman needs to be ahead of the game. The crowd of onlookers will pass by here shortly, and they'll be in a buoyant mood. Open this door wide, make it inviting.'

Ruby stared at him, then down to his foot, his highly polished shoe still wedging the door.

'You'll scuff your shoe, Mr Earl,' she said. He was too familiar, and for the first time she'd been alone she wished Fred or Beatty were with her. 'I'm not opening. If you are worried about payment for your friend's rent, please don't be. I am able to pay, even if I close for one half day.'

To her annoyance, Tommy scampered under his uncle's arm and into the shop.

'Rascal,' his uncle said, and Ruby turned to see what the boy was up to, but in that split second regretted it. She felt the gentle push of Earl moving inside the shop. He went to close the door but she picked up the wooden block Fred had made into a doorstop and rushed forward.

'Don't close it . . . You were right. The people – they'll be coming past soon.' She pushed the door wedge into place.

'Feel free to browse,' she said and sat behind the counter. 'I take it you're on leave again.'

Earl frowned at her in question.

She pointed to his pinstriped suit. 'No uniform.'

He said nothing, just stared and wiped a pinkie across his top lip with practised precision. Ruby waited for a reply, but none came so she turned her attention to Tommy.

He stood near a selection of books for children.

'You can choose one and sit with it until your uncle leaves, Tommy.'

Earl moved into the meeting room. 'Attractive to the eye,' he said and Ruby felt the hairs along her arms rise to attention. The man literally made her skin crawl.

He picked up an old newspaper and flicked it open. With slow deliberate movements, he pulled out a chair and sat at a table. 'I hear you serve tea and coffee here now. I've taken to drinking coffee. Never used to, was always a tea man, but tastes change. Make me a cup, there's a girl,' he said in a superior tone.

'But I –' Ruby stuttered. She was cross with herself for allowing him to assume control of the situation. He ignored her and lifted the paper in front of his face. She doubted he was reading anything; it was an act of dismissal.

With a huff loud enough to get through to him that he'd offended her, Ruby stomped into the kitchen and filled the kettle. She waited for the pop sound as the gas licked at the match and surged forward with a flame. She took the time to calm her nerves. Earl had quite literally made himself at home, and he was an unwelcome guest. Through the gap in the door she saw Tommy turn the pages of the book. She wondered about his reading ability. The child never attended school – or so it appeared, with his regular visits to the shop.

'Tommy, want a milk?' she called through into the shop.

'No, he doesn't,' Earl's voice growled through from the meeting room. 'He's business to deal with. Boy, it's time.'

Ruby chose to ignore him and walked into the shop

211

with a glass three-quarters full of creamy milk and a sweet biscuit. She put her finger to her lips as she handed it to Tommy and pointed to the far corner of the shop, out of view from the meeting room. Tommy hesitated, but the pull of the drink and biscuit was too strong and he sat cross-legged, sipping his treat.

'Where's my coffee?' Earl's voice yelled out.

'I'm coming. And please show a little respect. This is my shop after all,' Ruby retorted. She made the coffee weak in the hope he'd never return.

As she placed it onto the table he snatched at her wrist and gripped it tight.

'Ouch! Let go!' Ruby shouted.

'Quiet. Get this straight, girly. I'm in charge around here. I call the shots. You only have this place thanks to me. Show a bit of gratitude.' Earl snarled out his words and Ruby's dislike for him rose to another level.

'You will let go of me right now. I might be a girl, but I will not be bullied. I'll report you to your superior,' she said and rubbed at her wrist when he released her. Her legs trembled and her stomach rolled over, creating a nausea she suppressed by inhaling deep and slow.

'You've got a wild spirit and I'll tame it, have no fear,' Earl said. 'And next time, don't be so stingy with the coffee powder – or sugar.'

Ruby's temper flared and she could no longer stand the man's presence. To her relief, Fred walked through the door. She saw by his face he'd heard the conversation. Her wrist burned and when she looked down at it she saw a wide red weal running full circle around it; before Fred saw it, she snatched up her cardigan and pulled down the sleeves.

Fred entered the room, gave Ruby a brief glance then turned to Earl.

'I think it's time you left, sir. Go – and take your bullying ways out on our enemy. Show courage against grown men; don't try to frighten young girls. I fought in the last war and know a coward when I see one. Where's your uniform, man?' Fred's voice was the loudest and strongest Ruby had ever heard. His elderly hand shook with age rather than fear as he pointed at Earl.

Earl stood tall. His menacing eyes bored into Fred's face. 'That's for me to know, old man. I'm no coward, I assure you, and if you call me one again you'll not be able to walk—'

Ruby sensed she must calm the situation before it grew out of hand. She interrupted Earl's verbal assault. 'Fred, thank you, I'll be fine. You head home; I'll see you later.'

She gave Fred a hug and smiled as his stubble grazed her cheek. 'Have you lost your razor?' she said with a giggle.

'Cheeky girl. So long as you're sure,' he said and turned to Earl. 'Don't touch a hair on her head. Hear me?'

Earl scowled back at Fred, and Ruby encouraged Fred out of harm's way and waved him off.

Back inside, she smoothed her hands down the front of her skirt, composing herself. The atmosphere outside was warm and muggy; inside, it was tense. She re-joined Earl. He was a man who'd continue with aggressive reactions if she went back to him with attitude so, against her desire to throw everything at him, she opted for a humble approach.

'Earl, Fred means well and he's protecting me. I think it might be wise for you to leave. I'm a little sensitive today; it would have been my little brother's birthday. So, as you can see, I have not controlled my feelings properly and may have come across as a little rude. I appreciate all you've done for me with regard to this place.'

Whilst she was talking she waved and flicked her hand behind her back to attract Tommy's attention. She'd seen him move closer to take in the adult conversation, but Ruby knew he'd suffer the backlash of anger Earl would unleash once he left the building. Fortunately, Tommy saw her signal and ran. Unfortunately, he ran straight into a customer, knocking the wind from him. He hesitated and, unable to get into the street, turned around and ran to Ruby's side. She looked down at him and stroked his head. His frightened eyes stared up at her and portrayed him for the little boy he really was, and her heart went out to him. She knew from that moment she would protect him from his uncle. She needed to speak with his mother, and possibly his aunt.

A sudden movement and the utterance of a few unsavoury words from Tommy's uncle brought Ruby back to the present. Before Earl could open his mouth to question Tommy as to why he was still around, Ruby turned to the customer. For a fleeting second her stomach fluttered when she saw it was John.

'Good afternoon. I hope you weren't too winded by Tommy,' she said, her voice cold and businesslike.

John didn't smile. 'No injuries. Had he been a few pounds heavier it might have turned out a different story. Your son is fast on his feet, though.'

'John, he's . . . I –'

Within seconds, Earl moved forward, interrupting Ruby. He held out his hand and nudged Ruby to one side. 'The name's Earl. That's a fine piece of equipment, and not British services, I'll wager,' he said, giving John a hearty handshake.

Ruby took the opportunity to stand between both men, and noted Earl's fake smile lifted his painted moustache. It was so black compared to the last time she'd seen him, she was convinced that too was fake. She waited for him to claim Tommy and enjoy lording it over John by putting him straight about being his uncle. It amazed her when all he did was reach out and touch the camera around John's neck. The two men were complete opposites. One pretending to be a man and the other everything she imagined one to be. Ruby had never before been in a position where she could compare men; her father and grandfathers – and Fred – were the only men she'd held close in her life, hardly romance material.

'John Clayton. And thank you; it is a vital piece of machinery. As much so as a gun.'

John might have taken Earl's hand, but his eyes were on Ruby when he spoke and she hated the warm sensation rising from the base of her neck to her cheeks. He always made her blush, even when she tried to control her feelings of attraction towards him.

'Mrs Shadwell, and Tommy, I've come to apologise for my rudeness yesterday,' he said, and held out his hand to Ruby.

'John, I . . . um . . . yes, thank you, but I'm not M—'

An irritated Earl switched the conversation back to the camera before she could correct John about her being Tommy's mother. 'Yes, a lovely piece of equipment. You've met Ruby before?' he asked.

'Yes, we've met a few times. I took photographs of a bombsite and your wife pointed out I needed to be more sensitive; it was once somebody's home.'

Ruby gave a brief shake of her head. 'You caught me at a bad moment, and I'm n—'

'Where in the world are you from, John? That's an

accent I don't recognise.' Earl draped his arm across John's shoulder and guided him towards the community room. 'Tea for our guest, Ruby,' he said abruptly.

Another surge of irritation launched itself; she needed to get him away from John. Ruby gave a tut. 'Earl, let the man sit and enjoy a cup of tea before you interrogate him. And, no matter where you're from in the world, a cuppa is always welcome. John?' She directed her gaze to John, who nodded. He wore a strange look on his face, and she longed for one of his smiles to break the awkward atmosphere between them. The heat in her body made her uncomfortable, and her thoughts confused her. Why on earth would she fantasise about a virtual stranger stroking her cheek, or touching her lips?

Then she remembered Tommy, and set about getting him away from Earl.

'Tommy,' she called softly when she reached the kitchen, and beckoned him to her. She bent to look into his face. She stroked a piece of his lank hair back behind his ear. His whole being screamed out for love and attention. For care and nurturing. Something told Ruby she was the person chosen to set him on the right path.

'Run to my house. Stay there with Fred and Beatty. Tell them I said you are to stay the night. You can enjoy a bath and a bite to eat. I'll tell your uncle you left – said you had something to do. Or tell him the truth, that you're staying over for a treat.'

'I can't – 'e'll kill me. You don't understand. It's best I do as 'e says. See you anover day.' Tommy glanced over his shoulder, his nervous tension obvious.

And, before Ruby could argue, Tommy left the shop. She rushed after him, but watched as his scuffed shoes and skinny legs disappeared around the corner. She looked back into the shop, torn between wanting to chase after him and going inside to give Earl a piece of her mind. Her heart sank. Tommy might be frightened of his uncle, but she wasn't and, although he made her uncomfortable, she was not prepared for him to take over her life as he had Tommy's.

She strode with confidence back into the meeting room. Both men were deep in conversation. Earl turned to her. 'You took your time. Where's the boy?' he said.

'Gone to carry out your errand,' Ruby said, her voice blunt and firm.

'Our friend, John, is from Canada. Of course I know where it is, but you wouldn't have heard of it,' he said and sniggered, giving John a wink.

Earl's patronising assumption infuriated Ruby, and she placed the teapot on the table a little harder than necessary.

'As a matter of fact, I *do* know whereabouts in the world Canada is, *and* I know Queen Victoria chose Ottawa to be its capital city. I will confess I have no idea where that is, but I do know a little geography, thanks to having an education, much to the surprise of some people.'

Ruby bit back a triumphant smile which she suspected had a hint of smugness about it and John looked up, raising one eyebrow.

'Ah, but you know very little about war, and the important part some of us play in it,' Earl spat back.

'I understand this war – possibly better than you, Earl. I've experienced the sharp point of the enemy's intention,' Ruby retorted, but stopped herself from saying any more when she noticed Earl's knuckles whiten as he gripped his hands together. She wasn't stupid enough to ignore he'd use them if provoked too much.

'Mind you, I reckon you know far more than me, Earl. Being a travelled soldier and wiser to the ways of the world,' Ruby said in a pacifying tone – one she'd heard her mother use on her father whenever his temper required dampening. Although it took a lot to make her father's rise, Ruby noticed Earl's temper never subsided. Each time she'd met him, he came across as an extremely angry person.

'Yes, well . . .' Earl said, and preened his top lip once again.

John smiled at Ruby. 'You serve, Earl?' he asked.

With a slight cough, Earl ran his finger around his collar. He sipped from the cup Ruby handed him.

'I do. Not always in uniform, though. You understand?' Earl winked and tapped the side of his nose.

The action made Ruby more curious about his business

within the British forces, but she dared not aggravate him by asking questions. John could handle Earl, and she'd find out more by taking a back seat and listening to their conversation.

She moved into the shop and, as quietly as she could, she closed the door and turned the sign. Customers would be a distraction. She sat and listened.

'Ah, Secret Service,' John said, but Ruby picked up on a slight mocking tone. Earl did not.

'Well, least said and all that.'

Ruby peered through the gap between the door and its frame, and cringed as once again he tapped his nose.

'Silence is my code,' John said, and mimicked Earl's nose-tapping.

Ruby wanted to release a squeal of laughter. She walked into the room and, behind Earl's head, she raised an eyebrow. John did the same. Earl preened his top lip and now, bored with listening to him hint about his secret life, Ruby daydreamed whether he'd be able to fire a weapon in between preening.

Earl made her jump back from her daydream by slapping his hand onto the table.

'Enough about me. What about you and taking pictures? How does that contribute towards the war effort, John?'

This time, Ruby heard Earl mocking John. Something inside snapped; she could no longer bear hearing the snide remarks of Earl. She wanted to hear more about

Jean-Paul Clayton, but dared not tread that road for fear of Earl's ability to render her dumb and silent.

'I take it you also have things to do. I have to close shop. I think you need to look for Tommy; he's been gone a while,' she said to Earl.

John jumped to his feet. 'Let me take a photograph of you both. Stand together.'

Horrified by the very idea, Ruby stood where she was and looked over at Earl. Fortunately, he looked as eager as she, and he tapped out a cigarette on the back of his silver cigarette case. 'Can't do, old pal.'

Ruby knew the nose-tapping would follow and before she released the pent-up mirth bubbling inside, with relief she'd not have to stand beside a man she disliked and have their image captured forever, she moved to the front door and opened it wide. 'Enough of the questions, Earl. I think we should let Mr Clayton leave. I'm sure he needs to get back to camp.'

John settled his cap on his head, shook Earl's hand and followed through with a firm shake of Ruby's. 'Thank you both for your hospitality. I'll keep an eye out for Tommy and send him home.'

As they saw him from the premises and watched him walk away, Ruby stepped to one side and pointed to the street. 'And you, Earl. As I said, I'm shutting up shop and heading home. It's time for you to go – perhaps back to your camp too.' Ruby resisted tapping the side of her nose.

'I'll be back. You're too young to have to deal with foreigners, especially foreign servicemen,' Earl said, stepping onto the pavement.

'Don't put yourself out on my account. I'm sure you're busy with secret meetings. I'm not so important as our great country. No, don't worry about coming back, Earl. I'll cope.'

Before she could blink, he'd grabbed her arm again. He bared his teeth. 'The Canadian might not be who he says he is, and a danger to the country with that camera. He thinks you're my wife, and Tommy's our kid. We'll keep it that way. Understand?' He pulled her closer to his face. 'I know where you live, and who lives with you. Old and frail fall all the time. Dead by the time they hit the floor. Understand?'

Petrified at the thought of Fred getting caught up in this man's violent threats, Ruby nodded. Earl stepped into the doorway and pulled her closer. He jammed his mouth to hers and she squirmed her way free.

'Just for appearance's sake.' Earl let her arm go and walked away. Frightened of him returning, she shut the door, turned the key and walked away in the opposite direction as fast as she could, her heart racing as she turned over Earl's threat in her mind before heading for Eagle Street.

CHAPTER 21

Ruby talked herself into calming down. Earl had no true hold over her, and she would speak to Fred when she got home. She shook herself free from the fear and offered a smile to a regular customer as she crossed a road, grateful for the distraction.

'They look pretty. From an admirer?' the woman said, and pointed to the flowers in Ruby's hand. The small posy of flowers – made up of Michaelmas daisies and yellow roses collected from her garden – were in honour of her little brother, and she wanted to lay them close to his resting place.

'Would have been my little brother's birthday today,' Ruby said.

'Aw, duck. I'm that sorry. So sad . . .' the woman replied.

'It is, but he'd have liked these. He loved the garden,' Ruby said and lifted the flowers for the woman to smell.

'Lovely thought. You take care of yourself, Ruby, and you know where I am if you need anything.' The woman touched Ruby's arm and walked away.

Ruby gave a nod. 'Likewise, Maude,' she said and moved onto the land where her home had once stood.

She stood on the ground beside the now filled crater, and it took her by surprise to see the dark hole no longer existed. She'd known it would happen one day, but hadn't expected it when presented with its disappearance. The lack of a dark pit meant the end of hoping to see a familiar face stare back at her. A dull ache took residence in her chest. There was no relief, nor sadness, and Ruby made a mental note to speak with Helen as soon as possible, to find out what the plans were for the land. The grave of her family.

Burying her nose into the flowers, Ruby inhaled their sweet perfume. She kissed the petals and knelt down, leaning forward to place them on the charred soil. No tears fell, but a shuddering sigh heightened the ache inside. She placed her hand across her pounding chest and held back a scream or some form of verbal reaction. She could not – would no longer – allow despair to take over her life every time she visited the spot. She lifted her head to the sky, then dipped it towards the ground as if in prayer, but if anyone could read her thoughts they'd see they were far from generous towards their enemies as she renewed a vow to create a happier place, and not let them take away her right to enjoy life – to make her live with guilt every day.

Something rustled behind her and disturbed her thoughts. She snapped her head to her right and upwards, to see John standing a few feet away. 'Were you following me?' she asked and made no attempt to stand.

'No, I think it's the other way around. I've been here since I left your shop. Seeing you today made me want to return to see the green wallpaper, but look –' he pointed behind him '– it's gone and, for some strange reason, it saddened me. You made me see it in a different light. I've seen a lot of things differently since that day.'

Ruby's brief annoyance with him was squashed when he gave her a beaming grin. There it was – the way to her heart. John released the ache inside her chest and replaced it with another sensation – a butterfly tremble in her stomach. A happy moment.

'What sort of things do you see when you look through there?' she asked, and pointed to the camera. 'I mean, I know you see objects, and record things for the war, but why – what is it you see to make you want to turn it into a photograph?'

'In Canada, I saw beauty. Rugged land, trees higher than buildings, buildings which deserved the name skyscraper. Over here, I see pain, destruction, strength and endurance. Both humble me. Here, you look. Tell me what you see.'

John held out his camera to her, and Ruby stood up and took it from his hands. The black box was lighter than she'd expected.

'It's a Rolleiflex. I had my father's but this one is smaller and easier to use when I'm moving around.'

'How do you use it?' Ruby asked.

'Put your hands here.' John moved her hands into position and his touch came as a surprise. Ruby gripped the camera tight for fear of dropping it as her hands warmed in his. 'Don't grip so hard; that's right, now look down. I've adjusted for the light. If you take a photograph, it's with this button, here.'

John explained a few more details then walked a few feet away; he opened his arms wide and stood with his legs apart. 'Tell me what you see.'

Ruby peered down into a window at the top of the camera and shook her head.

'Nothing,' she said, and peered into the camera again, screwing up her eyes with determination.

With a laugh, John moved behind her and peered over her shoulder into the viewfinder. 'Look there,' he said and directed her finger with his hand to the viewpoint.

He walked away and stood in front of her again. 'Now what do you see?'

Ruby wanted to tell him she could see a man who made her stomach flutter every time she looked at him. A man with a smile which lit up his face and made his eyes twinkle. She saw lips she wanted to touch, arms she imagined holding her tight when her troubles haunted her, and she wanted to tell him she looked at the first man she'd imagined warming her on a cold winter's night. She saw love through a lens and clicked to capture it for ever.

'I did it!' she said.

With a clap of his hands, John applauded her and reclaimed his camera. 'I'll develop it for you to keep. A reminder of today. After all, it's only fair as I have photographs of you.'

'You have photographs of the old me, and the distressed me.'

Sitting on a wooden beam, John patted the space beside him. Ruby chose to sit on a concrete slab opposite. Sitting beside him felt over-friendly, too close to be able to regulate her feelings for him. She sat straight-backed, and envied his ability to relax. He fired triggers of pleasure she'd never experienced before, just by crossing his legs or adjusting his jacket front. Any movement sent shivers through her body and the urge to sidle up beside him was swiftly suppressed. She doubted he felt the same. To a man like John, she would be just a child of war to add to his collection of images.

'Ruby, please don't think I'm intruding into your life, but your unhappiness—'

Lifting her hands to stop him talking, Ruby gave a

soft smile. 'My unhappiness is easing. It's days like today which hurt. The flowers are for my brother. Ten today . . . I mean he would have been if this hadn't happened,' Ruby said and swept one arm around the desolated area.

John said nothing in return and she watched him fiddle with his camera. He was better-looking than most of the boys she'd admired at school. She noted his clean-shaven face, his lean jowls and the small pulse beating in his slim neck. Ruby longed to reach out and stroke his strong jaw line, to link her fingers with his. She jumped when he lifted his head, catching her staring.

'Do you mind I've photographed you with the flowers?' he said, his voice soft and concerned, his accent adding to his desirability.

'Not really. It means today won't ever fade.' Ruby turned away and looked at the flowers, their colours bright against the charcoal and brown of the ground. Her brother would have preferred a comic, but flowers were the gift you gave the dead. A comfort for the living.

'It's a shame you can't capture their colours. They'll live on in your photograph, but they'll be black and white for ever,' she said, and turned back to John.

'The way photography is advancing, one day everything will be as it really is – no more black and white rainbows,' he said.

Ruby gasped and put her hands to her mouth, instantly regretting the childlike movement. For some inexplicable reason, she wanted John to see her as a grown woman. She inclined her head as if in thought, then looked skyward as if searching for something.

'I can't imagine a black and white rainbow. How strange. Sad too, as a rainbow lights up the sky with its colours. I'd like to see one in black and white though, just to see what it looks like.'

'I've got a few. I'll bring one next time I see you. Talking of colours . . . The red mark on your wrist . . . I couldn't help seeing –' John said, and pointed to her arm.

Ruby gave her body a slight shake, as if shrugging off something undesirable. Then she seized the opportunity to tell the truth.

'John, I'm not Tommy's mother. Earl is not my husband, despite threatening me to make you think I am, after you left. He's also got it in his head that you might be a threat to Britain. He's a bully too.' Her words were rushed with embarrassment.

John stared at her, his mouth open with surprise. 'Ruby, he hurt you, and Tommy?'

Ruby nodded. 'He told me he'd hurt Fred if I didn't pretend to be his wife. He tried to kiss me.'

John swore, then looked at her with a guilty apology in his eyes.

Ruby screwed up her nose and clenched her hands together 'I need help, John. I can't ask Helen, Beatty or

Fred this time, and I have no one else. It's luck we met here. Meant to be, I think. I'd be silly not to ask you what I should do about it.'

Ruby noticed his jaw twitch as he listened. Then, striking a match against a brick, John lit a cigarette and puffed on it before he spoke again.

'Obviously, I'll help you, Ruby. You cannot live with this sort of bullying. He sounds a dangerous man. He's Tommy's uncle, you say?'

'Tommy said so, but now I'm wondering if it's a lie. The poor child is so scared whenever I speak about his mother. I thought I saw her today, but even that might be another woman scared of Earl.'

'Do nothing. I'll visit the shop tomorrow, after I've had a think about what we can do about this situation. Men like him are dangerous, and we must tread carefully. I'll help, Ruby. Go home, and don't worry any more. You have a friend in me, and Earl will never try to kiss you again.'

Without worrying who saw them, Ruby reached up and kissed John's cheek.

He gave a grin. 'Ah, if I get one of those for every time I speak about rescuing you from an evil bully, I wonder what will happen when I put my words into action.'

'I wonder,' Ruby said with a hint of daring in her voice, and returned the grin.

'Get yourself home before we get ourselves into something we can't control, Ruby Shadwell, and thank you for trusting me.'

'When I saw you, I knew I could. Thank you, John.'

John turned her by her shoulders in the direction of Spon Street, and Ruby waggled her fingers goodbye.

CHAPTER 22

After collecting bread and her ration allowance of butter, Ruby headed for Shadwell's, her mind calmer after talking with John the previous day. Arriving at the shop, she saw Earl talking with Beatty on the doorstep. It looked to her as if Beatty was guarding the door with her broom, and side-stepping to prevent Earl from entering before opening time. Taking a deep breath for courage, furious with herself that she'd allowed this man to have a hold over her shop, Ruby strode towards them.

'Well, hello, Ruby,' Earl called out, his voice loaded with false friendship. Ruby ignored him. Pretending she hadn't heard him address her, she focused on Beatty.

'Everything all right here, Beatty?' she asked.

'All fine and dandy. Ready to start the day – in half an hour,' Beatty replied, adding extra emphasis on the last four words. She stepped aside to let Ruby pass by and enter the shop and then turned back to face Earl. Ruby had to smile at the standoff between them, but she wouldn't allow Beatty to antagonise him too much longer. She didn't trust the man not to push his way inside and hurt Beatty in the process.

'I said hello, young lady.' Earl growled out his words to Ruby's back.

Swivelling around to face him, Ruby forced her lips into a false smile. 'I'm sorry, Earl. I didn't hear you, too busy chatting with Beatty. Where's Tommy – at school? Not that there's much schooling going on around here. Do you know, I heard there were six children having to do their English lessons in Mrs Dennison's back room.' The more Ruby chatted the more she saw Earl's face twist with anger. She knew she'd annoyed him by ignoring his greeting but, with Beatty present, Ruby hoped he'd keep his temper.

'He's with his mother,' Earl said and stepped inside the shop. It annoyed Ruby when he pushed her aside and moved into the centre of the shop, but she remained calm, thinking of John all the time she spoke.

'I'm surprised you're still around, though. What with all that is happening abroad. I thought you had –' Ruby tapped the side of her nose '– important secret work to do. I don't know how you do it; I find it hard to keep a secret. Do you bite the side of your mouth to stop blurting it out?'

Ruby allowed her dialogue to rattle along, ignoring the red stains rising on Earl's face. She busied herself preparing for the opening of the shop, and at one point gave a sly wink to Beatty, who in response scuttled away into the kitchen to prevent the onset of giggles. Earl stood in silence. From the corner of her eye she saw his eyes darkening and his jaw twitching. A menacing atmosphere fell and Ruby ended her semi-sarcastic chatter and moved in with a friendlier approach. She wanted the man gone, but had no reason to ask him to leave. She recalled the way her mother had spoken to awkward customers, and opted for the same pacifying tone.

'Feel free to browse, Earl. As soon as the kettle's boiled, Beatty will make you a coffee, if you're staying. I know you enjoy a morning coffee. Goodness knows, you must be pushed to the limit with war work.'

'Don't play games, girl.' Earl took large strides towards her and stared into her face. Ruby clenched her clammy hands together under the counter; she didn't trust herself not to slap his face away.

'I don't know what you mean, Earl. Have I upset you? As you said, I'm a girl; I have a lot of learning to do. Go and sit. Beatty will bring you a drink, and I'm sure we have a biscuit left in the barrel. Beatty will sit and keep you company; have adult chat with her – discuss the goings-on of Hitler and the war. It goes over my

234

head sometimes.' Ruby swept her hands above her head to emphasise the statement. 'I'll keep out of your way and get on here.'

'Shut your chattering. You don't fool me. Young, yes, but sly and cunning too. I've seen you around. Watched you at a dance pretending you're better than everyone else.' His eyes bored into her and she felt his rage. 'Crying on a soldier's shoulder – oh, yes, you might look shocked, Beatty, but your little slut here carries on with men on the bombsites. Nothing gets past me.'

Ruby's hands trembled and when Beatty took a step forward, with her mouth open in readiness to say her piece, she gave a slight shake of her head and Beatty stopped walking, her knuckles gripping the broom handle so hard they turned white. The bravado Ruby had felt earlier left when Earl stared at her. He was a dangerous man to meddle with, and she understood why Tommy was scared of him. His tobacco breath blew across her face as he puffed smoke in her direction. His pompous manner irritated Ruby but she held back, understanding the fine line between trying to be an adult and acting in a foolish manner.

Earl stabbed out the butt of his cigarette into the ashtray nearby and slammed his hand on the counter. The contents of the ashtray scattered across the countertop and Ruby made a point of playful tutting and wiping it away. 'Beatty's only just cleaned this, Earl.

You'll be in bother.' Again she attempted a light-hearted approach, but the moment Earl's arm lifted sideways with his palm open she knew she'd gone too far.

'Any more of your lip and I'll –'

'You'll what, sir?'

Ruby heard John's familiar voice before she saw him; it was loud and commanding. Neither she nor Earl had noticed him enter the shop, and Beatty had obviously kept her counsel, knowing Earl would be seen and heard threatening Ruby. Unsure whether to move from behind the counter, Ruby remained where she was. Earl turned to face John and Ruby watched as John straightened up and stood full height. Ruby noticed he was a fraction taller than Earl but, seeing the malicious look on Earl's face, she guessed he'd stood level with men far sturdier and taller than John.

'I asked you a question. You'll what, sir? Threatening a young woman is not good conduct for one of Britain's finest, is it?' John said and squared his shoulders as Earl attempted to stare him down

'Stay out of my business,' Earl hissed into John's face.

'Ruby is your business? I don't think so. Ruby is her own woman, so I am led to believe,' John retaliated, and gave Ruby a swift glance and a reassuring wink. Unfortunately, the wink fired up Earl's anger another notch.

'She might have sniffed around you, but she enjoys a hound, not a pup.' Earl bared his teeth and stabbed a finger John's way.

Lifting his camera from around his neck and laying down other personal items, John took a step towards Earl.

'Threatening young women is taboo in Canada. We don't bully women; we respect them, as do, I think, the majority of men in Britain. Sadly, there is always one who thinks he holds all the power, especially over women *and* children.' John's voice was firm, calm and in control. Ruby's breath hitched in her throat and she put her hand to her neck to regain a regular breathing pattern. Had John gone too far, or did he deal with men like Earl without experiencing consequences? It looked to Ruby that he had handled this kind of situation before, and she wondered if he'd faced the enemy at any time. His bravery suggested that he might have done, and she looked to Beatty, who remained quiet on the far side of the room.

'Beatty . . . Beatty, can you cover the counter for me, please?' Ruby called across her shoulder, then turned her head forward to keep a watchful eye on both men. Their growing animosity towards each other concerned her, and she knew she had to act fast before it became a physical event. As much as she'd like to consider John to be her hero of the day, she didn't want him to become an injured one. Earl's twisted nose and protruding jaw line made her suspect he was used to street brawling and sustaining injuries to the face. John's face was too good-looking to encounter such damage on her behalf. She inhaled and found her loudest pitch.

'*Stop!*'

Both men stopped their posturing and looked at her. Earl still wore a threatening stare, but John's face softened and he gave an apologetic downturn of his mouth.

'My apologies, Ruby, Beatty. I was concerned for your safety,' he said.

Beatty moved to his side. 'And grateful we are, young man. Thank you.' She turned to Earl before she bustled her way past him and stepped outside. 'Manners cost us nothing, and some need to think about using some.'

Ruby grimaced at the volume of dust Beatty created with her fierce use of the broom. John took advantage of Earl looking at Beatty, and handed her an envelope. 'I came to give you this.'

Ruby pulled out the contents. Two photographs. One of her with the flowers, and she noticed he'd done what he'd set out to achieve, and had captured the pain and anguish in her face. Her cheeks warmed with embarrassment. The other was the one she'd taken of John. She looked at what she'd captured in that split second of hitting the button. A six-foot, broad-shouldered male with happy eyes and a gentle smile. Handsome. Ruby knew her cheeks would be scarlet and, in an attempt to hide them, she put her hands over them, pretending excitement.

'It came out! I took a photograph. Look, Beatty. I took this. Isn't it magical?'

Earl stepped forward and snatched up the picture before Beatty had a chance to look.

'If you like a photograph of a vain man, then I suppose this one isn't too bad. I prefer this one; I think I'll keep it.' Earl took the photograph of Ruby laying the flowers. Anger welled inside her. Earl had assumed control once again, and she had to claw it back. She reached out her hand and took it back from him.

'It's mine. A gift from a friend. Nothing to do with you, Earl.'

Although her words came out clear and controlled, Ruby's insides churned with worry about the possible reprisals. Earl's glare back at her told her she'd done the wrong thing – belittled him in front of John.

Earl snatched it back. 'Manners. I was looking at it.'

He stared into her face and Ruby knew by the cold stare he gave her, he wasn't going to let her get away with it. Just as his hand reached out for hers, a loud shout went up outside the shop and Tommy ran inside. He called out for Earl and ran to him, grabbing at his sleeve. 'Earl, Earl. Come quick. I . . . um . . . it's um . . . Quick!'

Flustered, Ruby pushed past Earl, who'd chosen to ignore the boy, and bent down to Tommy. Distress was etched across his dirty, pale face, smothered in bruises – old and new.

'Tommy, what's the matter? What's going on?'

'It's urgent, Earl. Real urgent!' Tommy's face twisted into that of a terrified child, and Ruby pulled him close.

'Don't be scared, Tommy. You're safe. We'll help you. Tell me what we need to do,' she said.

Earl pushed her and she staggered sideways. Ruby watched the photograph flutter to the floor, and picked it up before Earl had the opportunity to take it from her again.

'Leave him to me,' he muttered and pulled Tommy from the shop.

'Do you need help?' John called after him, but Earl didn't respond.

Beatty went to a chair behind the counter and sighed as she sank into the cushion. She turned her attention to John. 'It's all go around here some days. Best to walk away.' Her words were loaded with a warning tone and Ruby glanced up at her. 'That Earl has a temper. We don't need to encourage it,' Beatty continued as she folded white napkins. Her eyes were focused on the job, but Ruby understood her meaning. John might have put himself in danger. Earl was not a man to be messed with, and John had called him out on threatening Ruby.

'John, thank you for the photographs – I will treasure them. But Beatty is right. Earl is a—' Her words faltered when Tommy raced into the shop. His lip was split and tears streamed down his face.

'Tommy!' Ruby yelled and ran to him, just as he fell to the floor.

John moved in and lifted Tommy into his arms.

'Bring him through here. We'll make a space on the floor. Grab those blankets.' Beatty barked out her orders and Ruby followed her into the community room.

'Tommy . . . Tommy.' Beatty softly called the boy's name and stroked his cheek. All three adults let out a sigh of relief when his eyelids fluttered and his eyes opened. Fear shone back at them all and in an instant Ruby knew this was Earl's doing.

'We'll get him back to ours. John, I think Earl will come back and I'd rather you leave. Going by this, his temper is at its worst and we'll all suffer. You especially; he'll be gunning for you. Beatty?' Ruby looked to her friend for support.

'The girl's right, young man. You don't want to become involved in a brawl. My advice: leave and stay clear. I'll calm him down and Ruby can care for Tommy. Now go, quickly.'

John's face no longer smiled back at Ruby; it expressed something she couldn't interpret. Concern? Upset?

'Beatty's right. Go now, while you can. And thank you.

Thank you for offering to help. I'll never forget it, but I don't want you getting hurt on our behalf.' Ruby turned back to check on Tommy. 'Come by this evening. Six-ish. When things are calmer.'

CHAPTER 23

'Sleeping like a lamb,' Ruby said as she removed the damp towels from the floor.

'Going by the colour of those towels, that boy's not washed for a year.' Fred pointed to the pile in her arms.

'He's exhausted. When I get my hands on that Earl . . . What does he think he's doing, letting the child run around in that state? And as for that Canadian lad . . . He's too keen, Fred. We need to watch him round our Ruby. She's only invited him round – he's due any minute now.' Beatty puffed her way through her speech and pointed to the clock.

'He's concerned about Tommy, and you know he is. If he's keen on anything, it's to give Earl a piece of his mind and a good hiding.'

A knock on the door gave Beatty no opportunity to reply.

'Right on time too,' Fred said.

Ruby, flustered, flapped her hands at Fred to open the door, but he took his time standing up and brushing crumbs from his shirt. The knock became a loud hammering, and Ruby's blood ran cold.

'It's that man! Fred, it's Earl – be careful,' Beatty cautioned and reached for the fireside poker.

'What will you do with that?' Ruby whispered at her, petrified Beatty might render a serious injury to Earl and find herself on the wrong side of the law.

'Is he here? Where's the boy?' Earl's voice echoed loud around the house and he pushed past Beatty. Fred followed, holding his elbow. Earl had used force on him, and a surge of anger ran through Ruby's body.

'What are you doing here? This is our home. How dare you?' She stood with her hand on the back of a dining chair, not wanting to lose her balance if he pushed against her.

'Get out!' Beatty shouted and lifted the poker. Ruby moved in front of her.

'Beatty's right – get out.' Ruby pointed beyond Earl's shoulder. 'This is our home. You have no right to come bursting in and shouting at us. Tommy is asleep. He fainted in the shop. He's been fed and washed.'

'Get him now. His mother's worried sick,' Earl shouted.

'She's not been so worried about him before. He looks like a Victorian waif, poor kid,' Fred interjected. Earl moved towards him with clenched fists, so fast Ruby feared he'd hit out at Fred.

'Get out of my way, old man. Move!' Earl snarled and spittle hit Fred's face. Fred wiped it away and Ruby noticed his hand tremble. As brave as he'd like to be for her, Fred was old and frail and could not match the strength of Earl. She had to distract him. She reached out and tugged his sleeve.

'Earl! Leave him be, I warn you. Fred was worried. We all are. Tommy's mother can come and fetch him in the morning. Tell her he's fine. He just needed to slow down and eat.' Ruby subdued the rage in her voice in the hope he'd calm down as he backed away from Fred.

'Bring the boy to me, and then I'll go.' He leaned into her body with his shoulder. 'You think you are so very clever, little slut. Well, let me tell you this – be careful, be afraid. Now, get the boy!'

'Did you know he's taken a beating? Your sister – I assume he's your sister's son – she wouldn't harm him, would she?' Beatty pulled herself tall and folded her arms across her stomach, the iron poker on full show. Ruby recognised the stance, and had seen Beatty win a verbal match with many a man who'd crossed her, but knew this time it would result in violence on both sides.

Ruby watched as Earl's fists clenched. Panic set in; she needed to defuse the situation. Two elderly people and a girl were not a match for the likes of Earl.

'Earl, calm down. I'll fetch Tommy. We only wanted to do something kind for the boy. He had a scare. I'm sure he'll be better off with his uncle… Beatty, fetch his things.' She gave Beatty and Fred a warning glance to stay where they were.

A sleepy Tommy, now dressed in clean clothes brought home from the shop, stood scrubbed and pink-cheeked. His mop of hair fell over one eye and everyone looked his way. Beatty produced a brown wool coat, and busied herself dressing him.

'Come here, little'un. Auntie B will help you. Poor little lamb.'

Earl watched on and Ruby saw his jaw clench more than once. He oozed impatience.

'Hurry up, woman.'

'Bye, Tommy. See you soon,' Ruby said and gave the boy a cuddle. For once he smelled of fresh soap.

They stood back as Earl dragged him by the arm and Tommy's steps were forced into a run beside his uncle. Once they were in the street, Ruby pulled back the net curtain just in time to see Earl clip Tommy's ear. 'I think the best thing we can do for Tommy is feed him if we see him, give him fresh clothes and stop annoying his uncle. Poor little dear's just had a clump for being here. His mother is either weak or uncaring. I can't work it out.' Despite her words, Ruby knew she'd try and do more for Tommy than just feed him. When he was around her she always felt a natural instinct to protect him.

She pulled the curtains as if to shut out the scene. Tommy's bag of toiletries and new clothing lay on the floor where Earl had thrown them on his way out, declaring he looked after his own, and if Ruby had any sense she'd look after hers.

The three sat around the table catching their breath when there was another knock on the door. Beatty gave a silent scream.

'It's John . . . Relax, Beatty. I'd almost forgotten he was coming. Earl won't be back tonight. He got what he came for – poor little Tommy,' Ruby said and patted Beatty's hand.

'I'm all of a dither. That man played havoc with my nerves,' Beatty said and then looked over at Fred. 'Your turn. I'm in no mood for opening doors,' she said and laid the poker back into its rack.

Fred grinned over at Ruby. 'Ready?'

'Wipe that grin off your face, Fred Lester,' Beatty said and Ruby appreciated her attempt at making things normal again. 'He's here to ask about the boy. We'll tell him, and then he leaves. I think Ruby's suffered enough drama for one day.'

Ruby's heart went out to Beatty. She clucked like a mother hen on Ruby's behalf, and for the first time in a long time Ruby enjoyed the fuss of a motherly figure.

'It will be fine, Beatty. Let him in, Fred, but no drinking, you hear?'

'I'm never drinking again,' Fred declared, and pulled a face at Beatty.

Nervous anticipation at seeing John again made Ruby's stomach roll with excitement. It also churned with worry in case Earl returned.

It startled Ruby when Beatty rushed across the room and claimed her favourite seat, then placed a newspaper on Fred's. The two spare ones were opposite each other with a wide corridor of space between them, and very obviously left for Ruby and John.

Ruby had a silent giggle and slowly shook her head at Beatty with an amused grin. 'Good evening, Fred.' John's voice sounded calm and gentle after the raging boom of Earl's.

'He's always polite, I'll give him that, but you be careful, young lady. He's a good couple of years older than you. Seen more of the world,' Beatty whispered.

'Shh,' Ruby whispered back, embarrassed by the attention given to John and her friendship with him.

'Come in, lad. Come in.' Fred ushered John inside and showed him into the room. 'Look who's come to pay us a visit, ladies.'

'John, lovely to see you. Come in, and sit down,' Ruby said as he entered the room with Fred close behind, and pointed to the chair opposite her.

248

'Good evening, ladies,' John said, but remained standing, holding out something wrapped in a piece of newspaper. 'I'm sorry I'm late.'

'No apologies needed; we're pleased to see you,' Beatty said and Ruby knew she told the truth. John was a breath of fresh air after the evil presence of Earl in their home.

'How's Tommy? I've worried about him. He's such a vulnerable boy. My mother would call him a lost soul.' John sat in the chair and made himself comfortable.

'You've just missed him; he's with Earl,' Ruby said, waving her hand in the general direction of the window, desperate for something to say before Fred and Beatty took control of the whole visit. Seeing John flustered her and she knew Beatty was watching her every move.

'Glad to hear the little guy has recovered, but not so much now Earl has him in his clutches again. Shame I missed him, though. I bought him this; it's a model airplane,' he said and held out the parcel. 'I passed a carpenter who whittles them from scrap wood to earn a few coins, and knew it would be the perfect present for an injured boy.' John unwrapped the package and held up the plane. 'It's nothing special, but I thought the kid would enjoy it. I'll leave it with you and maybe you'll give it to him when you see him again.'

Ruby took the plane from John's hand and his fingers brushed hers. It was a deliberate move and she spotted the hint of a smile playing at the corners of his mouth.

The usual rush of butterflies in flight she felt when in John's company tumbled around her stomach. She eased her hand away from his with a slow movement. She didn't want Beatty and Fred noticing the intimate moment, but was saddened she could no longer enjoy the pleasurable feeling of his touch.

'That's very kind of you, John. Tommy will love it. I think I'll keep it at the shop so he can play with it there. Can we offer you a drink?'

'That's kind of you, but I have to say no, thank you. I came to check on the boy and to say goodbye; I'm leaving tonight. I've received fresh orders – I'm being sent to another unit. It's temporary, but I'm not sure for how long. More into the thick of things, from what I gather.'

Fred patted John's shoulder. 'Good luck to you, lad.'

Ruby stood in silence. A cold shiver ran through her body.

With a sudden flurry of movement to and from the kitchen, Beatty moved faster than Ruby had ever seen. 'Take this with you. It's a pie. Spam and egg. Keep your strength up.'

Once again, Ruby watched Beatty fuss around like a mother hen, her protectiveness towards Ruby now transferred to John.

'That's generous of you, but I won't be able to eat it in time, nor take it with me. I won't forget your kindness, though. If I get an opportunity I'll write, if that's accept-able to you all?'

The butterflies in Ruby's stomach ended their dance and were replaced with a heavy, dull, brick-sinking sensa-tion. John was leaving. 'Of course we'd love to hear from you. Feel free to write, if you get the chance. I'm sure one of us will reply if you add a return address,' she said and hoped the disappointment she felt didn't reflect in her voice. 'We can only wish you good luck. I'll pass this along to Tommy. Don't let us keep you.'

Not wanting to rush him from the house but eager to stay in control of her emotions, Ruby held out her hand for him to shake. John frowned and took her hand and she noticed his clenched jaw. His head moved with the slightest of flicks towards the door and his eyes widened, and Ruby sensed they sent a message that he wanted to speak alone.

'I'll see you out,' said Ruby, and knew this was a chance to offer a small hint of her feelings for him.

They walked down the side of the house and stopped before they reached the street.

'John . . . Before you go, I want to tell you something.'

John looked down at her and Ruby desperately wanted to feel his lips on hers. The depth of feeling she had for him scared her. He put his finger on her lips. 'Shh. It will keep. I have to go. I'll write, I promise,' he said.

'Kiss me, John. Kiss me before you go.'

In what she knew Beatty would call a brazen act, she put her arms around his neck and moved her hips tight into his. She crushed her lips to his and he gave in to her demand. A few seconds later he manoeuvred her away from him.

'I've longed to do this, but would never presume you wanted the same.' John's lips teased her face with light kisses, and soon they lingered on her lips in another urgent moment of passion. John eventually eased himself away from her and Ruby saw tears glisten in his eyes.

'I'll try and come back to you, Ruby. I can't make any promises. Give me a smile to take with me.' John lifted her chin and kissed her again, and when they parted she gave him a shy smile.

'Stay safe, John. I'll wait for you, I promise. Just come back to me.'

Ruby leaned back into the shadows and listened to the last echo of John's footsteps as he walked away, before returning inside.

'All right, duck?' Beatty asked and glanced up from her knitting.

'Fine. Why wouldn't I be?' Ruby replied, a little sharper than she'd intended.

'Touchy. Show respect,' Fred said with a tut.

'Leave it, Fred,' Beatty warned, and gave Ruby a knowing look.

Before leaving for her bedroom, Ruby spoke to them

both. 'I'm tired, sorry. It was kind of John to drop by and ask to keep in touch with us all. It shows we made an impression with our friendship. I don't like the thought of him – or anyone we know – putting themselves in danger. I realise it is war, but it still upsets me they've put their lives in danger to protect us.'

'So, he's just a friend then?' Fred remarked and Ruby scowled at him.

'Will you give over, Fred?' Beatty's telling off continued as Ruby left them to go to her room. She pulled out the photograph she'd taken of John. She touched her lips and remembered their kiss, but it brought no comfort. The dull ache of loss had returned, and a black sorrow overwhelmed her. Every day was a challenge, fraught with worry about rationing, escaping bombs, and now she added Tommy and John to her list. Her heart sank when she thought of John leaving, and the possibility she might never see him again. Ruby prayed their kiss wouldn't be their last. Or that he'd move onto another girl, one closer to his age and not a cripple.

Placing his picture back in the drawer, Ruby readied herself for bed and cried into her pillow until the early hours of the morning.

CHAPTER 24

The morning showed itself to be as damp and miserable as Ruby felt, and she walked beside Beatty as far as Helen's office in silence. Beatty made small talk, and Ruby was thankful for her discretion in not mentioning John, or her reaction to Fred the previous evening.

'I'll be about half hour, Beatty. See you later. I hope Earl doesn't come causing trouble today; I'm really not in the mood. Just make him a brew and give him the newspaper to read.'

'He'll feel the sharp end of my broom if he steps out of line,' Beatty said.

'I think the defence unit should arm our women with them and send us to fight off the enemy. You're scary when you've a broom in your hand, Beatty,' Ruby said and dropped a kiss on Beatty's cheek and they both laughed before going their separate ways.

Helen's office was in a state of disarray when Ruby entered, and she stood back to allow a tall man carrying several boxes to leave the room.

Helen looked up from her kneeling position in front of a large filing cabinet. She was flanked by orderly piles of paper. The face which turned to look at Ruby wasn't a bright smiling one. Dark circles under sad eyes told of illness and distress.

'Gracious, Helen. What on earth is going on?'

'I'm leaving, and my files are moving to Housing and other departments. I was going to come and tell you later,' Helen said and rose from the floor, stretching her back and knees.

'Leaving? What – office or town?' Ruby asked.

'I've had a telegram. My sister's husband was killed and she needs my support. I telephoned her and it's obvious she needs the support of someone, and I'm her last living relative. I've agreed to move in with her. She lives in Yorkshire. Lovely house. Plenty of room and fresh air. News of Coventry last year sent her into a pit of despair . . . Now she's a widow, she only has me to worry about, and it's made her quite . . . I hate to say it, but mad.' Helen dipped her head, and Ruby could see she was burdened by grief and worry. She had no intention of adding to it, although not having Helen in her life would be strange.

'I'll be lost without you, but family comes first. Of course you must go to your sister,' Ruby whispered.

She watched Helen rub her eyes and pull her cardigan around her body. She stood with her arms folded. Shaking her head and returning to her task, Helen spoke soft and low.

'I have to go, Ruby. It's not that I don't care about you, but my sister needs my help too. Either way, I'll feel I've let one of you down, but you are thriving, and she isn't.' Helen sniffed, and Ruby knew she was crying.

Walking over to Helen, Ruby knelt down beside her and placed her hand in Helen's trembling one. Helen leaned back on her heels, released her hand from Ruby's grasp and touched her face – a tender, motherly touch.

'Live your own life, Ruby. I'll give Fred and Beatty all the information they need to help you with your finances. It's not hard, and the solicitor will help transfer guardianship. I have to go, I'm sorry.'

Rising to her feet, Ruby looked down at Helen and a pang of guilt flurried around her. Helen had to go, and Ruby had no right to try and stop her.

'I understand, I do. I'm not selfish, but I envy your sister. We can write and, who knows, I might get to visit Yorkshire one day.'

Helen also stood up and patted down her skirt.

'Who knows? You keep doing what you're doing, Ruby. You've clawed your way back and I couldn't be prouder. Give me a hug to take with me.'

Holding Helen, Ruby knew it would be the last time

they would have such close contact. With a heavy heart, she kissed Helen's cheek and walked away. Words were not needed. She refused to say goodbye; it was a word which was all too familiar in her life and wounded her every time she said it. She'd heard someone say her soul must be battered and bruised by now. Ruby had never thought of having a soul before the loss of so many in her life, but assumed the constant ache she carried with her was a damaged one. A place where she carried all her sorrow. If only she could empty it and move forward. Her life appeared to take one step in a positive direction, and then two steps back. How were you supposed to deal with such things when the very people surrounding you were dealing with their own demons and issues? And each time someone set you up for seeing light at the end of a very long tunnel they disappeared. Beatty and Fred, her beloved friends, were all she had left, and Ruby was determined to ensure their lives were happy, comfortable and peaceful and they had no reason to leave – until death took them, of course. The inevitable. Ruby shooed the thought from her mind.

In the meantime, Ruby Shadwell, you have a business to run.

Ruby thought of all her plans and projects, scribbled on a pad lying in a drawer in her office, and strode with a sense of purpose towards the shop. She bit into her top lip as she walked. Tears were not allowed to dampen her cheeks.

When she pushed open the front door she was pleasantly surprised to see the shop filled with people, and Ruby had to push her way to the counter to be greeted by a flustered, red-faced Beatty.

'Thank goodness you've arrived; it's mayhem,' Beatty called out over the noise.

'What's going on? Where have they come from?' Ruby asked, taking a set of bed linen from a woman and folding it into the basket she held out.

'I've no flipping idea, but keep them coming is what I say. I can't serve tea, though, so I hope you don't mind but I've asked Violet to help out.' Ruby peered into the community room; it was filled with women sewing or knitting, and Beatty's friend Violet bustled back and forth with refreshments. Shadwell's was filled to the rafters.

Ruby turned back to her customer. 'That's a shilling, please.' She smiled as the woman stared at her, wide-eyed.

'I heard you sold at a good price to help us back on our feet. Can't believe someone so young runs this place.'

Beatty leaned across to address the woman. 'She's got brains and beauty this one. Beautiful inside and out. Wants only to help others. Saved my life, I can tell you.'

Before Ruby could protest in embarrassment, Beatty returned to her own customer. Two queues had now formed and, as the morning went on, one became sales and the other for Ruby to buy items from a varied group of customers. Some asked to exchange watches or trinkets for more practical items, and knitted woollen socks were a favourite item exchanged. The women bought them to send to sons, brothers and husbands fighting abroad who complained of boots rubbing blisters. Ruby refused to take advantage of those desperate to send comfort to loved ones, and gave cash along with a free pair of socks. Their request had given her an idea.

During a lull, she wandered in to speak with the ladies enjoying their chatter and tea.

'Ladies, could I have a word, please?' she called out over the chatter. 'This morning has highlighted a need, and I think we can help. If you can knit, then socks for soldiers appear to be in great demand. I've a room filled with knitted things with holes, and Beatty often unravels one and knits Fred or me a new jumper or vest. How about I bring them into this room and you get knitting socks? I'll sell them for a small price, and we'll donate the money to a fundraiser of your choice.'

The women began calling out the places where they felt the money would be best sent.

'The Red Cross need funds.'

'They've got an agricultural one for seeds. They send them to the POW camps. My boy told me when he was last home.'

'The St John's thingy joined with the Red Cross. My

aunt held a dance to raise money for them. I think young Ruby here is onto a good idea. I'm all for it, girl.'

The buzz of excited agreement went around the room, and Ruby gathered a few ladies together to help her bring down the fifteen boxes of unwearable items.

It was agreed to close the doors for an hour whilst they organised themselves, and Ruby and Beatty took advantage of the time to slip home and collect four more boxes stored in Beatty's room. As they walked back to the shop, they bumped into Tommy. He still wore his new clothing, and the bruises on his face still showed purple and black against his pale skin.

'All right, Rubes, Auntie B?' he said and shared a wide toothless grin.

'We're fine, Tommy. How are you? We were worried silly last night,' Ruby said and knelt to his level.

'Auntie B. It's got a nice ring to it, lad. I like it. Is this sore? Is it a new one?' Beatty reached down and stroked a red gash under Tommy's eye.

'It's me own fault. Earl's always tellin' me that. I ain't nibble enough.'

'Nibble? Ah, nimble. Nimble for what, running from a beating?' Ruby asked.

Beatty shot her a warning glance. Ruby gave an apologetic expression. They'd discussed not pushing Tommy for too many answers about his circumstances for fear of driving him away. Both had agreed to keep a watchful

eye over him and, in their own small way, keep him safe
from the neglect he'd previously suffered.

'I'll walk you home later and have a word with your
mummy,' Ruby said.

'She's at work. Ain't no use tryin' to talk to 'er.' Tommy
shoved his hands into his shorts pockets. With a sheepish
smile he pulled out two small stones.

''Ere, I got these for ya both. Found 'em and look,
they sparkle.'

His grubby hands held out two small pieces of granite
stone. Ruby reached out and selected one. She held it up
to the light and saw the small specks of silver against
black shine back at her. She handed Beatty hers.

'What pretty stones, Tommy. They do sparkle, thank
you.'

'Yes, thank you, Tommy. I bet your mummy liked
hers,' Beatty said. Ruby went to frown at her, but changed
her mind. Beatty had a way of asking questions without
making them sound like an interrogation – an art neither
she nor Fred had perfected.

'I ain't –' Tommy stopped talking and looked to the
floor.

'I ain't what?' Beatty asked, repeating his words in his
accent.

'Ha, you sound like me,' Tommy shouted out and ran
ahead of them.

'Notice how he's changed the subject again?' Beatty

whispered to Ruby. 'He did it with the stones, when I mentioned his mum. I don't think he's got one – a mother.'

'I've often wondered. There's no way my mum would have let James run around in the state we found Tommy. Even grubby, James was never grimy – or starved. He's starving, always. Busy as she was, my mum fed us.' Ruby picked up her boxes. 'Let's get him to the shop, feed him and let the forces knitting group fuss over him.'

'Forces Knitting Group. I like it,' Beatty said and also picked up her load.

'Oi, you two slow coaches, comin'?' Tommy's voice called out to them as they crossed into Hertford Street.

Both women increased their speed, and Tommy jumped his way over bricks and rubble until they reached the shop. Everything about the last ten minutes felt right to Ruby. A gentle amble with a friend and a happy child skipping ahead. A scene she'd like to enjoy several years down the line.

CHAPTER 25

Entering the community room, Ruby was taken aback by the hive of activity and enthusiasm of the local women. They'd expanded in number whilst Ruby was out. Their ages spanned from toddlers, school children, girls her age, pregnant women, middle-aged grandmothers and women aged into years earning them the respect of being the city's matriarchs of many a family.

Young children sat at the feet of adults, hands held high, little fingers spread apart, supporting yarn unravelled at speed by the enthusiastic participants of the fundraising event. Ruby's heart swelled with pride. Not for herself, but for them. These people had endured massacre, and survived in a spirit of unity. They'd climbed back onto the tide of life and rode with the challenges of whatever came their way. Nothing could, or would, break them.

Tommy sat amongst them; he looked so happy and comfortable. Only his accent was out of place. His bright personality bounced from one woman to another as he handed them whatever they asked for, and Ruby sensed his longing to make this a normal event. He bent over backwards to please, just to receive a small amount of praise or a thank you.

'Tommy, if you aren't too busy, could I have a word. I've something for you.' Ruby held up the wrapped package containing the wooden plane from John.

Tommy leapt to his feet as the group around him gave shouts of encouragement.

'Cor, Tommy, a present. Is it your birthday?' one little boy asked.

'Nah. What is it, Rubes?' Tommy took the present from her.

'You won't know until you open it, will you?' she teased.

Tommy's playmate jumped up and stood beside him. It touched Ruby to see Tommy with a friend his own age, sharing an exciting moment.

'Open it, quickly. What is it?'

Wasting no time, Tommy ripped open the paper and gasped with delight. 'Is this mine? All mine?' His words came tumbling out on a breathless whoosh as he swung his arm in play.

'John, the Canadian soldier, said he was sorry he missed

264

you last night. It is a get well gift, and a sort of farewell gift. He's had to go away, so we probably won't see him again, but he promised to write to us. When I have an address for him, you can write and say thank you.'

'You'll 'ave to 'elp me, Rubes.'

'I will. Of course I will.' But Ruby spoke to fresh air, as Tommy raced around the main shop floor pretending to be a fighter pilot, and three other boys his age joined in the chase. She'd never seen him so free and easy, so happy. He leapt and giggled his way around with new friends. With a sinking feeling in her stomach, she knew Earl would arrive and suck the joy from the child, but whilst he was in her company Ruby set her mind to help him back into childhood, make him less fearful of the world around him. She'd speak with Earl and get his permission for him to stay at her home with one of his friends once in a while. One boy stood out as an ideal companion. His mother hadn't survived from her injuries after the bombing; his father had left him in the care of his grandmother and returned to fight. His manners and cheerful personality matched Tommy's and as Ruby watched them play she was determined for the friendship to blossom even further.

'He seems happy enough. Bless his little heart, I don't think I've ever seen him smile so much,' Beatty said as she stood beside Ruby watching the boys.

'Yes, until Earl turns up. Talking of him, Tommy's been

here long enough.' Ruby disliked the thought of breaking up his imaginary play, but it dawned on her he'd been in their company for several hours. 'It won't be long before Earl will come hunting for him, and I don't want a repeat of yesterday. We'd best send him home,' she said, and turned her attention back to the boy. 'Tommy, I think it might be time for you to head home. Your mum will worry about you if you're out for so long, and Earl will be sent to collect you.' Ruby gave him an encouraging smile.

She still had no idea whether his mother existed, but felt the need for the constant mention of her presence in case Tommy let slip more information about her. Tommy turned to look at her and his arm dropped to his side. He let the plane fall to the floor and for a fleeting second Ruby saw an expression of anger cross his face. He poked his tongue out at his playmate, turned away from Ruby and walked to the door. Whilst the boys played, Ruby had locked it against the public, not wanting their fun to be disturbed. He pulled at the handle, but it remained in place and Ruby earned another angry glare. She felt for the keys in her pocket, hesitated about letting Tommy out, and finally chose not to unlock it until she'd spoken with him in private.

'Tommy, don't get mad. I need to speak with you. Come upstairs to my office. Bring your plane; I'll keep it safe for you. If you don't want to take it home, you can leave it here with me, if you think it will be safer,' she said. Something told her he'd lose his new toy if he took it with him.

With another tug at the door, Tommy gave in to the realisation it wouldn't open until he'd done as asked, and with reluctance walked to Ruby's side. He handed her his toy, looked up at her and she pointed to the stairs. She followed him as he climbed each one and, as she did, she composed what she was going to say.

Once in her office, she stood by the door and pulled a chair beside the one she usually sat on and kneeled down and placed her hands on Tommy's thin shoulders.

'Sit down and don't look so scared. You've done nothing wrong.'

Tommy scrambled onto the seat and looked so small against the large cushions. She wanted to scoop him up and hide him away from the horrors of the world, to make his life as happy as the few minutes he'd just spent downstairs.

'Tommy –' Ruby spoke in a soft voice as she clicked the door shut '– I've asked you many times about your mummy, but your uncle never tells me about her, and you seem to ignore me. I have a problem, and only you can help. I need honest answers. Understand?'

Tommy chewed on a nail, and nodded. Ruby sat on her chair and chose her words carefully.

'The other day you were scared, beaten and exhausted.

When I took you home, Beatty and I cared for you and it worried us about how you got into that state. You'd not been at school –'

'There ain't none,' Tommy retorted.

'True enough,' Ruby said, not allowing him the opportunity to change the subject, 'but there are a few days when you can have lessons. If your mummy needs help to find out when they are, I can ask the other mothers for her. Would you like me to do that?' Ruby pulled her chair in front of him and sat down.

'No point,' Tommy said and returned his fingers to his mouth.

'Why's that, Tommy? Won't your uncle let you go?'

Tommy kept chewing at his fingers.

'Where is he today? Left, and gone to fight the war?'

Ruby knew she'd used sarcasm in her words, but Tommy wouldn't understand the tone, simply the question.

'Nah. 'e's gone ta do business back 'ome – London.'

'Ah, so it's just you and Mummy at home then? Do you want me to walk you back? I was going to ask about you and your new friend downstairs –'

'Douglas.'

'Douglas, I see. Well, I was going to ask your mummy if you would like to spend a day or so at ours, and maybe Douglas too. A little holiday, and a break for mummy, as she must be tired looking after you and working all day.'

Tommy slid off the seat and walked to the door, and Ruby rose from her seat, blocking his way out.

'Ain't gonna 'appen. You gonna let me out?' he shouted and kicked at the door.

With a sigh, Ruby knew she'd got as far as she could with him, and opened the door and followed Tommy downstairs.

Douglas ran to him, but Tommy pushed a grubby hand his way.

'See ya, Dougie.'

Unlocking the front door, she watched the two friends part, and Douglas's disappointed face summed up her feelings too. Ruby ruffled Tommy's hair as he brushed past her and stepped outside, resisting the urge to pull him back to safety.

'Come and play with your plane any time,' she said.

'Give it to Douglas,' Tommy shouted over his shoulder as he ran down the street.

Ruby relayed what had happened to Beatty on their way home, and both came up with different ways of tracking down his mother. They chatted about it over their evening meal, but Fred didn't share their enthusiasm.

'There's a reason the boy hasn't brought his mother to meet you. And why that Earl is cagey about where she is all the time.' Fred filled his pipe with tobacco, and Ruby went to reply, but he held up his pipe to silence her.

'Ruby, I know you want to help, but I think it's safer if you leave it alone. Don't stir up trouble for yourselves. You've seen what the man's like; not only that, he might make life more miserable for the kiddie. For what it's worth, my opinion is Earl's controlling both of them, and it doesn't pay to fight a bully if another is involved.'

'You're as worried as we are, Fred, I can tell, but we must do something,' Ruby said.

'I am; the poor lad has a life we don't understand, but it doesn't mean I'm going to meddle in his affairs – Earl's, I mean.' Fred puffed on his pipe.

Frustrated by his seeming reluctance to help Tommy, Ruby snapped out a response.

'Does it mean we are right in ignoring Tommy, then?'

With an irritated sigh, reminding Ruby of her father whenever she'd argue, Fred held out his fingers as he counted off several points he wanted to get across to her. 'Think about it. One, we know nothing about their lives before Coventry. Two, he's got an aunt to look out for him too, remember? And three, Tommy hasn't asked us to help him, no matter how many times we've offered or hinted. It's all too complicated for us to unravel and stick our noses into. No, I say we forget about the whys and wherefores and carry on as we are when the lad turns up. We go around the houses with his mystery every night, and after Earl's behaviour last time he paid a visit, I say leave well alone.'

Ruby opened her mouth to speak, but Beatty beat her to it. 'As much as I hate to admit it, after listening to the old fool, I actually think Fred's right. We keep planning how to care for the child, how to make his life better, but who knows if we're actually making it worse? He's got an old head on young shoulders and he's streetwise, that much is obvious. His aunt features a lot in his life, and seemed to have a bob or two in her pocket at some time in her life, but where is she now, eh? Maybe Londoners behave different when it comes to bringing up children.'

'But –'

'No, Ruby. For once I'm going to put my foot down. Beatty and I are far too old to be worrying about who is going to shout at you next, or knock the door down. Please do this one thing we ask. As your new guardian, I am *telling* you this is how it is to be from now on. I've respected you're more mature than most your age, but in some things you are not experienced enough to deal with the outcome. It is my place to make the decision which will protect you.'

Fred puffed out his words between inhaling and exhaling on his pipe. Ruby looked to Beatty.

'I think Fred's summed it up and said all there is to be said. We'll leave well alone and keep you safe. Tommy is someone else's responsibility. And, talking of responsibility, we've made you ours, despite you thinking it's the other way around, and I've a feeling we need to have a chat about a certain young soldier.' Beatty reached out and squeezed Ruby's hand. 'Fred's volunteered to make the cocoa, so I think we'll get to it, young lady. Let's sit in the comfy seats.'

Fred stood up and looked at Ruby with a comical face. 'Getting forgetful in my old age. Can't recall volunteering for anything in my life, let alone making three cups of cocoa, but if our friend Beatty here says I have, well, who's going to argue? I'll leave you two to it and do my duty.'

Curling her legs up under her on her favourite chair, Ruby felt the love in the room and knew this was the right time to have a difficult conversation.

CHAPTER 26

15th November 1941

October came and went with Ruby heeding the advice from Beatty the night they had their heart-to-heart in September. She'd shared her feelings for John, and her guilt about sometimes forgetting times with her family. Beatty encouraged her to write a diary and bought her one the following day. From the moment she received it, Ruby spent time relating back to the day her world had fallen apart.

Occasionally, there were lighter moments but, on the whole, Ruby noticed a pattern of solemn thoughts and days of deep contemplation. Fred, Helen and Beatty featured as her life-savers. A page for each family member held only cheerful memories, but each one was marked with a black cross and their entry date ended *14-11-1940*.

Ruby couldn't add an exact time they'd all died, and drew a line under each one ending her visits to that page. There was no going back, only forward. The journal became her daily habit, and each person who had entered her life giving a reason for her to acknowledge them received a short entry or, in some cases, several pages. Every night, Ruby spent time respecting the reason for Beatty's purchase, and gained strength from her efforts.

Earl claimed no pleasant comments, nor gained doodles beside his name, unlike Tommy, whose pages were filled with amusing stories, sad snippets and smiling sunshine images scrawled around his name.

Then there was John's page. He earned four pages from the onset, followed by more each time she thought of him. Around his name she'd scribbled decorations of the Union Jack flag, a camera, green leaves and one red heart. When she thought of their first meeting, she allowed words to touch the page she'd never say out loud, and would never share with anyone she knew. The more she wrote the more she fretted over another reading its content, and found a suitable box with a lock to store it and the photograph of John inside. She pushed it to the back of a drawer for peace of mind. She trusted both Beatty and Fred with her life, and knew they'd never betray her trust. Her reason for secrecy was purely from embarrassment at describing a man, who others would consider a stranger, as the person she'd marry, and of her willingness to carry his children. She jotted down intimate thoughts and shocked herself with their baseness, and wondered where she'd learned their meaning. Her hands wandered over her body after writing tender moments she'd shared with him whilst looking through the lens of his camera. Her fingers found tender spots she had no choice but to explore. After each silent, breathless discovery, Ruby also experienced a sense of shame, but nonetheless wrote down each experience. After she'd written, she was tempted to scrub them from the page, but again, it mystified her how memories of a brief hand-touching moment between a couple could bring such hot flesh moments. Had her parents experienced the same? Could they see her? Still the thought of even being discovered by those looking over her never stopped the thrill of imagining John's flesh against hers. Had Fred shared the same thoughts and desires about his wife before they'd married? And Beatty with the man who'd sent a surge of pulsating adoration throughout her body by just walking into the room – did she feel guilty and at times shameful of having no self-control? Some days, Ruby wondered if every female kept a diary, for she found it hard to imagine her thoughts being put into words just to release the pent-up excitement they induced.

Somehow, Ruby knew she'd moved on from writing

out imaginary married surnames into a world more intimate, and indescribable verbally – an adult world. At
last, Ruby realised she'd slipped over the invisible line
which marked the end of childhood, and ventured into
the world of all woman. Each day she learned women
were dropping standards, girls craved more from their
boyfriends, and every act was blamed on the war. Every
tale she overheard in the community room, Ruby learned
to interpret into language she understood, and although
the wedding night act, which Beatty and friends referred
to, was not something she understood, she knew, deep
inside, it was something she'd save for the sacred day
itself, unlike some who'd brought 'shame and upset' to
many a household, for giving in to their partners before
marriage.

Ruby's dreams were always of wearing a pretty lace
dress, much like ones she'd seen in magazines, and worn
with dignity. And always on the arm of one man. Jean-
Paul Clayton. Since he'd left, she'd taken to listening to
the war news on the radio in the hope of second-guessing
where he might be in the world. News which never
brought her joy, and only instilled a fear that John was
lying injured – or worse, in a country she'd never heard
of, or back in Canada enjoying the company of a female
his own age. John occupied her thoughts far more than
she'd like, but the thoughts refused to go away.

*

Drawing back her curtains after dressing in readiness for one of the many memorial services, Ruby looked out at the grey sky and let out a deep sigh. Reminders around every corner were not what she needed when treading the road to recovery. The past year had been a game of one step forward and one back. She looked down on black hats bobbing on the heads of people heading to various places of work or worship and, with one swift move, tore her own hat from her head. She raced downstairs and opened the back door to inhale fresh air.

'What on earth's the matter?' Beatty asked as she entered the kitchen. 'Are you ready?'

Ruby turned to face her. 'I'm not going.' She paced a few feet then back to the fresh air. 'I mourn them every day – not just my family, but all who died. I am going to use this day for the living. I've an idea and will open the shop. You and Fred pay your respects. I'll be doing it in my own way.'

Beatty tugged on her gloves. 'If you're sure. You have to do what's right for you, but don't bring necessary upset on yourself. Hunt us down if you can't cope alone. You hear me?' Beatty held open her arms. Her warm smile and loving eyes moved Ruby and she embraced her with a gentle hug.

'Fred will understand, so you think about yourself and do what you have to do. We'll come by after church,'

Beatty said and took a small step away from Ruby and peered into her eyes, reassuring herself all was well.

'I'll be fine, but feel free to check on me. I just need to do something other than cry in a crowd.'

When the last of the mourners wove their way past the shop window, Ruby set about the idea the grey of the day had triggered. A gentle wind meandered along the road, and Ruby felt it perfect for her project.

Pulling out the large ladder, she tied string from one side of the shop front to the other, where Fred had placed hooks for external shades, yet to be made. Then, armed with pegs and a box of items, she spent fifteen minutes pegging out multi-coloured socks in a row. They blew in the breeze and brightened up the grey surrounding her. She wrote each family member's name on a large piece of cardboard and drew colourful images around the names with pencils from the children's table in the community room. The cardboard cut-out was kite-shaped, and she'd attached pieces of colourful rags cut into strips from its tail. Their bright colours cheered up the lamppost opposite the shop. In the window she placed anything bright and cheery, and taped a large poster to the inside of one window, declaring they were in memory of all the bright souls who'd walked the streets of Coventry and might they live on through rainbow colours.

Satisfied with her work, Ruby went back inside and prepared plates of rich tea biscuits and set up the new hot water urn Fred had purchased after Beatty complained about how many times she'd had to fill the kettle in just one morning. Ruby had a feeling that once word got out about the decorations, several people would pay her a visit. Curiosity always won over the knitting group.

She glanced at the clock above the front door. Ten-thirty. Pulling out her ledger, she worked on the weekly figures. She thought back to when her father and Stephen sat side-by-side doing much the same, whilst she worked on a mathematical problem Stephen had given her. All seemed so long ago but, in reality, it was no longer that two years. Grateful for a good education, Ruby continued working on adding up figures, re-planning the shop floor and wondering how long it would be before the stock had outgrown the shop. By eleven-thirty Beatty and Fred could be heard laughing outside and she sat and listened, delighted her efforts had brought the result she'd desired. More laughter joined theirs, but fell silent as people looked to the wording inside the window. The front door clicked open and a trail of people followed Beatty inside.

She looked at Ruby, whose heart pounded inside her chest. She knew Beatty and Fred understood, but would the others? After their initial finding and laughter, the words appeared to have subdued them. Then it came to her; they were coming inside to pay their respects.

She jumped down from her seat and beckoned them into the community room. Beatty unpinned her hat and placed it on the counter; she pulled on a pinafore and began the job of preparing pots of tea for Ruby to place on the tables. Well-wishers spoke of her family and thanked her for reminding them of how their own had once brought laughter and light to their lives, and that they should never forget those times by wearing the burden of grief.

By midday the shop became silent once again and Ruby, with Fred's help, took down the decorations.

'Shame that young chap with the camera wasn't around. He could have photographed it all for you,' Fred said and handed Ruby a thick pair of red and blue striped socks.

Not wishing to get drawn into a conversation about John, Ruby lifted the socks and waggled them about. 'Almost patriotic. It's a good job some of these can't be seen under the uniforms.'

'If their feet suffer like mine did in the trenches, they'll be grateful for any shade, and I think the powers that be wouldn't care if they wore them on their heads when the fighting reaches its peak,' Fred said.

Ruby and Beatty laughed.

'That's me done in the kitchen. I've used the remaining hot water to soak some of the clothes we received yesterday. I'll deal with them tomorrow,' Beatty said.

They tidied the boxes away and pulled on their coats. Ruby had made the decision to keep the shop closed for the rest of the day.

A rattle at the door distracted them. All three let out a sigh when they saw Earl's face peering through the window. None of them moved from the doorway, knowing he'd not see them from that angle. With another rattle of the handle, Earl followed through with a rap on the door. They watched as he stood and lit a cigarette, discarded the match and walked away. The click of his shoes echoed in the street and eventually disappeared. Only then did they step out onto the shop floor.

'I've not missed him these past – what, three weeks?' Beatty said.

Ruby peered out into the street and stepped out. 'It must be. Coast clear,' she said. The others stepped out and she locked the door behind them. 'Tommy's not been around for weeks. Gone back to London, I expect. Let's get home before Earl comes back. I can't be doing with him hanging around, today of all days.'

Back at home, Ruby thought more about the plans she'd scribbled down that morning. With Helen in Yorkshire, she no longer had a contact for news about Eagle Street, and set her mind to finding out from the council office. As it was Saturday, she was frustrated there was another day and a half to get through before she could ask her questions.

'And that's where my family died. I appreciate the house couldn't be built back to front, with the crater at the top end of the garden, but if I could purchase it from the landlord, I –' Ruby inhaled after telling the fierce-looking council officer in front of her the reason why she was so interested in a bombed plot in Eagle Street.

'Miss Shadwell, how old are you?' The council officer who'd sat chewing the corner of his moustache during her speech eventually asked the damning question.

'Seventeen and a half, but I –'

'*But* you are – too young. I'm sorry, any purchase you make would have to be in another's name, and the deeds would be registered to them,' the man said in a tone which suggested she was wasting his valuable time.

'So, it could be done? You know the landlord, and could approach him on my behalf? I own Garden Cottage in Spon Street, and would swap it with Eagle Street if he preferred. I'll ask the bank manager to prove I've money to purchase the land, if not.' Ruby spoke with great enthusiasm after hearing words of hope.

'Swapping houses is not how things are done, Miss Shadwell.' The officer's patronising tone annoyed Ruby, but she kept quiet as he continued talking. 'Owning a property at your age is unusual, but it does mean someone already supports your interests. I'll look into your request, and maybe your guardian will attend the next meeting with you, should there be a positive response from the landlord. Happy with that? I'll write to you of the outcome.' The man lifted a pile of paperwork and patted it, edge down on the table, clearly indicating their meeting was over. Ruby rose to her feet and held out her hand, but not before wiping it down her dress. Her nerves had made her palms sweat and she wanted to make the right impression.

'Thank you. I appreciate your help, and for understanding my reason for wanting to do this. I'm young, but know that I want to remain in Coventry.'

The man shook her hand and gave her his first smile of their meeting. 'I do understand, and it is an admirable reason. As I say, I'll do my best.'

'Thank you. That's all I ask,' Ruby said and left the meeting under a cloud. Age. Age prevented her from acting alone once again. Beatty and Fred would support her decisions, but she'd never be able to surprise them with anything until she was twenty-one. A birthday which seemed like a lifetime away. Although the war had brought her more freedom than she'd ever experienced, she still needed her independence.

CHAPTER 27

7th December 1941

A letter from Helen landed on the doormat – Ruby recognised her handwriting. A second letter bore the postmark, *Military Post, 10th November 1941*. It was addressed to *Miss R Shadwell and family, Garden Cottage, Spon Street, Coventry*.

She ripped open the envelope, pulled out its contents and snatched up a slice of the cold toast sitting on her plate and took a bite. Chewing slowly, she opened the single sheet of paper and admired the neat handwriting.

Dear All,
Forgive the short note, but things are moving fast around here, and I am sitting on a truck waiting to move out to pastures new.

284

I would like to thank you for your friendship, and want you to know my mother appreciated her son's welcome to your city. If ever you are in Toronto, she said you are to drop by. I warn you, Toronto is a large place to try and drop by without an address. Maybe, when the war is over, you could come and walk in Allan Gardens. Please, all of you, make the trip over and see the beauty of my country. I travelled up to Scotland and, in some small way, it reminded me of home, with the pine trees and lakes. Toronto has large buildings, rightly named skyscrapers, too big for the pretty villages I've seen in England. I digress. I recently had a bumpy ride into a country I cannot name for security purposes, and Ruby, I saw more wallpapered walls, and remembered your words. I took time to find out more about the occupants where I could. It's a sad, cruel war.

Our driver has arrived, and I'm afraid the pot-holed road will not allow me to write with a steady hand. If I get the opportunity, I will write again. Should you wish to write to me, please send letters to the address below, and they will forward them on.

Stay safe in Coventry,
My regards
Jean-Paul Clayton

C/O
Canadian Army Film and Photo Unit
Canadian Military Headquarters,
2, Cockspur Street,
SW1
London, England.

Ruby stared at the letter for a few moments, hunched over, and imagined John huddled in a corner and thinking of them – her. Ruby liked to think the reference to the gardens was for her alone.

Next, she tore open Helen's letter.

Dear Ruby,

All is not well with my sister, but at least I am here to keep watch over her. We walk each day but it is all she does. Her mind wanders and she thinks I'm a friend of a friend. The death of Bill has taken her mind. I will never return to Coventry. She needs me for everything, and I can't see it changing any time soon.

I hope all is well with you; write and tell me your news.

Take care of yourself.

With fond affection,

Helen

Poor Helen.

Ruby thought about her friends as she put pen to paper, undecided as to whom she wrote first.

Garden Cottage,
Coventry

Dearest Helen,

How lovely to hear from you, but I am sorry to read your sad news about your sister. Please take care of yourself.

The shop is thriving, and the community room is heaving every day. We've sent a hundred pairs of knitted socks to soldiers, and raised the amazing sum of twenty pounds for local causes by selling handmade items.

I've given a bit of thought to John, the Canadian. I've met with him a few times and please don't think me foolish, but I quite like him. He's different to others I speak to and treats me as an equal. He's abroad now, I think, and I have to write to their headquarters in London, and they will pass the letters onto him.

Please take care of yourself, and write back when you have news.

Fondest wishes,
Ruby

Taking a deep breath, Ruby set about composing her second letter, and the increase in her heart rate surprised her. Writing a letter to John brought about the same excitement as sitting in his company.

Garden Cottage,
Spon Street, Coventry.

Dear John,
Thank you for your letter. Receiving post always makes us feel as if life is returning to some form of normality, and the outside world hasn't forgotten us. Considering it is only the beginning of December, and we think you wrote this from outside of England, your letter did not take too long to reach us. Beatty and Fred send their regards. My life is busy here, and I've not seen Tommy, nor Earl, for many weeks now.

I hope I can call you a friend – pen-friend, as I'd like to hear from you again. Tell me about your life before the war. Let's not allow the atrocities smother the good times – I assume you had good times in Canada.

Coventry mourned on the first anniversary of the Blitz bombing, but I did so in my own way. I wish you had been here to photograph the shop. It was covered in knitted socks to commemorate the bright

*souls who once walked our streets. It went down
well, and no one told me off for not going to the
formal church memorial service. I'd intended to go,
but something told me I had to do it my way. And
I did. Maybe I'll do the same in April, when we go
through the next anniversary of mourning.*

*I went to the council to see about buying my old
house. They are rebuilding, and I want the landlord
to release it to me, even if he won't sell. It is my
intention to live out my life here, and give Coventry
the best of me. Not that it is much, but it will be the
blood of a Coventarian to continue a life tree of sorts.*

*I will leave you with our good wishes, and hope
this letter finds you safe and well. Ruby*

Satisfied the letter told John all she wanted to say, she
sealed the envelope and headed to the post office.

As she approached the entrance, Ruby thought she
heard the familiar voice of Earl coming from a side alley
nearby. The more he spoke, she knew it was him, and
he was talking to another man with a similar accent to
his own. She allowed a woman to go in front of her on
the pretext she might have left her purse at home, and
rummaged through her bag.

'The place is full of stuff. Money too,' Earl said.

'Easy pickings are always welcome,' said the anonymous
man.

'I've got a runner going in soon. Easy, as you say. By the way, I've got access to a couple of extra ration books, and four petrol coupons, if you can shift them. I've got a cow coming our way next week. There'll be a leg in it for you.' Earl laughed, and dropped his voice. 'But not around here – understand? This is my patch.'

Ruby shuddered as she imagined his threatening face and side-of-the-nose tapping action, then anger wormed its way with realisation of what he'd said.

The man was a crook, a spiv, and had nothing to do with the army. If he did, it was only to steal for the black market. She shuffled forward as the queue moved up a notch, and waited her turn. Her mind was in turmoil. She needed to speak with Fred. He'd know what to do – who to tell.

CHAPTER 28

'I tell you, that man needs locking away,' Beatty declared as Ruby relayed the overheard conversation when her friends returned from a trip to Birmingham to visit an old friend of Beatty's.

Fred scratched the day's growth around his chin, deep in thought. 'We have to be careful. It's only hearsay. Our Ruby overheard two men talking. The police won't be interested when there's blatant looting happening under their noses. If we see Earl again...'

Fred looked at Beatty when she gave a loud sigh, interrupting his flow of words.

'If we see him again. I won't get too excited about it. Creep,' she said.

'Fred, I just thought – he said about money being kept on the premises. What if he's talking about the shop? We only bring the tin home on Friday.'

Beatty put her hand to her mouth as Ruby spoke.

Fred glanced at his watch. 'Get your coat; we'll go and get it now.'

'You've only just got home. It's too dark,' Ruby protested.

'No matter. We'll sleep better. Get the torch with the cover; it'll help light the floor and we won't have to pull down the blinds, or light up the shop.'

They linked arms and walked as fast as an elderly man and a crippled girl could through dark streets and avoiding fallen masonry. Two fire-watchers called out a greeting, but the pair saw no one else until they turned the corner into Hill Street. Ruby gave Fred a glance and he nudged her to turn off the torch and they stepped back into Bond Street, into the darkness of an alleyway before the man lingering outside the shop saw them. A few minutes later the man ambled past them and headed away from the area. Ruby held her breath for fear of the night air vapours giving away their whereabouts. Once the sound of footsteps receded, Fred took a step out of the alley. 'All clear,' he whispered.

They moved around the corner again, when Fred suddenly stood still. He held his arm across the front of Ruby as a barrier to prevent her moving forward.

'For a minute, I thought –' Fred didn't complete his sentence, but pointed at Tommy, walking the other way. 'It is – it's the boy.'

Ruby peered into the darkness and made out a shadowy figure ahead. She leaned forward, ready to run after Tommy, but Fred kept his arm in front of her.

'Whatever's going on, we must fetch the police. I think they've taken what they wanted – I think you heard Earl correctly. There's nothing we can do here. It's too dangerous. Looters are not to be dealt with by the likes of you and me.' His voice, an urgent whisper, warned her not to move.

'The police think Earl's responsible for quite a few criminal offences around here,' Ruby said as they relayed the evening's events to Beatty back at home. 'Tommy is small and nimble. And, as we know, fast on his feet. He's the ideal person to use. A bedraggled child with a few bruises wins the heart of a shopkeeper, susses out the layout, stock, comings and goings of the owner. They smashed the back window and he scrambled inside.'

Beatty stared at her, her expression confused. 'If it weren't you two telling me all this, I'd have said it was a made-up story. Whatever next?'

Ruby gave a short sniffle. 'I've lost the money and a few items from the glass cabinet – the ones I bought from them last time they were visiting – but no one was hurt, and we have to be thankful for that, I suppose.'

'Let's hope the boy's not cut himself,' Fred said, and Ruby frowned back her agreement.

'Why didn't he tell me what was going on?' Ruby questioned herself rather than the others.

Fred sat on a chair and pulled off his shoes. 'Like the policeman said, he's afraid.'

'If they find him, what will happen to him?' Beatty asked.

'They said he'll be returned to his mother. But they've got to find him first – and her – as I've yet to be convinced she exists. I've never really understood her never showing her face, but what if she's part of the gang? He won't be off the streets for too long. He's a good little earner for them,' Fred said, and Ruby heard the anger in his voice. Anger she also felt.

'Sadly, unless Tommy is found, he'll turn out like Earl and there'll be another little Tommy running criminal errands. You stay there, Fred. I'll shut up the chickens,' Beatty said and went into the garden.

'Charlie Fayers has boarded up the window, and I'll square up with him tomorrow. I'm done in and ready for bed. 'Night both,' Fred said to Ruby.

''Night, Fred. Sleep well, and thank you. I'll wipe the dishes and head up myself. I want to get to the shop early tomorrow to clear up before we open.'

'You get some sleep, young lady. No staying up fretting about Tommy.' Beatty's firm voice followed through as she stepped indoors.

Ruby didn't like to tell her it was Jean-Paul Clayton

who she usually fretted over, and it probably wouldn't alter until she knew he was safe.

News soon drifted around the women of the knitting group about the break-in and, armed with brooms and pans, the glass shards were soon removed and, in true British style, the teapot filled. The warmth of friendship touched Ruby.

Pearl Harbor had been bombed the night before, and the men stood discussing the implications – war with Japan – whilst the women in the room made Tommy's situation the topic of their conversation. Some argued he knew better, even at such a tender age, but the majority condemned both his mother and uncle. By early afternoon, Ruby had heard enough and closed the shop early. She stood in the silence, allowing it to wash over her, bringing with it an ease to the tension of the past few hours.

The world pounded her down with war talk, people to distrust, and the quandary of falling in love at such a tender age, with a man she might never see again. She wanted to gather up the better parts of her life and run away to a quiet corner of the world.

A tap on the door disturbed her thoughts and she looked up, frightened the men or Earl had returned. Instead, John's face stared back at her. Her fingers fumbled with the keys as she unlocked the door.

'John!' She tugged him into the room by the sleeve, and locked up behind him.

'Hello, Ruby.'

When she turned around he stood with his arms open and she needed no second invitation to run into them. He folded her into his body and his lips found hers. When they pulled back for air, she stared up at his face.

'I thought I'd never see you again!'

'I'm back for forty-eight hours, so I came to visit my favourite girl.'

'Ah, so you have others hidden away?'

John kissed her again, and this time his tongue teased her teeth apart and Ruby caved in to his non-verbal instructions.

John stroked her hair as he spoke. 'What happened?' He pointed to the boarded-up window.

'I had a break-in. We think it's the work of Earl.'

'That man again!'

'Let's not worry about him; he's not important. This is.' Ruby went to him and tiptoed up to enjoy another kiss.

'Come with me,' she instructed and led the way upstairs to her office. She removed her coat and draped it over the back of a chair. John went to her and pulled down her hair and stroked each curl into place, grazing her neck with his fingers as he did so, and Ruby let out a sigh. A louder one followed when he played three fingers against her throat. By the time he'd cupped the right-hand side of her face in the palm of his hand Ruby had no breath left to offer. She was his.

His fingers fumbled with buttons, hers flexed across his arm muscles until they'd crossed a line she didn't understand. John's words urged her further into something she couldn't comprehend. Jean-Paul Clayton had won her heart and if his intention was to weaken a woman already willing to be moulded by his attention – lust, love, whatever those around them would call it – Ruby surrendered. She waved the flag of permission. And when his kiss attacked, she returned the role of the invader and her lips equalled his on the battleground of pleasure. If classified as a war, the one of Shadwell versus Clayton signed off as a draw. She lost herself in his embrace. John's kisses, his reassurances of care, his urgency to love her, burst through a dam of self-restraint, both parties satiated by acceptance. Love conquered all when both parties loved. The passion between them was undeniable, and when Ruby allowed John to take her for the first time she rejoiced in it and understood it was a greater force than herself which urged her onwards.

Another expulsion of air left her lips, but this time pleasure overcame pain. Over and over their lips met, neither one of them wanting the moment to end, waiting for the second wave of want to sweep them into another bout of desire. Their breathing matched speed and urgency, and then, to Ruby's surprise, John pulled away with one abrupt movement and composed himself. She watched him move with routine, tidying his clothing, flattening his hair and silently cursing himself.

She watched as he paced the floor, then dropped to his knee in front of her.

'Ruby . . .' his voice sounded out her name with deep passion '... I am so sorry. I . . . it's not what I wanted to happen.'

Before Ruby gained control of her own breath, John was on his feet again. She felt the sting of rejection in that one swift movement.

'John?' She could barely whisper his name.

'It's wrong, Ruby. Wrong.' The distress in his voice puzzled Ruby.

'But it didn't feel that way, John. Wrong isn't the word I'd choose for what just happened.'

With another glance at his flushed face, Ruby questioned her ability to speak. His mouth, so intent on expressing his fierce need and desire, had left a sensation of bruising. John rubbed his mouth, and something told Ruby hers had done the same.

'As God is my witness, I didn't mean that to happen.' John's words stung.

'As whatever God there might be, I did.' Ruby spat her words back with anger.

'Blasphemy doesn't become you,' John shot back.

Ruby curled herself into her seat. 'And righteousness is not something you are good at, Jean-Paul,' she whispered.

'John. My name with you is John.'

'And it will be again, when you don't feel guilty about what just happened. I'm young, but not stupid. I know the difference between general love and whatever that was between us. Lust? Passion? Whatever it was, one of us has to guide it in the right direction. Can you? As the man, the experienced one, can you take me into a future of new experiences? Can you take responsibility for your actions?'

Standing tall and unnecessarily adjusting his clothing, John failed to look her in the eye, and Ruby sensed a goodbye statement in the atmosphere. She drew on her inner strength to prepare for his rejection, and reminded herself of the age difference between them.

Don't give him the easy way out, Ruby. There's no excuse for him taking advantage of you. Her thoughts recharged their battle call. *One of us has to take control or step away to protect ourselves from emotional destruction.*

'No ties, no regrets. Is that how we leave this? We have nothing to bind us into something we can't handle. You are far too old for me. I'm not what you need. I'll put it down to one of life's experiences.' Ruby's words rushed from her mouth and she felt each one tug her heart as she expelled them. Composed and determined not to cry, she pinched her lips together, still feeling the burning of want and need from John's.

A slap of John's hand against the arm of her chair made her jump, and Ruby suppressed a screech of surprise, but launched into the second part of her speech before he had the opportunity to say anything.

'I'm not a lover or a woman of experience. I'm at the beginning of my adult life. What I mean is . . . I want what you offer, and can match it, but I don't want it for a day, a night or a week. I want what I feel for life, but clearly that's impossible, so I have to be realistic. You have to walk away, and I will return to my life and accept whatever it throws at me. I know other girls my age are still dreaming of Prince Charming coming to the rescue, but life gave me no option; I had to grow up fast. I hadn't planned on falling in love. I thought it would come later – in my twenties, when I . . . oh, I don't know what I'm trying to say. Please go, John. Don't hurt me. I can't bear any more pain.'

John waited until she'd finished speaking, his head tilted to one side, and Ruby watched as he held his arms out to her again, inviting, and confirming he was going nowhere.

'It's impossible. We're impossible,' she whispered.

'Life's impossible. Complicated. But it's to be enjoyed, and for how long? Who knows?'

With legs eager to reach his embrace, but a mind warning her of the dangers of her next move, Ruby battled to remain standing firm.

'I read something romantic in a book once. Something about being allowed to drift free and always remember. Can you do that for me, John? This war has twisted everything into a mess of confusion. I'll always want you, need you, in my life. You are the man who helped me see life through a different lens, but I can't let you carry on feeling sorry for me. Nor can I let your loneliness lust after me. I'm not that person.'

A finger pressed against her lips. John's dark eyes gazed into hers. 'Ruby, stop talking – thinking too hard. Why would I feel sorry for you? I admire you. I don't know what you are expecting of me, or what you want from me, but I know this much. I have to live each day meeting fear, to photograph fear, and to face fear, and yet the only time I've felt truly afraid is now, standing in front of you, listening to you sending me away. Like you, I've imagined, thought and hoped, and now you've asked me to walk away and simply remember you. Well, I've also heard an expression: love conquers all. Let's speak to Beatty and Fred about how we feel.'

Ruby turned her head away from his gaze. 'I can't,' she whispered.

John went to her and tilted her head upwards to his. 'Can't talk to them, or love me?'

'Both.' As Ruby said the word, she walked to the door and pointed down the stairs.

'I can't because that is my life, down there, with people who come together because of me. I realise now, I've given them hope of a fresh start. A simple thing, but I did it, and made it my responsibility. Coventry is where I have to stay. My heart won't let me leave here . . . with you. Besides, we barely know each other.'

John sat down on the chair Ruby had vacated, and she watched him reach inside a chest pocket and he pulled out a photograph. 'Then let's learn more. These are the most important people in my life. My parents. My sister.' He held out the picture and Ruby took it from him. She moved to a chair beside him, and lowered herself down.

'You have your mother's eyes, and your father's height. Your sister looks like you too. I wish I could show you mine.'

For another hour she listened to him relay the life of Jean-Paul Senior, his bank manager father, and his mother, Ida. According to John, his mother made the best cakes and bread. John had no pets, but longed for a dog. They were just establishing that John's photographic career stemmed from joining his father whenever he recorded architecture or the beauty of High Park, when a sharp rap at the door interrupted him.

'Ruby! Ruby, are you in there?' Beatty and Fred's voices called out.

Pulling her clothing in tidy order, Ruby looked to John for guidance. 'They're worried; I didn't realise we've been here so long.'

'Go to them. I'll be right behind you. We'll face this together.'

Beatty beat Fred through the door.

'Thank goodness. I was worried sick. Oh, I see you've got company. Look who is here, Fred.' Beatty stepped to one side and let Fred through the doorway.

'John . . . I thought you'd left the country,' Fred said, and pulled his cap from his head.

'I was – am. I'm back just for a couple of days, and chose to spend my time checking on Ruby. I heard about the break-in.'

Ruby couldn't believe she'd heard John lie about knowing about the burglary, but was grateful he gave a valid reason for being in the shop.

'It was selfish of me, you two. I should have told John to come back to ours with me, and not sit chatting here forgetting you'd be worried. I'm so sorry,' Ruby gushed out her apology. She felt guilty about two things but could, and would, only apologise for one.

'I think we'll leave it that you're safe, and say no more about it,' Beatty said.

'And will you be back, John, or have you seen enough of Coventry?' Fred asked, then looked at Ruby. She felt a giveaway blush but, before either Fred or Beatty made the situation more awkward with questions, Ruby offered up a snippet to show them John and she had exchanged personal information.

'John has entertained me with his life in Canada. His father works in banking, and his mother, Ida, is a home-maker.'

Beatty huffed. 'Rich folk then.'

Ruby watched her friend hitch her bosom over folded arms, wrapping them across her expanding waistline. She adored the protective side of her, and knew Beatty was teasing John, but his expression showed he'd not worked it out yet. Sweat beaded across his top lip, and he fidgeted from one foot to the other. She knew how he felt, and also wanted to get away.

'Comfortable. They live a comfortable life. My father lost a lot of money during the depression, especially in twenty-nine. He's worked hard and only really got back on his feet around four years ago. He's a proud man, and works hard.'

Now standing with her legs astride, looking every part the formidable parent, Beatty nodded her approval. 'Hard times. Well, I'm glad he reaped the rewards of his hard work.'

'Ruby? Are you in there?'

Beatty's voice cut into the dark dreams, and Ruby roused from semi-nightmares with gratitude. She pulled the eiderdown away from her, and registered the sweat-drenched clothing sticking to her body.

'I am. Come in.'

Bustling inside and drawing back the curtain to let in a stream of fading light, Beatty tutted when she turned and saw Ruby. 'The state of you. You look dreadful.'

'Thanks,' Ruby replied in a dull voice loaded with sarcasm.

'I take it your friend has gone?' Beatty stood over Ruby with her hands on her hips.

'He has. He left me a gift.' Ruby held out the necklace.

'Unusual,' Beatty said as she turned the tiny camera around in her fingers.

'I found it in my pocket after he'd gone.' Ruby pulled herself upright and swung her legs over the side of the bed.

'I'm so confused with how I feel. He said to talk to you – for us both to talk with you about our feelings for each other, but I didn't want to, and now I do. I think I love him, but it's a different kind of love than I felt for Mum and Dad, or I feel for you and Fred. It's like an ache which won't go away. I thought love was supposed to make you happy.' Ruby's words came in a rush, and she slumped forward after sharing her confusion.

Beatty sat down beside her and placed an arm around Ruby's shoulder. 'Love never gives us a day or time when it comes knocking. It's a confusing thing to deal with. We love to love, and love to hate. Love comes to us, and we walk away. Sometimes, it comes when we are at our most vulnerable. Even though you're a young woman, you have feelings. I'm inclined to think you're too young to fall so deeply, but who am I to judge how another loves? My concern is for you. John is only a few years older, twenty-two I think he said, but he is from another country, and will want to return when the war is over – can you leave here to be with him? You have to decide which path to tread. If you want to carry on chasing around with the boy then do so, but be aware of the consequences. Understand?'

Beatty's red face and twisting hands told Ruby she was talking about what she always referred to as the birds and the bees, and Ruby nodded she understood.

'It's too late to talk about it, Beatty. I know all about it – everything.' Ruby emphasised the last word and Beatty sat up straight.

'I see.'

Rising to her feet, Ruby peered into the mirror.

'And has he said he intends to come back to Coventry?' Beatty asked.

'He said he'd be back to see me as soon as he's back in England. I don't know when it will be, or where he is, and it's frightening.'

'Frightening for many reasons. Let's see what happens

next,' Beatty said and got up from the bed. 'This war has a lot to answer for,' she muttered as she made her way downstairs.

Ruby heard mutterings between Beatty and Fred, and knew Fred was fed just enough information to stop him feeling left out of Ruby's care. She was grateful she'd such thoughtful friends in her life. They would need her in their old age and, in the silence of her room, Ruby's future was decided.

CHAPTER 29

1st May 1942

The long snowy days of winter were long forgotten, and spring wavered on the edge of summer's rising. Radio news kept the household up to date with the horrors of the war still raging, and informed them of another city bombed the previous day. York had experienced the wrath of the enemy, and Beatty, Fred and Ruby stood in silence, remembering their own day of death and destruction, and all three hoping Helen was safe.

Ruby had worked through into another phase of her life. She'd received a letter from the council informing her the landlord was retaining the Eagle Street plot and, once rebuilt, he'd give consideration to renting it to her when she was of age. She wrote back and informed them she would not live there alone, and the tenant named on the documents would be either Fred or Beatty. She put the idea from her mind as she focused upon her new position within the local Red Cross Voluntary Aid Detachment. The shop kept Beatty, Fred and the many women who gathered there busy, and they ran it like clockwork. Ruby's job was reduced to the book-keeping, and when she'd spoken about getting involved in more war work they'd agreed a change would be good for her. Earl and Tommy no longer visited and life was calmer for them all, and Ruby needed to train her mind not to think of the danger John was in every day.

Standing rolling a bandage, Ruby looked around at the small group of VAD females she worked with; some were Beatty's age, others were much younger. Ruby worked alongside three the same age as herself and marvelled at their ability to present themselves more and more glamorously each day. Compared to some, Ruby thought she looked an old maid.

'Pat, how do you get your hair to stay in the curls around your cap?' she asked the girl working opposite her.

'I can show you later, if you like. Mind you, if I had pretty hair like yours, I'd leave it alone. You just need a bit of mascara on your eyelashes, and a bit of lippy. Red is in. What do you reckon, Dolly?'

The plumper girl of the two looked up from her task. She gave a shy smile. 'You worked wonders with me,' she said.

'I'll have a think about it, but I've a feeling Fred will have something to say.' Ruby laughed.

'Him? He's nobody. You're a free agent. If I had your luck, I'd –'

Ruby didn't remain in the room to hear what Pat would do. Her leg ached, her job bored her rigid and the company of some of the girls made her enjoy her own more and more. Pat's statement that Fred was nobody to her, and the thoughtless comment about her being a free agent and lucky, caught her unawares. She'd stood listening to mindless gossip and endless chatter about boys and their wandering hands for weeks, but could no longer bear the humdrum of every day. Guilty feelings of walking away from a worthwhile position would come later, but for now Ruby stomped off her anger with a walk to the shop. As she passed her supervisor she told her she had severe pains in her leg from standing too long, and was allowed a two-hour break.

'And they let you leave? Just like that?'

'It's my leg, Fred. I can't stand or keep up with the others.'

'Never held you back before.'

'It held me back at school. It made me different – stand out from the rest. You only knew the after-Blitz me.' Ruby snapped out words she'd said several times over as many days. She was beyond sighing, huffing and explaining why she'd left the VAD. Beatty said she found it hard to understand, and expressed her concerns about Ruby having no friends her age. No matter how many times she tried to tell them she didn't need them, she was shot down with reasons as to why she did. Dancing and letting her hair down didn't count in Ruby's world, but Beatty and Fred pushed their individual reasons as to why they should.

With an iron will, Ruby decided it all had to end that day. The hope of returning to some form of normality appeared to be drowning under an avalanche of repeated conversations. She took a deep breath.

'I'm going to Yorkshire. To see Helen.'

Fred stopped polishing his shoes, and Beatty stood open-mouthed. Both spoke at the same time.

'Alone?'

'I won't be alone. I'll be with Helen.'

'The journey . . . I mean the journey.' Beatty's voice was filled with anxiety.

'I forbid it.'

Ruby jumped as Fred's voice rang out loud and clear. It was firm and decisive. Beatty reached out her hand to him and they stood together, facing her.

'You can't stop me.'

The moment the words left her lips, Ruby regretted them. They sounded childish, and her aim was to show them she was adult enough to take the trip.

'I'm . . . we're your guardians. It's not safe for you

and we'd be wrong to agree for you to travel alone. Maybe Beatty can come with you – stay overnight in a guest house and bring you home the next day, after you've seen Helen. What do you say?'

Ruby didn't want to say anything. Disappointment crowded her thoughts, and she shrugged. Losing her parents had given her a freedom she'd never considered before their deaths, until Pat had mentioned it. Now, she had two people reeling her in, and taking on the role for themselves. She scrambled through her thoughts for the word which represented how she felt. Resentment. Ruby resented their decision to make up their minds for her, but accepted the time had come to give up her freedom. When she turned twenty-one, no one would make decisions on her behalf but, until then, Ruby knew she had little choice in the matter.

'You're right; I'm being hasty. I'll wait. In the meantime, I will be patient and focus on the business. You two take tomorrow off and visit your cousin again, Beatty. I appreciate all you do, but have lapsed into leaning on you far too much. I'll cope.'

'At least we'll know where you are,' muttered Fred, and earned himself a gentle cuff from Beatty.

'That will be nice. We enjoyed our last visit. I know you're frustrated with life, and your leg, Ruby, but all will settle into place one day. You'll see.'

*

The next morning dragged into midday, as Ruby sorted her way through a batch of tatty magazines and comics. She'd reached the final pile when the bell Fred had attached to the door gave a ping and announced a customer's arrival. Stretching herself from her kneeling position, Ruby stood upright and faced a well-dressed middle-aged woman.

'Can I help you?' she asked the woman.

'Na. But you can 'elp me.' Tommy's face peered round from behind the woman.

'Tommy! How are you?'

A clean Tommy stepped out into the room. He had dark rings under his eyes, and still looked underfed, but his smile hadn't altered. 'Betta.'

'Better? Have you been ill?'

Ruby looked to the woman, who'd yet to speak.

'It appears Tommy has not been well for some months. He claims you know him, and I assume you are Miss Shadwell – Ruby.' The woman's voice was clear and educated, and Ruby doubted they were related.

'I am, and I do. I've not seen him for some time, not since his uncle Earl took him back to London.'

Something in Tommy's face made Ruby stop talking. Fear. It was definitely fear.

'Evelyn Pearce.' The woman held out her hand, and Ruby shook it.

'Is there an adult I can speak with, with regard to this young man?'

'I'm sorry; my guardians are out of town. Can I offer you a cup of tea, and a seat? I assume you've travelled from London?' Ruby beckoned her to follow.

'Leamington Spa, actually. A tea would be most welcome, thank you.' The woman followed on into the quiet community room.

'Blimey, where's the crowd?' Tommy asked.

'A lot of the ladies have received their call-up papers, Tommy. Those who haven't, have got jobs in the factories to cover the lack of men. Working flat-out, day and night. I only open this part two days a week now, for the knitters and fundraisers.'

She placed a cup and saucer in front of the woman, and sat down at the table. Tommy sat in one corner with a glass of milk and Ruby hunted out his treasured plane.

'I kept it back, in case you came to visit,' Ruby said as he yelled his delight at seeing it again. 'Keep the noise down while we talk.'

'I'm here to ask your guardian – your grandfather, as I understand it from Tommy, if they would consider giving him a temporary home. We have no room; the orphanage is full to overflowing, as you can imagine.' The woman gave an exaggerated sigh. 'It would be until we can find a permanent place for him within one of the evacuee communities.'

Tommy stopped roaring out aeroplane noises, and Ruby replaced her cup into its saucer.

'I'm sorry . . . a home? His mother, uncle . . . Are they –' Not wishing ill of the dead, Ruby truly hoped something dreadful had happened to Earl. She found it hard to forgive him for many reasons.

She watched as Tommy over-exaggerated his concentration on the plane.

'Tommy is an orphan, Miss Shadwell. Sadly, the man claiming to be his uncle is in fact a rogue. An abuser. He is no relation. Tommy ran away from an orphanage when he was barely five. Originally from London, he fell into the clutches of a crook, and the man kept him on a tight leash in Leamington Spa. He taught Tommy to steal and then sell the items on.'

'Oh, Tommy, you should have trusted us enough to say! You must have been petrified. I can't believe you were so close, and not in London. I thought you'd gone back there with Earl, but it all makes sense now.'

Tommy looked up at her, and the love she felt for him came rushing back. Tommy was more than a child she wanted to watch over; he was a little boy sent to comfort her, and she to comfort him. Ruby went to him and knelt down beside him, stroking his head.

'Na. I didn't know 'oo ta trust. You wus kind, but 'e'd been kind at the start.'

Ruffling his hair, Ruby rose to her feet. She went back to the table. 'I know we'll give him a roof over his head; I own the house. My guardians love Tommy as much as

I do, but I'm worried about the man he called his uncle. You gave the impression he is still around, and we can't have him making life any more difficult than it already is – you understand?'

Evelyn Pearce pulled out papers from her attaché case. 'He was arrested and is behind bars, and will be for a very long time. Tommy wasn't the only child he had locked away in his house. They were found when a bomb hit the house next door and it exposed a wall.'

'Locked away?'

'Like animals, Miss Shadwell. Animals.'

Tommy fell silent, and Ruby put her arms around him.

'Oh, Tommy. You're safe now. We'll look after you, and Auntie B will spoil you rotten. You try stopping her. I take it they are the papers for them to sign.' Ruby pointed at the small pile in front of Evelyn Pearce.

'Yes, he has a new ration book allocated, and it will come to my office. I'll need your address for my records. When is your guardian due back?'

Ruby scribbled it down. 'Early evening. I've two guardians, and neither one will hesitate to sign. You can leave the papers with me, and we will put them in the post tomorrow. We can manage without his ration book for a few days, but any longer we might have to fetch it from you. Tommy can stay for as long as he needs.'

Evelyn Pearce looked at Tommy, showing she'd like a private word with Ruby.

'Tommy, go and run with your plane inside the shop. No going out of the door, though.'

Once the noise of whatever aeroplane Tommy was pretending to be reached a loud enough level, Evelyn Pearce rose to her feet. 'Tommy's abuser is not able to get to the child, and I think the company of someone such as yourself will be good for him. He's possibly still light-fingered, as it's become a daily habit, so please be aware.'

'Oh, I know Tommy well enough, Mrs Pearce. He'll be fine with us. Fred, although he's not my grandfather, he's taken on that role, will do the same for Tommy while he stays. He takes no nonsense. He's put me straight on a few things. And Beatty, she's a natural mother hen. They've both got hearts big enough for all the children in need,' Ruby said, and as she spoke her words resonated with her. Fred and Beatty only ever looked out for her, and she reminded herself to show a little more respect towards the fears they showed whenever she shared her impulsive ideas. A trip to Yorkshire could wait.

'I'll leave him in your care. Unfortunately, I have nothing to hand over other than the child. We've had a frantic twenty-four hours, and I forgot his wash bag.'

With a shake of her head, Ruby walked the woman to the door. 'As you can see from the shop, I can find him clothing. And we can buy what he needs on the way home. He'll not go without.'

Closing the door behind Evelyn Pearce, Ruby looked at Tommy, running around the room. 'Well, this a surprise.'

Tommy stopped running and looked over at her. 'I'm sorry we stole from you.' His voice quivered.

Ruby waved a dismissive hand. 'I'm more than sorry we didn't know the truth. I need you to promise you will always tell the truth from now on. And if you are scared or worried, you tell me, Fred or Beatty. You hear?'

'I hear.'

'Signed and done,' Fred said, and handed the papers to Ruby.

'The lad's asleep. Tomorrow we'll have a move around and he can share Fred's room. Are you sure you'll be all right down here?' Beatty addressed Ruby. 'I've set him out fresh clothes for the morning,' she said as she walked through with Tommy's laundry.

Looking at her friends, Ruby smiled. From the moment she'd told them about Tommy's background, and his situation, they'd both agreed he was in the best place. She glanced at the wooden plane sitting on the table and a pang of sadness crept its way into her thoughts. She missed John.

After settling onto her bed, she composed a letter.

Dear John,

I hope this letter finds you well – and safe. I wear your necklace every day, and often wonder where your travels have taken you. I scour the news for hints, but will probably never know if I am right or not. I miss you so much.

You'll never guess who turned up today – no other than young Tommy. The most dreadful thing has happened to him. Tommy was a runaway from an orphanage, but was too scared to tell us. He was held captive along with other children and by none other than Earl, who is not his uncle but a criminal preying on young children. Luckily, Earl was caught, and is now in prison. What a wicked man! Thankfully, Tommy is now safely in our care.

My life has its dips and highs; at the moment it is in a dip. Although, as you know, I am not eligible for call-up papers, I did volunteer for basic duties for the Red Cross VAD, but circumstances changed and I left. I've found my leg aches more, and I'm better sitting for hours rather than standing. I'm now back at the shop and I'm working on a new project, which I have kept secret, but wanted to share it with you first as you'll appreciate the sentiment behind it. As a photographer, you taught me the importance of keeping a record of events through images. I've a selection of notebooks and have *written out memories of Coventry and family life as I remember it before the bombs fell. My aim is to speak to more people and create a memorial book for their own families. I love writing and feel it is a worthwhile task. Some might call it foolish, but it gives me a purpose.*

Come back to me soon, Jean-Paul Clayton.
My love
Ruby xx

CHAPTER 30

July 1942

'Tommy, it's time for your reading lesson,' Ruby called out to Tommy, working alongside Fred on the vegetable plot at the top of the garden. He'd filled out and no longer looked pale and scrawny. Freckles scattered across his nose and cheeks and no matter how many times she and Beatty tried to trim his hair into a tidy style it fought back in unruly waves. He'd been called cherubic and angelic-looking, but the household knew he was far from either of those things. The local policeman had caught him up to no good on three occasions within the first two weeks of him staying with them. The fourth time had been the last straw for Fred, and they'd agreed to contact Evelyn Pearce about looking for another home for him. It had broken Ruby's heart, but she knew, unless

Tommy settled down, they could do nothing for him. Earl had burrowed too deep inside the child's mind.

Tommy, not averse to eavesdropping, had overheard their concerns and broke down in a frenzy of sobs. He'd fallen asleep on Beatty's lap after gulping out promises that he'd behave if he could stay with them a while longer.

A letter from Evelyn Pearce informing them there was still no place for Tommy was relayed to him, and a new routine was established. Tommy's freedom was curtailed, and he spent all his waking hours in the company of another during the day. Fred taught him the merits of keeping a tidy garden, how to use woodworking tools and cleaning small mechanical items to sell in the shop. Beatty showed him how to polish shoes, peel potatoes and lay a table for mealtime. Small tasks for idle hands. Ruby took him to the shop every day and taught him his letters, and allowed him to play with other children visiting with their mothers. At home, for one hour after the evening meal, she made him read to her. The book he'd selected from her growing collection was *The Tale of Peter Rabbit*. She'd argued it would be hard for him to learn and read out aloud but, determined as ever, Tommy proved her wrong. His accent held him back from proper pronunciation, but Ruby felt his struggles were hard enough and didn't want to put him off by continuous correction, so kept quiet.

Weeks went by with no news from Evelyn Pearce, so Beatty and Fred took it upon themselves to visit her in the last week of July, and request his ration book and identification papers. Upon their return, they called both Ruby and Tommy to join them around the table – a place where major decisions were often made between them.

Serious-faced, and with many papers in front of him, Fred spoke first. 'Brace yourselves.' He grinned. 'Beatty and I have decided to marry. It's to save Beatty from gossip, which appears to be spreading about us living in sin.'

Fred's face went scarlet, and Beatty looked at her hands in her lap. Ruby had heard rumours but had ignored them, giving them little thought. For Fred to be so blunt and open about the subject rendered it serious, and she made a concerted effort to listen. Tommy stared into the middle distance, bored by the summons and subject. The fact he was sitting there suggested to Ruby he was involved in some way.

'Evelyn Pearce has a sharp tongue and didn't hold back on her thoughts of our household. Living in sin, indeed! She's quite happy for Tommy to remain under our roof as it means less work for her, though,' Beatty snapped and Fred gave her a soft smile.

'I can't deny Beatty means a lot to me, and I'd often thought about our situation and how others see it, but now it's been flagged up, and Tommy could lose a stable home because of it, well, we've made up our minds.'

He and Beatty shared a smile, and Ruby's heart went out to them. She looked over at Tommy; at the sound of his name he'd perked up and appeared to be more interested in what they all had to say.

'When you say Tommy could lose a stable home, did they intend him to remain here?'

With one of her famous huffs, Beatty launched into a tirade of personal thoughts about the woman who'd become so overwhelmed with orphan children she felt it better Tommy remained in Coventry under the care of those who knew him best.

'I told her,' Beatty continued before anyone had the opportunity to draw breath, 'I said it's folks like us these kids need, but younger. Fred and I can't adopt the pair of you at our age.'

Ruby jumped to her feet, and she saw Tommy look at them with surprise. 'Adopt? Why would she mention adopting me? It's Tommy under her care,' Ruby said.

'She had to ask all sorts of questions. I accused her of being nosey, and I think she added ten more on for bad behaviour.'

Beatty drew breath and Fred took the opportunity to have his say.

'We explained our situation, and she advised we adopted you both. You are vulnerable. She feels there will be changes to the law after the war; with so many children desperate for homes and families gone, it has to be done. They'll have to be processed, according to Mrs Pearce.'

'I ain't got no bovver wiv it.' Tommy spoke for the first time. 'Rubes'll be me big sista.' He laughed and pointed at Ruby.

Ruby remained silent, but she gave a simple smile back to Tommy. One with no great meaning, but which obviously spoke volumes to Beatty.

'Ruby might not want us as her parents. Looking at that face, I think that's the case. Ruby?'

All heads turned her way, and Ruby felt her cheeks burn. She disliked hurting her friends. 'I love you both, but I don't see you as my parents. I'm sorry . . . I can't agree to being adopted by anyone. I'm not a child any more. Haven't I proved I'm adult enough by running a business, and providing a roof over the heads of others? Is it law yet?' she whispered.

'Ruby, stop. Look at you, pale as a sheet. We end the discussion here —' Fred cut into the conversation '– we'll adopt Tommy, and remain your guardians. It suits us all, and protects you both, and that is all we want to do.'

Ruby looked at Tommy, expecting to see him offering up a toothless grin, but instead a large tear rolled down his cheek and dropped onto the table.

'Tommy?'

'Goodness, lad, whatever is the matter?' Beatty rushed to Tommy's side, and only just beat Ruby.

Beatty put her arms across his shoulder, and Ruby knelt to his level.

'Tell us. What's made you cry?'

Gulps and sniffles followed by a loud blow of his nose on Fred's handkerchief settled into a final sob.

'You don't like me,' Tommy stuttered out to Ruby.

'What makes you say that? Of course I like you. In fact, I love you – for some reason or another.' Ruby made her voice light-hearted, adding a jovial tease and ruffling his hair.

Tommy pushed her hand away. Turning his head to look her in the face, Ruby was taken aback by his words. 'Na, you won't be me big sista. If you loved me, you'd be me big sista.'

She looked to Beatty and Fred, then back at Tommy. 'I do want to be, and will be a big sister to you. I'll be a sister, auntie and mummy rolled into one, I love you that much, Tommy. What I won't have is the same name as you. I have a very special reason to keep my name.'

His small arms snaked their way around her neck. 'Promise?'

With a kiss on his forehead, Ruby scooped him up

and a surge of affection engulfed her. She buried her face into his hair and she whispered her promise.

'Come and sit on my knee, Tommy. We need to chat about so many things.' Beatty held out her arms.

Clambering down from Ruby, Tommy went to her and snuggled into her lap. Ruby was surprised to see him pop his thumb into his mouth, but said nothing.

'So, you'll be Beatrice Lester soon.' Ruby gave Beatty a grin.

'I suppose I will.' Beatty gave a laugh. 'Who'd have thought that, eh, Fred?'

Tommy wriggled upright on her lap. 'And I'll be Thomas Lester. Thomas Lester the orphan thief. I 'eard you call me that yesterday. Orphan thief . . .' He grinned and looked at Fred.

Fred gave a shake of his head. 'We'll hear no more talk like that, my lad. It was idle talk on my part, and I'm sorry you heard me. Besides, that's all behind you now. My dad's name was Thomas. If you take my name it will carry on, but we're happy if you want to keep your own, Tommy.'

'Na, you're all right. Me mum never wanted me, and no one knows 'oo me dad is – a wrongun like me mum is all they said at the 'ome. I want to be more like you, not a thief.'

Ruby felt Tommy needed steering away from the subject of stealing. 'I know, you will be Tommy Lester,

327

our family jester,' she said, and then spent the next five minutes explaining what a jester was, much to the amusement of Beatty and Fred.

Beatty held onto Fred's arm as they walked away from the register office as Mr and Mrs Lester. Tommy trotted alongside them in his Sunday best, and Ruby walked with Helen, whose surprise visit had delighted them all.

Back at Garden Cottage, they gathered around the table to watch Fred and Beatty cut their cake.

'It was extremely generous of you, Helen. It's beautiful,' Beatty said, and handed Fred a knife.

Helen waved a dismissive hand. 'It's a small token, but remember, only the top half is to be eaten. I don't think even the chickens would enjoy the pretty cardboard bottom layer.'

'I beg first slice,' Tommy said, and held out his plate. Ruby took it from him and laid it on the table.

'Manners, Tommy. Fred and Beatty have another part of the wedding ceremony to perform. They have to cut it, and take the first slice.' She watched his lip drop in disapproval of the news she gave him, and laughed. 'But you will get second slice, right, Beatty, Fred?'

'We'd better get the job done then, before the boy starves,' Fred said and placed Beatty's hand over his as he guided the knife through the layer of white icing.

Their guests politely applauded the newlyweds and

raised a glass of extremely watered-down sherry as a toast, and the handful who'd been invited into their home offered congratulations, clutched at a thin slice of cake and left.

For Ruby, Beatty, Fred and Tommy, life moved on as usual. They excused themselves from Helen in order to change out of their Sunday best and, by the time a light lunch had been enjoyed, everyone had forgotten it was a wedding celebration. Exactly how Fred and Beatty wished it to be remembered. They were far more excited about signing the guardianship papers for Tommy in pre-adoption preparations the following day.

Ruby and Helen took a walk to the local park and sat on a bench watching people working amongst the plants and trees. It made a change for Ruby not to be sporting her gardening clothes and hoeing row after row of soil.

'What are your plans now, Ruby? I've never known a girl with so many brilliant ideas floating around her head,' Helen asked, and took a bite of a slice of cake they'd taken with them.

Ruby relayed her idea of the memory books and keeping a record for the Coventry residents.

'Will you write something for me?' Ruby asked. 'Your feelings of that night, and after. You can write about meeting me; I don't mind. I'd like to include you in mine.'

'I think you've thought of something wonderful, and

what you've created in the shop is lovely. A happy corner where people are fundraising. Fred and Beatty are good for you. They look happy enough, and Tommy's a little dear. But how about you, Ruby? How's life treating you? Not publicly, I mean. But inside. How are you coping nowadays?'

Standing and stretching out her back, Ruby looked at Helen. 'I fell in love. Fallen – I've fallen in love. If that's what the feeling is, outside of a family. Yes, I think I'm in love,' she confessed shyly.

Rising to her feet, Helen went to Ruby with her hands on her hips and her head tilted to one side. Ruby noticed a twinkle in her eye. 'And? I assume it's the Canadian.'

'John. Jean-Paul Clayton, to be precise. Yes, he's a photographer for the Canadian army, and away somewhere – *in the thick of things* were his words.'

'Ah, that will explain the long face. I thought there was something playing on your mind. You smiled a lot at the wedding, but I could see something worrying you.' Helen reached out and took Ruby's hands in hers. 'You understand he might never return – for several reasons, and one being he might have toyed with you whilst in town. Understand? Use it as a hard lesson learned, Ruby. He moved on, and you must do the same. You are young. Too young, some might say.'

Slowly, Ruby shook her head from side to side. 'He's coming back to me. He promised.'

Helen gave a slow nod. 'He said that, and I am sure he meant it at the time, but Ruby, promises often get broken. Don't pin your hopes on him, that's all I'm saying. Don't wait for ever.' She gave Ruby a hug. 'I must get to the station. You take care of yourself, and keep writing. I love reading your news. And don't forget, you are still young.'

'I'll never be allowed to forget,' Ruby muttered as they walked back to Garden Cottage.

After Helen said her goodbyes, Tommy played marbles with Fred and Ruby remembered playing with her siblings and crouched down to join them. Beatty pulled out a chair and they spent time in the evening warmth. A family cobbled together, but a tight family nonetheless.

'We've an early start tomorrow. Are you sure you won't come with us for the day out, Ruby?' Beatty asked.

'No, I'll open the shop. You take Tommy and enjoy the day together. It will be good for him. It's a big day in his life, eh? A brand-new start, and you get me as your big sister!' Ruby teased Tommy with a flick of a tea towel.

'Yeah, I've been thinkin' about that, Fred – can I 'ave a dog instead?' Tommy said and ducked as the tea towel flicked his way again.

'Now, now, you two, no teasing each other,' Beatty scolded.

A wonderful sense of belonging washed over Ruby,

and she could see the same had happened to Tommy when he went over to Beatty and clambered on her lap. The boy had found his place, and although he was long-limbed and claimed he was too old for most things, a cuddle with Beatty was never refused.

CHAPTER 31

26th September 1942

August came and went and, with it, a cease in the bombings. The irregular attacks in towns and cities across the country had taken its toll, and as September rolled in the British people dared to breathe. The Lester/Shadwell household had created their own routines. Ruby spent her days gathering stories and writing them into her journals, and Tommy proved he was willing to change, and blossomed under their care. Ruby listened to him and Beatty negotiating his bath time for the evening, and giggled at his cheeky replies. He'd brought laughter into their home.

'Damp out there today.'

Ruby looked up at Fred as he entered the kitchen. She dried her hands on the tea towel and relieved him of five eggs and a small bunch of flowers.

'It was a misty start when I looked out first thing. Are these for me?' Ruby asked and laid down the flowers on the draining board.

'I think my wife has had enough gifts from me this week,' Fred teased as Beatty walked through to join them.

'Giving flowers to another woman is not something I'll overlook, Fred Lester.'

Ruby watched Fred place an affectionate kiss on Beatty's cheek, and smiled. Although they'd said their marriage was purely to give a roof over Tommy's head, it was obvious they enjoyed their new status as husband and wife. Ruby placed the eggs in their container and tugged on her coat. She picked up the flowers.

'Thanks, Fred. I'll be off and tell Tommy I'll take him to kick his ball up at Radford Common later.'

As Ruby headed to the cemetery for the first time since witnessing the mass funeral, she hesitated whether to forego the visit and turn around. She'd chosen not to lay the flowers for James's birthday, as she had the previous year. After a chat with Beatty, she'd made up her mind to visit Eagle Street on non-anniversary days, when the memories might not be so painful, heightened by the date. So far, it had worked. However, today she had another reason for hesitating. It was a year since she'd taken the photograph of John, and the day she'd learned what it felt like to wish for a future with a man who was not her father. Shaking off a feeling of nostalgia, she took the path along to the graveside and laid flowers there amongst the many hundreds of tributes from other families and friends. For the first time it felt the right thing to do – to imagine the place as the family grave, and not the site of their old home. As she walked away a peace settled around her, and Ruby headed for Eagle Street for the last time. She'd withdrawn her request to purchase, and knew this trip would be more difficult. After considering her future, Ruby decided she should not tie herself to painful memories by living where her nightmares existed.

The street was no different than the many times she'd visited before, and a selection of dead posies lay in front of her. Each one was a remembrance gift, no longer sharing their bright and cheerful colours, but instead reminding the world of yet more death. Unable to bear looking at them any longer, Ruby gathered them all into her arms and walked away. She made no speech, gave no loving messages to her family as she'd done on previous occasions; this time she felt none of the raging angst and fear. The flowers angered her for letting her down and not retaining their beauty. She wasn't stupid; she known they'd die, they always did, but today their shrivelled petals spoke volumes. She buried her nose into their death and they failed her again. No beautiful perfume filled her nostrils, just the stench of decay, and she gagged. She wanted them away from the area, to not visualise them as the last thing she saw of her old home.

They were not meant to be part of her memories, but in the silent hush of mourning and through the hubbub of everyday noises she heard the familiar click of a camera and she knew someone had made them just that – a permanent reminder.

She swung around and was shocked to see John.

'Ruby.' John said her name soft and low, but she raised one arm to prevent him talking or coming closer. She couldn't reply. He moved towards her and held out his arms to take the flowers from her, but she pulled them back tight against her chest, using them as a barrier.

'Don't.' Her throat finally released a word.

John took a few steps backwards, looking at her in shock. 'I remembered this day . . . last year. You and the flowers. I wanted to come and take a picture for the last time. I was heading your way, and wanted to see if anything had changed here. When I saw you just now . . . Ruby, I cannot describe how I felt, what I saw. It was powerful, moving. Your face shared something which wasn't grief, nor anger. The light –'

Ruby threw the flowers to one side and watched as their petals scattered across the mound of rubble and rubbish beside them, then turned her face to John.

'The light? Powerful and moving?' Ruby's anger would not subside. She tried to calm down, but instead she gave him a penetrating gaze, desperate to get across what he took from her with that one click of a button.

'Do you want to know what I saw? I saw a man take something private and make it public. I saw someone capture the one thing I wanted rid of – the stain of death on petals, *and* the moment I'd decided to leave my family in peace for ever.' Ruby went to turn away to hide her tears. She cried because he'd returned to her, and for her past life. She cried for the confusion of emotions she couldn't comprehend. Her mind was a whirl of conflicting thoughts. She wanted to be angry with him, but her love for him was powerful and overrode the anger. Eventually, she calmed down.

'Ruby, can we go somewhere less public?' John's words broke through the awkward silence as he pointed to their left. Ruby glanced at the family of three walking through the bombsite, looking over at her and John.

'Why? What's the point? So we can make love, and you can walk away? I need something more permanent, John. I can't bear the thought of you never coming back to me. I don't want to hold flowers with brown petals in your memory.'

'Yes, so we can make love again. Yes, so I can prove I want permanent too. Am I forgiven?' John asked.

Ruby nodded – a shy nod of embarrassment for creating such a scene. Then, as his lips touched hers, she chided herself for allowing the serious side of what had happened to be overshadowed by a kiss.

'In one way, but not another. Yes, for coming here and

remembering I might need a friend, but not for the photograph. I don't want a reminder set to paper; it will not allow me to move on. If ever I opened a magazine or newspaper and saw it, the guilt of walking away from them –' Ruby pointed to where the crater had once been '– and leaving their souls unattended . . . well, I . . . I'd hate myself all over again. I've moved them to the cemetery with my gran – in my mind, and until I heard your camera take that away I was coping.'

Reaching out and taking her other hand, John turned her to face him again. He reached out and tucked a random curl back into place.

'I cannot open the camera here, as I will lose a lot of important – tragic – images from Dieppe, Puys, where I've just returned from. I'm heading back to HQ to hand them over, but I promise – *promise* – I will not print yours. I will destroy the negative. Erase the moment.' John's eyes filled with tears. 'I seem to always be asking for your forgiveness, but I truly need it right now. You've taught me another valuable lesson, Ruby: I must not take for granted I have the right to capture pain.'

Touched by his desperate plea and taking more notice of his fragile state, her heart went out to him and, with no hesitation, Ruby pulled John in for another kiss. This time it was celebrated with a wolf-whistle from a passing van of American soldiers, cheering John on.

Before she could say any more, John's lips were on

hers. The ache and tension within her body released itself as she gave in to the kiss. With one swift movement, John was down on one knee. Her hand went to her mouth when she realised what he was doing.

He looked up at her with pleading eyes. 'Ruby Shadwell, marry me. Make it permanent.'

And there it was – the moment Ruby had dreamt of every night since she'd met John. His proposal. His promise of life ever after. Love had found Ruby a reason to live. Her mind flashed back to her mother's smile, knowing she'd approve of John and her smile would have beamed out her approval of this very moment. She imagined her father's polite cough, always offered when he was embarrassed by emotional gestures of affection, of Lucy and James whooping with delight, and Ruby pressed her hands together; this was not a time for tears but a time to celebrate her and John. Her emotions raced along at the same speed as her heart. She'd experienced many life-changing moments, but with John down on one knee, loving her with such a fierceness, she doubted she'd ever experience anything like it again.

Aware his knee probably ached against the rubble, and not wanting him to think she was hesitating for the wrong reasons, Ruby pulled him to his feet.

'Yes. Yes, I'll marry you. I love you and cannot imagine life without you.'

Her arms went around his neck and he pulled her to

him so close she felt they were one body. She heard a cheer and clap from the onlookers but blocked them out. The dark fog of her temper lifted and her mind filled with a peace she'd not experienced for years.

Eventually, they pulled back from one another. John gripped her arm as if in fear she'd walk away, but Ruby stood with no intention of leaving him again.

'The shop's empty,' she whispered, and put her hand into John's, allowing him to lead her away from the past and into a future filled with hope.

CHAPTER 32

15th November 1942

My dearest John,
   I don't know where you are in the world, but want you to know I'm always thinking of you. Fred and Beatty send their love, and Tommy said love is soppy for boys, so just to say 'ello. He is settling down really well, and is a lovely child. His mother has missed out, but we count our blessings. He's cheeky and cheerful, just what we needed in our lives. Today, as you can imagine, is a painful one, but bless him, he drew me a picture of a bright sun with us four standing holding hands. As with true child's honesty, I have one leg so short I wonder how I'm still standing.
   I've given us a lot of thought. You mentioned the war ending, and our lives beginning. When that

happens – I refuse to say if – when it happens, what an exciting time for us both. My ring sparkles in the sunlight, and Beatty said she's a little jealous as she skipped the engagement part. I know she is teasing. Fred talks about his girl's fiancé, as if I'm his daughter. Thank you for understanding my request for using the Shadwell name, and Ruby Shadwell-Clayton sounds la-di-da but oh, so right! I cannot wait until the war ends and we set our wedding date. I know we wanted to marry straight away, but I understand Beatty and Fred's reasoning now. Besides, we might have enough ingredients for a proper wedding cake by then!

The business is thriving, and I'm in talks with another landlord about a second shop. I will move the jewellery and clocks into that one and Fred will be with me, leaving Beatty and her friend Violet running Shadwell's Buy and Sell. I've decided to choose another name, and Tommy suggested Tick-Tock Repairs. I'm not sure it's what I'd envisaged, but as it keeps him happy I use it as the temporary one. His tale-telling is less and less these days, and it's good to know a story has truth to it when he shares them with us, unlike in the past.

I received a lovely letter from your parents yesterday. They look forward to us visiting after we are married, and returning the visit to us in England.

They are extremely understanding of your staying here in Coventry. You must have written quite a letter explaining my – our – reasons, and I love you with every bone in my body for giving up Canada for me.

The day is as grey as I expected, but I will go to the cemetery and speak with my family. I am sure some folk think I'm a little touched in the head when they hear me standing there chattering to a mound of earth. The amusing thing is, it is doing that which keeps me sane!

Take care, my darling, and I look forward to seeing you again and enjoying one of your kisses. The last one still sends shivers down my spine – as does . . . well, you remember.

My loving wishes. Always, stay safe.

Ruby xx

January 1943

My darling Ruby,

Your letter cheered me up, and thank you for writing to let me know my parents have written. Their letters to me are supportive and they love me enough to allow me my dream of marrying you. If our lives are to be filled with the magic of our last night together in October, I cannot wait. When I am restless, I calm myself down with images of your beautiful body lying next to mine. It was wonderful.

I'm told I will be travelling a lot more soon, and will get as many letters written to you as I can. I wish I could share with you the sights I see – not the dreadful ones, but when I am home and the war has ended, I will get permission to take you to London to see some of those which are not so top secret.

Take care, my darling,

John xx

Dearest John,

I miss you. I love you. There is nothing more to say.

I've written to thank your parents for their wonderful Christmas gift. The food hamper was filled with so many treats, I thought Tommy was going to faint!

We had peaches and evaporated milk, tinned ham and chocolate for Christmas Day tea. It was a banquet.

I have news. It isn't sad or dreadful, but it is rather frightening. I've been rather off colour for a few weeks, and spoke with Beatty. Darling, dearest John, I am pregnant. I am carrying your baby. This is not what we'd planned, and I have a lot of *explaining to do to a few people, but I am not ashamed. Never will I be ashamed.*

Fred and Beatty are standing by me, and are extremely supportive. It came after a lot of telling me how foolish I was to give myself to you, but they soon calmed down. They are fussing around me and Beatty is a little over-protective, but I let her fuss. I've not told Tommy yet, nor have I written to your parents. I will leave you to explain to them, unless you tell me otherwise.

Can you believe it, darling – we are to be parents – us holding a little one of our own. I have no fears for giving our child a good upbringing. We have a roof over our heads, and I have money in the bank, thanks to my financially aware father. Don't be afraid for us; the raids have stopped for a long time now, and we're rising from the ashes so to speak. Oh, John, I do hope you are not angry. Come home to us soon.

Much love, my darling xx

March 1943

Dearest John,

I hope my Valentine's card reached you. Baby and I are doing well, and the dreadful sickness has thankfully passed. I fainted twice, but it was because

I'd not eaten properly. I pray this baby is born with both legs as long as yours. I have quite a mound and my back aches due to the limp, now little one is growing. And it certainly is growing.

I get extra milk, vitamins and cod liver oil – horrid stuff. I wash it down with my free orange juice. The government are looking after us, John, so don't fret. I do wish I could read a new letter from you. I've heard nothing since I told you about the baby. I pray it hasn't frightened you away. Then I get angry with myself, as that would make you a dishonourable man, but I know you are not. You are kind and courageous.

Tommy has won an award for school attendance, and reading. How wonderful it is to see him turning a corner. He is such a kind child and helps anyone in need. The little waif has turned a corner and I am as proud of him as I imagine a mother would be – as I will be with our child.

My love always,
Ruby xx

February 1943

Dearest Ruby,
I wish you could have seen the smile on my face when I read your letter. There was shock too, but

it soon turned to joy. Parents! I cannot think of anything more wonderful than a child created from you and me. Take care of yourself, darling. I cannot write much, but hope this reaches you so you can read I am ready to come home and care for you both. Eight weeks and I'll be back on British soil.

Your loving fiancé,

John

March 1943

Dearest John,

I was so pleased to receive your letter. I cried so much it scared Tommy, and he wouldn't leave my side. He considers it his duty to look after me and the baby until you come home, especially as I've agreed to be his guardian should anything happen to Beatty and Fred. He now considers me his sister, which is sweet. I'm afraid you will be given the role of a big brother when you get home. He's making a banner to hang up for when you arrive. He has worked hard on his handwriting, and I'm so proud of him.

Although I've not seen it yet, I love and cherish our baby; it represents life. The blood of our families flows through its veins.

Take care, my darling,

R x

March 1943

Dearest Ruby,

You are in my thoughts. I wrote to my parents about our news, and wait for their reply. They are good people, loving and kind. They will not be angry – a little surprised and shocked that their son misbehaved, but in general I think all will be well.

Tell Tommy I'll be honoured to be his big brother and I look forward to my first letter from him.

I am sorry this is not longer; it's time to pull out and move onto my next project.

My love to you and our child. Say hello to all.
J x

April 1943

Toronto, Canada

Dear Ruby,

Jean-Paul wrote to tell us about the baby. To say we were shocked was an understatement, but now that shock has passed we write to tell you how delighted we are – but we are also filled with sadness beyond our comprehension.

Our dearest boy has been declared missing in action during the bloodbath of the Battle of the Atlantic. As his fiancée, we wanted to inform you of this huge sadness, and we have asked the London Unit to keep you informed as next of kin in England. Pray for good news.

Dear girl, please look after yourself and your precious cargo. Upon your instruction, we will come to see you both when he/she is born. We are grateful for your love of our son, for the happiness you gave him. This is a delicate subject, but how are you coping financially? We can arrange for funds for the child; never fear, we will not fail in our duty as grandparents.

Our fond wishes, we know how precious your love is for our dear Jean-Paul.

Jean-Paul Snr and Ida Clayton

CHAPTER 33

September 5th 1943

The warmth of the sun on her shoulders lifted Ruby's mood. The past few months had been a lesson in coping with John's disappearance, and of how to learn to walk without pain in her hip. The baby's kick often reminded her to respect Beatty's and Fred's request she ate something, and the task of learning to knit with the group of ladies at the shop filled the lonely hours. The idea of a second shop was dropped until she could focus on the long-term future of Shadwell's without breaking down in tears. The pregnancy made her cry. The news of John made her angry. Her tears wouldn't fall for him. From the day she'd read the letter and handed it over to Beatty she'd never shed a tear. She refused to believe he was dead, so why cry for him?

She'd read all she could about the Battle of the Atlantic, and often wondered why he was at sea, but then, knowing John, he'd wanted to capture the action of his fellow Canadians and talked his way from the army to the navy portfolio.

Ruby spent every day pondering the words she would say to John's parents in a letter. She'd persuaded Fred and Beatty to write on her behalf, to send hope as a family and to reassure them the baby was to be born into a loving home and she was in good health.

Some days she thought about writing to them and asking if she could live with them, just to be a little closer to John, and on other days she wanted the baby for herself, and not to have to share it with relative strangers. People who might deem her an unfit mother once they met her. All of these things churned away inside her.

This morning she'd risen early and taken a slow walk to stretch out her limbs. She'd watched people going about their business and envied their ability to move with ease. A homing instinct took her to Eagle Street; although she'd vowed never to return, she felt the need to sit there with her memories for a while. She walked to the empty site and noticed fresh grass filled the space, and smiled. The darkness had lifted. A sharp pain speared through her back, a reminder she'd still got a few streets before she could rest. She placed her hand on her pregnant mound, and spoke softly to the child resting inside.

'Can you feel their love, little one? This is where I began my life, and I think they are here to guide us through this, my little angel.' Another pain told Ruby it was true. 'Ouch. Let's go find Beatty. It's time for you and I to meet.'

12th September 1943

Dear Jean-Paul and Ida,

Forgive me for not writing before, but my world fell apart after your letter, as I'm sure Beatty and Fred explained in theirs.

I have news. Wonderful news. On the 7th of this month, I gave birth to a healthy baby boy. He weighed in at a bouncing seven pounds, at five to eleven at night. He is dark-haired like his daddy. All fingers and toes are complete and, I'm thankful to say, he has not inherited my shortened limb. In fact, we marvelled at how long his legs are, so definitely like his daddy. He is a feisty feeder, and a content baby. It was a long labour, but worth the effort. As to be expected, my emotional dam burst, and I cried for so long the midwife called for the doctor to visit me, but he said it was the combination of sadness for John, and joy.

I hope you will forgive me, but I have given our child the surname Shadwell. I have to register his

birth, and named his father for his birth certificate.
John had agreed we were to be Shadwell-Clayton
when we married to ensure my family name
continued. His name is to be John Shadwell-Clayton
(John junior). I know it isn't his father's true name,
but for me it is. I do hope there is news of John
soon, for all our sakes.

   With affection,
Ruby

June 1944

''appy Birfday, Rubes.'

'Yes, Happy Birthday.'

'Happy Birthday, duck.'

'Thank you, all.'

Ruby looked at her family around the table. All were going about their daily breakfast ritual, something most people took for granted, but Ruby no longer did. Tommy was ladling porridge into his mouth before heading for his lessons, now taken with a teacher in the community room, as he shoved forward a homemade card.

'It's from me an' Johnny boy.' He grinned up at her, and Ruby leaned in to kiss his forehead.

'Git orf, soppy. Give me baby brother a kiss, an' leave me be.'

Fred laughed at their antics, and continued to scrape

a thin layer of butter onto a slice of toast whilst bemoaning his small portion, and Beatty beamed at her as she poured tea into Ruby's cup.

'I swear that baby will be taller than you by supper.'

Ruby dropped a kiss onto her son's head and whispered to him as she took him to her breast.

'They might not be related to us by blood but they're as close as any family will ever be. Tommy has decided you need a big brother, and I think it is a wonderful thing. Your daddy's family arrive today, and will meet us both for the first time. They are very brave as they are coming by aeroplane. Oh, darling boy, I know they will adore you, but we have to hope I don't disappoint them. Oh, John, Mummy is scared. So scared.'

Ruby's breathing would not calm, and no amount of soothing words from Beatty helped. John's parents were in the house, and talking with Fred downstairs. She took each step down with care, and at the bottom of the stairs checked baby John over for the umpteenth time. He was perfect, and no one could help but fall in love with him. His dark lashes lay on plump rosy cheeks, and his lips still suckled in his sleep. Deep inside she'd buried her heartbreak, and she allowed her son to give her the strength she needed as she stepped inside the room where his grandparents waited to greet them.

'Oh, my, you are every bit as beautiful as Jean-Paul

said you were. Come here, darling girl.' Ida Clayton rushed towards them and embraced Ruby, who clutched her child for dear life, with warmth and genuine affection. But it was the man across the room who captured Ruby's attention as he spoke and walked to Ruby to give her his loving embrace.

'Everything he said. The boy has good taste. Thank you for our grandchild. For allowing us into your lives.' His voice and tone were the same as she'd heard from his son.

He stood tall and good-looking, a mature version of the man she loved. His image brought *her* Jean-Paul Clayton, alive again – a vision of what he would look like and, in all probability, what her son would look like at that age. She looked to John's mother and smiled, then held out her son to enjoy his first snuggle with his grandmother.

'We have a gift for him. For both of you,' Ida said, and looked over at her husband with a gentle smile.

'It's something Ida and I created, and we want you to keep it. We know you'll love it as much as we do.' He walked to the hallway and pulled open the door.

Ruby turned back to Ida, holding baby John. 'Did Jean-Paul look like this when he was born? Dark hair and lashes, chubby cheeks? Beatty called his skin olive. I just want to kiss him all day!'

Ida laughed. 'He did. A handsome baby. A boy from the onset. And as for kissing him, I could never help myself. Your son has brought back good memories and, holding him, I know his father will return to us.'

'And then maybe I'll get kisses all day too.'

A silence hit the room and Ruby heard gasps from Beatty and a whoop from Tommy, and a grunt of approval from Fred, but she dared not turn around. Dared not believe John stood behind her. His hands touched her shoulders and he manoeuvred her around to face him, and Ruby thanked goodness she'd handed over her son to his grandmother, for her arms flew open wide to embrace John.

'You're home. You came back to me – us. Oh, John.'

Ruby allowed the tears to flow. Tears of happiness and the unleashing of grief she'd held back no longer necessary.

She gripped his hand and looked into his eyes. 'Are you well . . . sick . . . injured?'

'I was rescued and flown back to Canada. I have an injury to my back, and am classed as officially medically unfit, but I'm much better now I'm back with you. I've missed you . . .' He kissed her with a fierceness and no concern for the others in the room. 'My girl. Oh, my Ruby, I'm home. I got here and I'll never leave you again.'

Tommy held out his hand. 'Oi, big bruvva, shake me 'and so I know you're real.'

John obliged then turned his attention to Beatty, holding out his hand.

Beatty looked at him, and Ruby saw the tears rolling

down her cheeks. 'Handshake? Come here and give your stepmother-in-law a hug.'

Fred stood back and Ruby turned to him. His face held a look she'd seen before, when she'd told him he'd be the one to walk her down the aisle.

'Fred?'

He gave a slight cough and held out his hand. 'Nothing to see here. John, welcome home.'

John's father moved to Ruby and planted a kiss on her cheek. 'Nice surprise? As we said, you can keep him. We have fallen in love with you already. Jean-Paul's a wise man.'

'He certainly is, and I agree his place is here with you, Ruby. He came home to us two days before we planned our trip, and it is because of him we've been able to fly to England. Isn't it wonderful?' Ida said.

'It is, and thank you.'

Ruby tugged John's arm. 'Come and meet him. John Shadwell-Clayton – our son. Hold him.'

Ruby took the baby from Ida's arms and gently laid him into the protection of his father's. Father and son locked eyes, and Ruby witnessed their love for each other surge to the fore. Their child grasped his father's finger, and John lifted the chubby hand to his lips. Their likeness was undeniable. The boy was a Clayton through and through, and with Shadwell blood in his veins – in Ruby's eyes – he was the perfect new generation. A triumph of love over war.

EPILOGUE

8th May 1945

'Do you have his flag? John's hat? Tommy, are you ready?' Ruby called out to both John and the boy she now classed as her son. 'Keep your 'air on, Rubes,' Tommy called back. 'I'm trying to get Johnny 'ere to keep still. 'e's bouncing all over the place.'

Ruby laughed. Her little boy had more energy than any of them, and whenever a day out was mentioned he let loose his excitement. A sniffle across the room caught her attention and she turned to see Beatty sobbing into a handkerchief.

'Beatty, are you crying? Oh, what is the matter?'

Turning to her guardian, Ruby looked at the woman who'd seen her give birth to two children and watched her like a hawk, waiting for the third to make its appearance in a few months.

'Fred would have loved this. Today, and your wedding next month – on your twenty-first. Our celebrations as a family.'

'He would, and it saddens me he never got to walk me down the aisle. But at least I'm not marrying in church, so it won't be such a painful moment. Don't forget, though, he's here, Fred's with us, Beatty. Fred will be celebrating the end of the war with us all.'

Fred had fallen ill in the winter of forty-four and succumbed to pneumonia a few months later. It hit the household hard, despite them knowing how old and unwell he was. John had helped Ruby nurse him when Beatty took ill shortly after Fred, and the influenza weakened her lungs. Ruby had taken over Tommy's care. At eleven years old, he'd turned a corner and studied hard. His aim was to open the second shop Ruby had once dreamed of, and become a clock repairer. Fred's skills as a patient teacher gave Tommy his own skills, and the praise from them all drove into him a tremendous ambition. After Fred's death, John had stepped in to support him as a father would his son, and they all knew the dream would become a reality. He'd once shared with them his memories, and Ruby understood more about why Earl had such a hold over him.

Tommy told them of how one morning he'd peered through the bars of the cot he'd slept in for two and a half years. Nothing around him had changed that day, but he said something told him to look for change or his life would always be like it was – uneventful. A nun took him to the doctor when he had a bout of sickness, but this time it was outside of the orphanage grounds instead of the doctor coming to them. Tommy said that was the turning point in his life. He noticed an exciting world – London buses, people, shops, noises of every kind kept his head spinning as he looked out from the bus window. Even at such a young age, he knew he wanted the life outside of the dismal building in which he lived. He said his violent outbursts of anger whenever anyone came to select a child put people off and unfortunately he was never offered a trial run in a home. That day on the bus he saw the error of his ways. If he could break free of the orphanage, he could break free of his miserable existence and look for his mum, so good behaviour was required.

A few days later, when the Grange family asked if he'd like to join them for a family walk in the park, with tea in their home afterwards, a calm and polite child replied yes, and his carers heaved a sigh of relief. The man he met when he ran from the park, from the suffocating demands that he sit still and listen to the words from the Bible Mrs Grange recited, offered to show him more of the city, and Tommy took his hand. Earl promised him so much and, although the Grange family were kind and attentive, Earl offered excitement and adventure. A trusting Tommy took Earl's hand, but that Christmas, in the dank basement of a stinking slum miles away from where he'd started out, Tommy regretted his decision. According to Tommy, Earl's threats of an early death were accompanied by a good hiding, and he'd witnessed others being carried out from the cramped room, never to return. Although he wanted to run, Tommy decided to become a loyal worker and earn Earl's trust enough to find a way to escape. It never happened as the more he earned for Earl, the more threatening Earl became, so he accepted his way of life and then stumbled across Ruby.

Ruby switched her thoughts back to Beatty, who was still crying into her handkerchief.

'And next month I'm no longer your guardian. You come of age and won't need me any more.'

Shocked Beatty had harboured such upsetting thoughts, Ruby bent and kissed her brow. She dropped another kiss on the cheek of the little girl they'd named June after her own mother, at the insistence of Ida. June Ida Beatrice Shadwell-Clayton, born nine months after her father returned to Coventry.

'We'll always need you, Beatty. You are more than a guardian to me, and my little ones see you as their grandmother – Nanny B. I'll always need you for your wise words and guidance. Don't cry. Let's enjoy the end of war with good memories and thoughts. John is recovering every day and we are such a united family it makes my heart burst. Beatty, never think you have no place in my future because of my age. John struggles and you listen to my concerns. That's all I need from you, a listening ear and loving reassurances we'll be all right. You listen to my worries about John, and it helps.'

'He's the best thing that ever happened to you – aside from Fred and the shop.'

'And you, Beatty, you are also something good in my life. You help John as much as I do. I know you help in the night, when he sleepwalks and cries out. Without your help, I'd be worn to the bone. Never think I've not got a place in my life for you. You live in my heart, understand?'

Beatty nodded. 'He had another bad night last night. What with madam keeping you busy, I sat with him and listened. He saw some dreadful things. Dreadful.'

'I know. I didn't realise how much it had damaged him, but it has. Thank goodness for his new line of work.'

John's injury took its toll on him, and was worse than first thought. His mental health also gave him troubled nights when he suffered tormenting nightmares of what he'd seen during the fighting. When the end of war was announced, he grabbed his camera and spent his days photographing people rejoicing, but never ignored the faces filled with raw emotion. His love of photography helped him through the difficult days. He kept his promise and took Ruby to London to see his work. Some she could not bear to look at for longer than a few seconds, but others made her proud of what he'd captured. She encouraged him to enter competitions, and one photograph, which Ruby allowed him to print and publish, after finding out he'd not destroyed the negative, won an award. *The Girl with Dead Flowers* hung in his gallery in what was Shadwell's Buy and Sell. The shop now bore the sign, *Clayton's Photographic Studio*. Ruby insisted it bore only his surname as it was his dream. She no longer needed the validation the Shadwell name would live on.

Today, the building wore a string of bright coloured, hand-knitted socks to commemorate the day, all gifts from friends remembering the community rooms.

Only a handful of streets flew bunting. Tables were pushed together, and what foods were available were shared amongst neighbours, but it was a tired and weary city which tried to rejoice. Their losses were overwhelming. Winston Churchill gave the news of victory in Europe, but many found it hard to celebrate.

John, Ruby and Beatty discussed how they wanted to spend the day, and they decided to head for Radford Common with a picnic, and let John Junior toddle and play with a new kite sent from his grandparents in Canada.

A large bonfire stood proud on the common, and families gathered to share their stories. Ruby recalled the night the common gave her shelter, and of how she'd watched the city burn in the distance. John stood beside her with his arms around her shoulders.

The war had given her losses, gains and heartache, but today Ruby accepted the challenges of the future, and at last could envisage them settling into their new home, a new build planned for a plot of land on the outskirts of the city. A long discussion about space and the size of the house to be built on Eagle Street had made Ruby rethink her dream and accept real life. So long as she had her loved ones around her, it didn't matter where they lived, providing it was still in the city. Bricks and mortar crumbled, but love in the Lester/ Shadwell-Clayton household stood firm.

ACKNOWLEDGEMENTS:

To Charlotte Ledger, the incredible team at HarperImpulse / HarperCollins (home and abroad), a huge thank you for putting up with my naïve questions, and for giving me another opportunity to write for the company. I cannot express how much this all means to me.

To my agent, Kate Nash. Thank you for standing beside me and urging me forward. From the day you handed me two chocolate hearts to seal the deal at the London Book Fair, I knew I'd made the right choice! Also, to Justin, thanks for the encouragement given when we met in London.

For Mum: This is me, Glynis Peters. The woman whom you rarely see when the edits are in, but still manages to nag you to do the right thing by your health from behind a closed door. Thanks for cheering me along. Love G x

To my dear friend and #1 fan, Kay Stamp.

This year you are fighting breast cancer. When I needed a female character who is feisty, determined, loving and courageous I thought of you. Ring the bell my lovely, ring the bell. X

To my children, their partners, and my grandchildren – you are amazing, incredible people, and I love you to the moon and back – and then some. X

To my close friends, you know who you are, and where you are in the world, thank you. Just when I needed you most . . .

To my readers, your support means everything to me. I am nothing without you, and I truly hope you enjoy Ruby's story.

During my research process I read stories which touched my heart and humbled me. The strength and courage of the people during WWII must never be forgotten.

A Q&A WITH GLYNIS PETERS

What was your inspiration for the book?

I was researching the London Blitz and came across the Coventry one. I'd never really taken in the story of Coventry and the devastation the city suffered during the war. The courage of the residents resonated with me to the point that I just had to write something. One of my character's 'spoke' to me, and the rest became my last book, *The Secret Orphan*. I haven't been able to stop reading about the place or the characters since!

Have you always wanted to be a writer?

I have. I loved writing essays, poetry and short stories at school, but I was born into an era of vocation or marry, so I chose nursing – and marriage . . .

Are any of the characters based on you or people you know? If so, which ones?

No. I never travel that path – you never know where it might lead! The characters are 100% fictitious.

How do you find time to write? And where do you write when you do?

I fit writing around caring for my elderly mother and with my husband now retired, we have a great work life balance which leaves me free to follow my career. My husband created a beautiful office for me within a spare bedroom. I also write in our static caravan. People watching for characteristics is part of the entertainment!

Do you have any advice for readers who want to follow in your footsteps and write their first novel?

Write it. Then find a way to develop it and ask two people from the writing / reading world to beta read for you. I value my editors, their suggestions often lead me down a far more exciting route, or I stick to my guns and maintain my voice, but either way, I value their input. Never give up on your dream. Mine came true when I was sixty-one and I didn't expect a new career at that age. You never know who is watching you, so be yourself, avoid confrontation on social media, and build a platform with readers. Chatting and engaging with readers is a must, they help you grow.

What would you like readers to take away from your story?

A lasting memory of a character or scene. Just a little piece of the novel which gives them an emotional hit – be it a sad one or an uplifting one.

Who are your favourites authors and have they influenced your writing in any way?

I've always been a fan of Catherine Cookson and Barbara Erskine. They have different writing styles which I try, in some small way, to combine into my style by incorporating history, romance and family saga into each story.

If you could run away to a paradise island, what or who would you take with you and why?

Ah, I'd take my husband. We've been together forty-four years and he's taller than me, great at DIY and cooking. I'd have someone to talk to, to make me a home and catch my fish! I'd also make sure he had my Kindle in his pocket!

Keep reading for an extract from Glynis's international bestseller, *The Secret Orphan* . . .

CHAPTER 1

14th November 1940: Coventry, England.

Boom.

Boom.

The ground vibrated with each explosion. Unfamiliar sounds surrounded Rose Sherbourne as her body received blow after blow from displaced items of furniture. She jumped when shattering glass hit falling bricks, and everything around her crashed under their weight. *Boom.*

Another explosion, followed by the sound of metal hitting metal, echoed out around Rose's ears and her breath came thick and fast. Through the opening of what was once the front room, a sudden blast of hot air blew both her and her mother off their feet. Rose's body fell against something hard and a searing pain shot through

375

her back. For a few seconds she could not see, and she blinked, only to feel fine dust fall on her cheeks and into her eyes yet again. She wiped it away with the back of her hand and prepared herself to scrabble upright.

Boom.

A wall fell around her and, unable to move both with fear and because something was pinning down her right leg, Rose took a moment to catch her breath. Above her an intense whistling sound screamed from the sky, followed by an eerie whooshing sound. A continuous whistle followed. Rose held her breath. The sound meant only one thing; another bomb would explode within seconds and all she could do was pray it was away from her home.

Boom.

The rest of the wall fell, and she watched helplessly as brick after brick fell to the floor and her mother's body bounced as it was forced into the air for a second time. Rose tried to move but she felt a crushing sensation, a gripping tightness across her chest. She tried to struggle free from the bricks pinning her to the ground. Her chest hurt each time she tried to cough free the dust she'd inhaled when she hit the floor.

A piercing sound screeched above and once again the planes dropped their unwelcome packages.

Thud.

Thud.

One by one.

Two by two.

Rose counted them down.

One by one.

Two by two.

She could hear return fire and engines drifting off into the distance.

The sky fell silent.

The enemy were heading back to wherever they'd come from and a stunned Rose blinked away the dust, trying to make sense of what had happened. Indescribable noises came from above and she raised her eyes skyward and saw a large bright moon taunting her with its white light. There was no roof.

Bombed. The bombs had hit her home.

Rose's ears tingled inside and with each noise she felt a strange vibration along her jawline. With focus upon her face she sensed heat. Her cheeks burned as if it was a hot summer's day.

There'd been a thick frost all day, but it did nothing to suppress the heat from the raging flames nearby. With relief, Rose noted they were not close enough to burn her, but they were fierce enough to make her skin tingle and sweat.

She set her mind to where she lay and which room she was in when the bombs had hit. She needed to work out an escape route before she suffocated. Fear raged through her tiny body, and a sense of loneliness overwhelmed her. She lay back with exhaustion and as she focused upon the light of the moon, questions raced around her mind.

Why hadn't Mummy taken her to the shelter when they heard the siren sound out its warning?

Why, instead of running to safety like they usually did, did Mummy hum Rose's favourite piano piece – Beethoven's *Moonlight Sonata* – and twirl around as if showing off a new dress? She'd acted excited – strange.

With a sob, Rose remembered how her mother had screamed at her to keep playing, and how her voice had growled it out with such a fierce urgency it had frightened Rose. When Rose pleaded for them to go to the shelter her mother cuffed her around the ears.

Rose's body started to tremble until she thought her limbs would never stop no matter how hard she tried to control them. She tried to shut out the screams she could hear around her. High pitched wails of wounded neighbours. The endless shouts and pleas from the street, the screams of other children calling for their parents. Not everyone had made it to the shelters, or if they had, the shelters had failed to protect them. Either way, Rose drew no comfort from knowing she was not alone with her struggle.

She tried to turn her head away from her mother's contorted face. Rose knew she was dead. A tear trickled down the side of Rose's face. She was alone.